Mountain of Shadows

AND OTHER TALES OF ALHAZRED

Mountain of Shadows

AND OTHER TALES OF ALHAZRED

Donald Tyson

WEIRD HOUSE

Ghoul Bane, Mountain of Shadows, Brazen Vessel, Isle of the Dead, Dance of Durga, The Caliph's Necromancer, Revenge of the Djinn, Hand of Nilus, Red Claws, and *Ancient Evil,* were originally published in Tales of Alhazred © 2015

Blood Ties, The One Who Walks, and *Day of the Dead,* are original to this collection © 2022

Text © 2015-2022 by Donald Tyson
Cover art © 2022 by Cyrus Wraith Walker

Editor & Publisher, Joe Morey
Interior design by F. J. Bergmann

ISBN: 978-1957121-33-8

Weird House Press
Central Point, OR 97502
www.weirdhousepress.com
Join the Weird House mailing list at our website!

Table of Contents

Ghoul Bane

I.

"You are ugly, Alhazred." The voice was deep and rough, but the tone was not unkind.

I looked up from the letter I was drafting to a seller of acids disputing his recent price increase. Beyond the glow from my oil lamp, my library lay in deep shadow. I smelled a scent like damp earth. "Thank you for that sentiment, Uto. I'll cherish it always."

The patch of darkness I spoke to detached itself from the wall and took the form of a crouching naked ghoul. The manhood that dangled between his black thighs was impressive, but not as impressive as the hooked talons on the ends of his long fingers. "There was gossip that your face is disfigured, but I did not imagine how severely. The glamour you usually wear hides it well. My heart is sad for you."

By reflex, I raised my hand and touched the place where my nose should have been. There was only a hole there now. My nose had been cut off along with my ears, and my cheeks deeply scarred, by the late ruler of Sana'a in Yemen, land of my birth. In my foolish youth I had served as the royal poet, and had committed the indiscretion of lusting after King Huban's beautiful daughter, Narisa. His punishment of me had been creative. After disfiguring me, castrating me, and feeding me my own body parts, he had cast me out in the desert to die. Yet here I was, in my house on the Lane

1

of Scholars at Damascus. And the king? He had suffered an unfortunate accident, the result of a falling roof tile.

"To what do I owe the pleasure of having you break into my house, Uto, leader of the White Skull Clan?"

I used a formal address as a matter of politeness. It is good to be polite when a ghoul stands near you in the shadows with his claws spread. So far as I knew, I was on good terms with Uto, who from time to time supplied me with fresh corpses for my necromantic experiments from the burying ground he and the members of his clan inhabited.

He made the harsh, rasping noise that is laughter for ghouls. "Do not fear, my friend. I have come to you for help."

Setting my goose-quill pen in its onyx holder, which was carved in the shape of a little owl, I regarded him for several moments. It was unheard of for a ghoul to admit that he might need the help of a man. The situation, whatever its nature, must have been dire indeed to bring Uto on such an errand.

I indicated a chair on the opposite side of my desk. "Sit and tell me what it is you need."

He came forward, blinking against the brightness of the lamp flame, and settled his buttocks awkwardly into the seat of the chair. This in itself was also a remarkable event. Uto was the only ghoul I had ever known who used a chair. He had acquired this and several other human habits from his frequent interaction with the necromancers who lived in the Lane of Scholars. His clan was the primary source of raw material for their experiments.

Around his neck hung a string of beads made from polished bone, and on one wrist, a copper circlet of twisted wire. It is a curious contradiction in the nature of ghouls that even though they prefer to walk naked, all wear little bits of jewelery as adornment. Some find leather belts useful for carrying various objects, but Uto seldom wore a belt.

I moved the brass lamp to the far corner of the desk so that it would not shine between us. The eyes of ghouls are extraordinarily sensitive to light, so much so that they cannot bear the rays of the sun but move about on the surface of the ground only at night.

"Something is taking my people," he said without preamble. "I want you to find it and kill it."

"Taking them where?"

"They vanish. There is no trace to show what happens to them."

"From whence do they vanish?"

"From the Place of Skulls. From our warren beneath the graves. Even from their own dens."

"No one has seen the thing that takes them?"

"No one."

I sat back in my chair and mulled this over in my mind. "Why have you come to me?"

"You are a master of magic. We need your arts to find this thing so that we can kill it."

It was flattering to be called a master of magic, but scarcely accurate. True, I was doing my best to acquire the art of necromancy, but there were many older necromancers in the Lane of Scholars more skilled.

"Why did you not go to Harkanos?"

The ghoul shrugged. "He is a good man, but he is only a man. You are a ghoul, Alhazred of the Black Spring Clan. You know our ways."

After being cast forth by King Huban into the great desert known as the Empty Space, I was adopted into a clan of ghouls known as the Black Spring Clan. It was due to their acceptance of me that I survived. Alas, my clan was no more, but I still thought of myself as a ghoul.

"You were right to come to me. I will do all in my power to help you."

"When will you come?"

I stood from my chair. "Now."

"What of your companions? Will they help us?"

It was widely known that I shared my house with a young girl and a mercenary.

"They are not here at present. I will come alone."

"It is good," he said, standing in his usual slouching crouch. "This is a matter for ghouls, not for men."

2.

We went silent and unseen through the lampless and almost deserted streets of Damascus, moving through the darkness as only ghouls can move. I was not as skillful as my companion, but my time among the Black Spring Clan had taught me how to creep in stealth in a manner beyond the abilities of normal men. The drunken revellers returning home from the alehouses and the occasional pair of armed soldiers on patrol did not see or hear us as we passed. I wore a black desert thawb, and on the belt around my waist my dagger, sword, and the bleached white skull of Gor, the ghoul who had been leader of my clan and my closest friend. I had sworn an oath always to wear his skull lest I should ever forget amid the palaces and streets of men that I am a ghoul.

When we reached the gate of the city nearest the Place of Skulls, Uto showed himself in the light, and the gatekeeper silently allowed us to pass through the wall without challenge.

"He has been well bribed," I murmured as we left the city behind us.

"He knows it is better for the health of his wife and children that he let us pass when we will," Uto muttered without turning his head.

He led the way. The burying ground was no great distance from the wall of the city. It occupied a hollow between several low hills that were bare stone on their crowns, and resembled the bald heads of giants projecting just above the surface. The graveyard was large. Hundreds of low mounds with stones at each head and foot lay scattered both inside and outside its low stone wall, for the burying ground had spread beyond its original boundaries until there were more graves outside the wall than within it.

My eyes are uncommonly good, but I was thankful for

the crescent of waning moon that rode in the eastern sky. Apart from the stars, it was our only light. The crowns of the surrounding hills and the stones on the graves shone silver-gray in its glow. If we came upon the thing we sought, at least I would have some illumination by which to use my sword.

For his part, Uto needed no such aid. He led me to a section of the burying ground that was older than the rest, and occupied by small crypts and graves completely covered with slabs of cut stone rather than merely marked with rough stones at the head and foot. Centuries ago it must have been the place of burial for the wealthy merchants of the city. Now it was overgrown by rank weeds and brush.

Standing beside one of these ancient slabs, I stared about me. The burying ground was deserted. Not even a small animal moved across the graves.

Do you see anything, my love?

Sashi stirred within me at this silently voiced query. *Nothing, dearest one. We are alone with the ghoul.*

I realized Uto's large black eyes were on me, and wondered if he had heard gossip about my familiar spirit, a djinn of the desert who had united with me and presently dwelt within my body.

"I thought you were taking me to your clan."

He grunted and bent over the grave. Grasping a corner of the rectangular slab in his powerful hands, he slid it aside. It rotated on a concealed pivot to reveal the dark mouth of a tunnel. I descended a flight of stone steps, and he followed, after replacing the slab in its former position.

The ghoul warren ran beneath the level of the graves and was lofty enough that I could straighten my back. At intervals it was lit by small flames that burned in crude bone lamps. Although ghouls could see in light that was too dim for a man to even notice, they could not see in total darkness. The fat that fuelled the lamps was probably human, I thought. Ghouls used the remnants and products of human corpses wherever possible for their needs.

5

I followed closely after Uto's hunched back through the bewildering maze of passages, the smell of the ghoul warren strong in my throat. It was strangely reassuring, reminding me as it did of the security I had felt while part of my own clan. From time to time we passed other ghouls, squeezing by their naked bodies in the narrow tunnels. They stared at my disfigured face but none of them spoke.

"Where are we going?"

"There is someone you must meet who will tell you more about the vanishings."

He led me into a den with rounded earth walls, its floor covered with straw. An ancient ghoul hag sat on her haunches beside an oil lamp, threading beads onto a string with a needle. Her breasts sagged like empty sacks over ribs that stood forth under the black skin of her chest, and her wizened face was like that of an octogenarian ape. In spite of her advanced age, her fingers were nimble enough. She glanced up as we entered.

"You're an ugly one," she said, her voice dry as a wood rasp.

"So I've been told."

We settled ourselves on our haunches opposite her.

"This is the one I told you about, old mother," Uto said.

She stopped threading her beads and stared at me intently for several seconds. One of her eyes was wider than the other, and she turned it forward to look. I saw that the other eye had a milky whiteness across it.

"He's no ghoul."

"I am Alhazred of the Black Spring Clan."

"Never heard of it."

"It was a clan of the Empty Space, many hundreds of leagues from Damascus."

"Was? What happened to it?"

"A merchant took offense and poisoned our meat. My clan died."

"Yet you lived?"

"I lived."

"Enough idle talk," Uto said with impatience. "Tell

6

Alhazred what you know of the thing that takes our people."

She set her necklace aside. "Learn this, Alhazred of the Black Spring Clan, I am not of Uto's blood. Before his clan came here, another clan of ghouls occupied the warren beneath the Place of Skulls and harvested the dead, as is our way since before time began. I was young then, and beautiful, and many ghoul males desired me."

Uto grunted.

"You doubt me? Well, so you may; it is not important. There came a time when members of my clan began to vanish from the warren and from the burying place above. One by one they were taken, at first only a few in every cycle of the moon, then more, until at the last several were taken each night."

Uto turned to me. "When my clan came here, in the nights when my father's father was a young ghoul, they found only her, living in the warren."

"All were taken except you?"

She nodded, peering at me with her good eye.

"Why were you spared?"

"At the end, when only a few of us remained, I left the warren and hid in the burying ground. There was a newly dug grave awaiting its corpse. I crawled into it and covered myself with dirt. The thing did not know I was there. I heard the screams as it took the last of my clan. Then it left this place, and I dwelt alone for many years before Uto's clan came and made me one of them."

"Did you ever see this thing?"

"Never."

"Is this unseen thing that has recently taken ghouls the same that carried away your clan so many years past?"

The old female shrugged her bony shoulders in the gesture so typical of ghouls, a blend of fatality and acceptance. "How am I to know that? It takes them in the same way it took them when I was young and beautiful, more in each new cycle of the moon."

"If it is the same bane, it will take more and more until the

White Skull Clan is destroyed," Uto said. "We must stop it."

"We will bait a trap," I told him.

"A trap? Good. What will we use as bait?"

"Me."

3.

The crescent moon stood higher in the starry sky, but several hours yet remained until the first light of dawn. I sat on the stone at the head of one of the graves in the burying ground. Around the grave I had scratched a pentacle of protection, using the most potent words and symbols of power I knew. Uto sat on the stone at the foot of the grave. From some tree, an owl sounded a soft and mournful cry.

"Are you certain all your ghouls are gathered together?"

"I told you already, Alhazred, I ordered them to remain in the main feasting hall for the rest of the night."

"Then we are the only easy prey of your ghoul bane."

"Are you certain your circle will protect us?"

"No."

"It is no matter. I am ready to die, if only I get a chance to rend this thing with my claws."

"Let us hope it does not come to that."

We sat in silence for many minutes, listening to the night wind in the leaves of the trees.

"How do you suppose this thing is able to move through my warren unseen by anyone?" Uto murmured.

"This I have been thinking about. It may be a creature of the outer spheres, not of flesh. It may move between our world and the next, invisible to us because it is not wholly of our reality."

"Then how are we to fight it?"

"It must assume form and substance before it can carry off your people. At that time it may become vulnerable."

The moon climbed higher. In another hour the first rose of dawn would tint between the eastern hills. In my heart, I gave up hope that we would confront the creature this night.

8

Be on guard, my love.

Sashi? What do you see?

Something approaches.

"Something comes," I murmured aloud to Uto.

He leapt to his feet, his fingers spread to strike, and turned this way and that. "Where? Where is it?"

Beside the large cypress tree, Sashi said in my mind.

What does it look like? I asked her.

Like mist, or smoke, with tendrils trailing behind it as it moves. It floats above the ground. There is a churning at its center.

I relayed this description to Uto.

"How can you see it? I see nothing."

"The djinn who dwells in my body sees it."

"Ahhh. I have heard of your djinn."

It hesitates. It seems to wait. Now it is gone.

"Gone? Gone where?" I said aloud.

It vanished into the air, my love.

When I told this to Uto, he cursed in the colorful way of ghouls for several minutes. "How are we to fight what we cannot see?"

We remained on our guard, but the thing did not return.

"I fear the night has been wasted—" I began.

Uto cocked his bald head. "Do you hear that?"

I listened but heard nothing other than the night breeze.

"It comes from below. The sound of a battle. I must go there."

He rushed forward and rebounded from the invisible barrier above the circle. Cursing, he pressed against it before realizing the futility of his efforts, then began to kick dust over the circle.

"Stop, you fool; you'll leave us without a defense."

"My people are dying. I hear their screams. I must go to them."

He burst from the circle and ran to the entrance to the warren with me close at his heels. At every instant I expected the invisible creature of mist to take us from behind, but we reached the tunnels without incident. I heard the faint cries of distress when I was under the earth and ran behind Uto, but he was too quick for me and I lost him in the maze of the warren.

There was no one to ask for directions. All the ghouls of the clan were gathered in the great feasting hall, and I had no notion how to find it.

Do you know where we are, Sashi?

I'm sorry, my love, I am as lost as you are.

I wandered this way and that, down one tunnel and across another. The distant screams of the ghouls stopped but the warren remained deserted. I wondered if the thing had taken them all, and how I was to get out of the warren before it found me. An awareness of the weight of the yards of earth over my head pressed down upon me and squeezed my breath from my body. I began to sweat and shiver. I am not usually given to fear of confined spaces, but the uncertainty of whether the thing lurked in front of me or behind preyed upon my mind.

4.

Uto stepped out of a side passage some distance in front of me.

"Thanks be to the Old Ones," I said, wiping the chill sweat from my face with my hand. "What was that screaming about?"

"The bane took two of my people, a female and a young one," he said.

"Did they see the creature?"

"No. The mother of the child noticed that he was missing from the feasting hall, and when the mate of the female said the same about her, the rest of the fools panicked."

He had almost reached me. I drew my sword in one motion and set its point in his heart with a powerful thrust, then jerked the blade loose and danced back. He stared at me with amazement, and looked down at the black blood that gushed from the mouth of the wound. I crouched and held the bloody point of my sword up before me.

Blood welled from the corners of his broad mouth. He coughed. "Have you gone mad?"

"Cold steel ever has power over your kind," I told him. "Is that why you prey on ghouls and not on men? Because ghouls use no steel?"

Uto's squat black body wavered like heat rising from the sands of the desert, and in his place stood the old mother of ghouls. She glared at me with hatred from her good eye. "How did you know?"

I gestured at the string of red beads that hung around her neck with the point of my sword. "Uto's beads are white."

She fingered the necklace with her talons and hissed in rage. Even with her lifeblood pulsing from the wound over her heart, she advanced toward me. "I will savor your flesh."

"How long have you hidden inside this old one?"

She cackled horribly, the gore running down her chin. "Many generations of her kind."

She continued to advance, and I to retreat, holding my sword between us.

"You need a living host of flesh to anchor you to this world," I said with sudden insight. "Without it you cannot attain physical form."

"The old one and I made a pact," it gurgled. "In return for permission to hide and sleep within her body, I heighten her endurance and prolong her life."

"Is that what you do between your killing cycles? Sleep?"

She nodded, her black eye never leaving my face.

"Does anything of the old female remain?"

"Not much," the creature admitted.

"What were you going to do after you'd killed this clan? Sleep again?"

"Until the next clan comes to claim this burying ground for its own, as Uto's clan did so many years ago, and the cycle repeats itself."

11

Something stirred at the edges of her black skin.

The creature comes forth, my love.

The expression of cold, hard cruelty on the face of the old female ghoul became vague and confused. She clutched at the wound over her heart and staggered against the side of the tunnel.

"How do you take your prey? Do you open a rent in this world through which to drag them?"

My questions found no response from the old ghoul, who appeared to be dying.

"Do not abandon me," she croaked. "I need your strength."

She did not speak to me, but to the empty air between us.

Alhazred, it strikes.

At Sashi's warning, I slashed the air with my sword and jumped back, only to feel the chill earth press against my shoulders. I had run out of tunnel.

The old ghoul raised her finger and pointed at me, cackling with demented glee.

A soft thing pressed against my face. The softness changed to needles of fire. In the darkness at the side of the tunnel, a rent appeared that was like a tear in a curtain, and through it I saw flickers of redness, like embers glowing in a grate on a hearth. As I looked at it, the gap widened.

I drew my dagger from its ivory sheath with my left hand and slashed the air with both sword and knife. Even though I could not see my foe, I felt resistance as the sharp steel cut invisible substance.

A shadow reared up behind the old female ghoul. She sensed a presence, but before she could turn, Uto had her in his talons. He tore out her throat and slashed her back. I saw the white of her spine in the gaping cuts as she fell forward with a dolorous moan. As the last of the air left her lungs, the thing that pressed its needles into my face also departed. I wiped the back of my left hand across my cheek and saw blood on it.

Uto rose from his fighting crouch and came to me. His talons dripped gore, but his face wore a smile of contentment.

"Your head is covered with a thousand little drops of blood," he said.

"The thing almost had me. Steel was not enough to stop it."

"I heard what you said about it needing a living host to hold it to this world."

"Thanks be to the Old Ones I was right."

He turned and regarded the pitiful, shriveled corpse of the hag. "How many generations did she live, do you think?"

"There is no way to guess, but you may be certain of one thing: yours was not the first clan she charmed her way into. She and the bane of ghouls played that game many times."

He kicked the corpse in its face. "I would offer you a portion of the meat, but it will be days before it is ripe."

"No matter; I'm not hungry."

He came close to me. I resisted the urge to step back. He laid his bloody claw on my shoulder, staining my black thawb with red.

"You have done a great service for the White Skull Clan this night. It will never be forgotten. If you have need of anything, ask a member of my clan and it shall be yours."

"The only thing I require now is a guide out of this maze of a warren."

He chuckled and set off along the tunnel, stepping on the dead face of the old female as he passed. I followed in silence. As I passed the corpse, I looked down. Her wizened features bore a peaceful expression.

"Such is the end of all flesh," I murmured to myself.

Uto heard me and grunted derision. "The end of all flesh such as hers is in our bellies."

Against this practical statement I could find no argument.

Mountain of Shadows

1.

"I thought you had sworn an oath never to go on another quest."

From the heaving, rolling back of my camel, I looked across at the scarred mercenary who rode beside me. "It was more of a determination than an oath."

"I was growing bored with Damascus," Martala said from my other side. "It's good to be on the road again."

"Keep your road, girl," Altrus said. "Give me an alehouse where I can sit and drink, and a featherbed in a brothel where I can sleep."

We were seven days to the north of Damascus, crusted with road dust and saddle sores. I had forgotten how much I hated camels. As if to remind me, the beast I rode turned its long neck and spat on me. Cursing, I lashed at its head with the heel of my hand, but it extended its neck until it was beyond my reach. It was a measure of our weariness that neither of my companions laughed at me.

"Are you certain this talisman will protect you from Nyar—"

"Don't speak his name," I said quickly. "Even in this empty waste, never voice his true name aloud, for to speak it is to summon him."

Altrus snorted in contempt but did not dispute the censure. He was a man without fear. The name of the Crawling Chaos was no more to him than a word. It was a

15

mark of his respect for me that he allowed me to close his lips.

"How do you know this talisman will protect you from ... *him?*" he went on, after a time had passed in silence.

"Nothing is certain in this life. It is reputed that the talisman is infused with the living substance of the Keeper of Gates."

"Who?"

Martala leaned forward in her saddle and framed a name silently with her lips.

"What? Who is that?" Altrus asked, staring at her in puzzlement.

"Yog-Sothoth," I said, suppressing my irritation, and turned to the girl. "You can say the name Yog-Sothoth."

"One you can say, another you can't say," Altrus muttered. "I'm glad I'm not a necromancer. All the little rules would drive me mad."

"Yog-Sothoth is the lord of gateways, and has absolute power both to open and to seal them. If I can use his talisman to close the way against my foe, not even his power will be able to breach it."

We rounded the rocky shoulder of a low hill. In the distance reared our destination, the Mountain of Shadows. It stood tall against the horizon, true to its name, its black stone unbrightened by the sunlight falling on its slope.

"I can't be certain the talisman will keep away the one they call the Crawling Chaos," I went on. "Yet if there is even a chance, it is a weapon I must possess. The next time he comes to amuse himself by toying with my life, I want to be prepared."

"No man can arm himself against the gods," Altrus said with fatalism.

"He is greater than the gods," Martala said. "He is an Old One."

"How is it you first came to learn about this talisman? You never told me."

"Uto, leader of the White Skull Clan of ghouls, overheard

a rumor of its existence whispered in the deep places of the earth by something not human."

"Why would a ghoul come to you with such a tale?" Altrus asked with suspicion.

"Last month I did a trifling service for him. He is in my debt."

"Do you trust him?"

"As well as I trust anyone. I am not by nature a trusting man, as you know."

His eyes lingered on the ravages of my face, and I saw a trace of pity there before he looked away. Both my companions were aware of my disfigurement, and while we were alone together I felt no need to hide my true appearance beneath the spell of glamour I wore while walking the streets of Damascus.

All through the morning and into the afternoon we approached the foot of the black mountain across the dreary plain. The setting sun found us climbing the foothills on our weary beasts. Camels are not bred for climbing. Their complaints increased in both frequency and stridency.

"Tomorrow we must tether these animals where there is water and forage, and leave them behind us," Altrus said.

"I never expected to ride them to the peak of the mountain."

"Is this talisman on its peak?"

"That I don't know. It is supposed to be here, somewhere, but what it looks like or where it lies concealed, I could not discover in my researches among the old chronicles."

"We're being watched," Martala said.

I looked where she pointed. Atop a great boulder that was the size of a house I saw a brown desert rat. It sat on its haunches with its forepaws gathered together against its breast, like a scholarly monk, and eyed us intently without moving as we rode past.

"Bold vermin, be gone," Altrus shouted and waved his arm. The rat did not even twitch.

Altrus opened his purse and drew from it a copper coin. He threw it at the rat with murderous intention, but his aim was poor. The coin struck the stone near the rat's feet with a metallic ring and flew away, the rays of the sun glinting on its polished sides as it tumbled through the air. The rat stared at the mercenary with its black eyes, and I almost imagined I saw contempt in its posture. With a leisurely flick of its long tail, it turned and jumped out of sight on the far side of the boulder.

"I have heard it rumored that the Crawling Chaos can spy upon his enemies through the eyes of desert creatures," the girl said.

"Where would you hear such a thing?"

"Your neighbors in the Lane of Scholars have servants. When I walk with them to the marketplace to buy your food and drink, we talk."

"Better for you to choose a less perilous subject of conversation."

"We are always discreet."

"Where Nyar— where *he* is concerned, the very bricks of the walls may listen."

2.

We left the camels tethered at the place where we had made camp the previous evening, beside a spring that bubbled from the rocks into a deep pool. I would have hobbled them, but Altrus pointed out that this would leave the beasts defenseless should they be attacked by wolves. I was forced to trust that the presence of water and grass would keep them in that place, even should they break their tethers. The prospect of recrossing the desert plain on foot did not appeal to me.

After climbing for hours a succession of slopes, we came upon a kind of pathway more suited to mountain goats than to men. It wound its way over knife-edged ridges and along the sides of deep chasms, never wide enough to walk two abreast.

"At least this path shows that the mountain is inhabited," Martala observed.

"One of its inhabitants waits for us behind that rock," Altrus murmured.

The girl and I accepted this information without comment. We were both aware of how keen was the mercenary's foresense of danger.

I bowed my head and feigned a cough as I put on the spell of glamour that conceals my disfigurement. I am not embarrassed by how I look, but strangers tend to react with hostility when they see my true features.

A man in a long black robe stepped into view from behind a boulder. He was slender of body but mature of years, with a shaved skull, and full lips that were almost womanly. He stood in the path, regarding us with impassive dark eyes, his hands concealed in the sleeves of his robe at his waist. His posture was very like that of the rat.

"What do you seek in this place?" he asked in a cultured voice. To my surprise, he spoke in Greek.

I answered him in the same language.

"We are contemplatives. We intend to meditate and pray on the summit of the mountain."

There was no need to translate the words for my companions. Both had a traveler's knowledge of the Greek tongue.

His eyes examined each of us in turn, but his face betrayed no indication of his thoughts.

"You are welcome to sleep and eat at the Monastery of Saint John during the term of your devotions."

"That is most generous. We accept your hospitality."

He nodded. "I will inform my brothers of your arrival. Continue on the path. You will reach the gates of the monastery before sunset."

He closed his eyes and muttered words under his breath, then seemed to listen.

"Your sleeping chambers are being prepared for your arrival. You will dine with us this evening."

Before I could thank him again, he slowly lifted off the ground and floated upon the air above my head. It was an impressive display of levitation. He drifted up the slope and was soon hidden behind the hills.

"Now that's what I call magic," Altrus said. "Why don't you ever do anything like that?"

"I have no need to make such vulgar displays."

Martala giggled but said nothing.

We continued along the path.

"This is a strange location for a Christian monastic order," the mercenary said at length.

"We don't know that the monks are Christian."

"They speak Greek. What else can they be?"

I shrugged my shoulders after the manner of a ghoul. It was a gesture that said nothing and asked for no response.

After a while, we came to a rushing torrent of water that cascaded down the steep slope in the belly of a narrow gorge and thundered across the path. The frothing white cataract was too wide to leap across and too swift to wade. Off the side of the path, it fell sheer in a waterfall for several hundred feet before crashing upon the rocks far below.

"There's no way we can cross it," Altrus shouted near my ear. The thunder of the water made conversation difficult.

"We'll have to go back and find another route."

"Alhazred, look." Martala grasped my arm and pointed into the air.

Above our heads floated another of the black-robed monks. This one was older than the monk who had spoken to us. He did not deign to acknowledge our notice of him, but merely traced a sign upon the air with his hand.

The rushing stream slowly lifted itself away from the path, attracted by his hand the way straw is drawn to polished amber.

"I think he means for us to go underneath it," I shouted.

They regarded me without enthusiasm. There was ample room to walk beneath the arching torrent, but should it suddenly fall back into place, anyone caught beneath it was certain to be swept over the cliff edge to the rocks below.

"I'll go first," Altrus shouted. He went forward, hesitated, and then with one quick glance upward at the floating monk, ducked his head and hastened beneath the water.

"You go next," I told the girl.

She seemed inclined to argue, but I cut short her words with a gesture, and she followed the mercenary to the other side.

I went after them. The rocks of the path were slick and worn smooth by the action of the torrent. The thunder of the mass of water passing above my head made me dizzy. Altrus caught my hand as I emerged from beneath it and pulled me to a more secure standing place.

Immediately, the torrent dropped back to the rocks with a crash that threw up glistening droplets and soaked the three of us to the skin. I wiped my eyes and looked at the sky, but the monk was already gone from his place. We stood for a time, gazing at the rushing water in the gorge.

"We'll need a rope," Altrus said.

I nodded to show that I understood. As usual, he was thinking three steps ahead. If the talisman was kept in the monastery, and we stole it, we were unlikely to have the aid of a flying monk when we chose to leave the mountain.

The path became steeper. In places it consisted of steps cut into the rock of the mountainside. Iron rings had been driven into holes in the rock to act as handholds. Even so, it was a perilous climb. I paused to breathe with my hand in one of these rings and looked out across the plain over which we had traveled. I could see the entire breadth of it even though it had taken us days to cross it. The shadows of clouds crawled over the sands like caterpillars.

"Do you think the talisman is kept in the monastery?" Martala asked me. She, too, had paused to rest.

"Unless there is some cave or shrine on the peak, it seems the most likely place for it."

"How will you recognize it?"

"I don't know."

"Do you even know what it looks like?"

"No."

Her expression spoke her misgivings more eloquently than words.

Eventually we came upon a gate set in a stone wall that crossed the path where it led through a narrow defile. I grasped the brass knocker and worked it against the door three times. As I was about to repeat this performance, the gate swung inward and a monk gestured for us to enter.

We continued up several long flights of stairs cut into the rock to the monastery, which was itself carved into the side of the mountain.

The serious monk with the dark eyes who had first greeted us on the path met us at the top of a broad marble stair in front of the monastery entrance. "Our abbot wishes to speak with you."

Two monks stood on either side of him. Their posture was not threatening, but their intention was clear. We were going to be taken to the abbot.

"We would be delighted to speak to your abbot," I told him in Greek, with a smile. "I wish to thank him for his hospitality."

3.

The abbot met us in a long chamber hung with tapestries and divided midway along its length by an intricately carved wooden screen that was set in a frame against the walls and ceiling. The only windows were in the front portion of the room, which extended back deep into the mountain. As a consequence, the area behind the screen was gloomy with shadows.

The wall hangings depicted various scenes in the life of the prophet Jesus. I recognized them from my study of the Christian holy books. One showed Jesus exorcising a horned and winged demon from a kneeling man. In another, the Devil tempting him on a mountaintop. Still others showed him scourged, fainting beneath the weight of the cross, and crucified. In the last, a man caught in a cup a stream of blood that flowed from a wound in his side.

The abbot was a little man of around sixty years of age. His eyebrows were white as milk, and thicker than any others I have ever seen. They almost looked like tufts of white feathers. Beneath them, his eyes shone blue and bright. He wore a black robe trimmed with white and gold, and a tall cap of the same colors. Around his neck hung a golden medallion with a hole in its center. Its surface was curiously engraved with interlocking dragons fighting, or perhaps mating—it is difficult to tell with dragons.

"Welcome, friends, welcome to the monastery of St. John the Divine. My name is Father Joram, and I am the abbot. You are most welcome here. We get so few pilgrims to our mountain."

I walked up to him with my hand extended and a broad smile on my lips. "The exalted and noble Moawiya, the Caliph at Damascus, wishes me to extend my warmest greetings on his behalf. He has heard about your wonderful monastery and is most impressed."

He took my hand. His fingers were cool and dry, and surprisingly strong. "You know the Caliph?"

"Indeed, a dear friend of mine. When he learned of our intention to make a pilgrimage to this mountain, he expressed a wish that I inquire into the practices of your order."

"I am flattered, but I confess to some surprise that so great a man as the Caliph should have an interest in our lowly community, or even know of its existence."

"Priests of your Christian faith have lately come to him with a petition to establish a monastery at Damascus, and he wishes to understand the nature of the various monastic orders before deciding which order to approve."

From the corner of my eye I saw Altrus look at Martala and raise an eyebrow. All that I had just told the abbot was false.

"But you say that you were coming to the mountain to pray in any case?"

"The holiness and purity of the Mountain of Shadows is known across the length and breadth of the Caliphate. It is said that one of Mohammed's teachers prayed on its summit for seven years, before being elevated directly into heaven."

"Indeed. That is most interesting. Our order has occupied this mountain for over two centuries, and our records show no such holy man."

"No doubt his presence was too inconsequential to chronicle."

"I'm sure that is the reason," he said, but his voice was doubtful.

"The Caliph particularly wishes to know of any sacred objects that may be venerated by your order."

The abbot spread his hands. "We are simple monks. We venerate no objects."

"But surely you have sacred things that are precious to you?"

"A few relics from saints. Bits of bone. We have the skull of Saint Timothy set in silver, and the finger of the apostle Luke contained within a vessel of crystal."

"Your humility is a credit to your faith."

He bowed his head slightly in acknowledgment of the compliment. As he did so, I looked beyond him into the shadows that lay in the far end of the room. There was something standing back there in the arch of a shrine; a statue of some kind. My eyes are better in darkness than those of most men, but not so good as the eyes of a true ghoul, and the details of the figure escaped them.

What do you see, Sashi? I silently asked the djinn who resides within my body.

It is the figure of a man wrapped about in something. More than that I cannot see. The screen obscures it.

I went to one of the windows and gazed out. "What a magnificent view you have."

The abbot came to my side with a smile of pleasure. "It is quite splendid. We tend to forget how impressive it is, until we are reminded by travelers who see it for the first time."

I caught Altrus's eye and nodded at the old man, then at the window. He came forward and took the monk gently by the elbow.

"Look there, holy Father. You can see the route we used to cross the plain."

When the abbot turned his back to converse with the mercenary, I quickly drew my dagger and caught the sun on the flat of its polished blade, then directed the ray of light to the back of the long chamber and through the wooden screen, playing it up and down. It lit the standing statue of a naked man entwined all about his body with the coils of a great serpent. The mouth of the snake and the lips of the man touched, as though in a kiss. Something flashed and glittered on the forehead of the serpent, but before I could see what it was, I was forced to sheathe my dagger.

"Forgive me, friends," the abbot said, turning to face me. "I must attend to my duties. Brother Manasseh will escort you to your sleeping chambers and will call you when the evening meal is served in the dining hall."

He tugged a silken cord that rang a bell. A young, shaven-headed monk with projecting ears entered. The youth stared at Martala with wide blue eyes. I wondered if she was the first woman to enter the monastery.

As we followed the monk along the great balcony that extended the full width of the monastery, I deliberately lagged behind, and Martala and Altrus fell into step beside me.

"I saw something flash behind the screen," the girl murmured.

"A jewel of some kind," I told her, and described what I had glimpsed by the reflected sunlight from my dagger.

"Is it the talisman?"

"It may be."

"What about the medallion around the old man's neck?" Altrus said. "That has the smell of magic about it."

"That, too, is possible."

"We can steal them both," Martala said.

"Let us not act in haste. First we need to see the rest of the monastery and the peak of the mountain. Who knows what shrines may be there, or what they may hold?"

٩.

The flat peak of the Mountain of Shadows had two shrines. One was pagan and, to judge by the extreme weathering of its stones, almost as ancient as the mountain itself. The other was smaller and of cruder construction. It bore a Christian cross on its keystone. Its altar was stained with rust, attesting to blood sacrifices at some time in the not-too-distant past.

"I thought the Christians didn't sacrifice beasts," Altrus said as he rubbed his hand over the altar stone. It left reddish powder on his fingers.

"There are different sects. Heresies, they call them. Some of them believe extraordinary and grotesque things."

"Like what?"

I waved my hand vaguely in the air. "Some monks cut off their own pricks and balls to avoid carnal desires. Others believe that sexual excess is the path to spiritual attainment."

"All Christians are mad."

"So are those who follow the Prophet."

Martala called my name and waved us over to the pagan shrine.

"What have you found?" I asked her.

She pointed at a large, flat stone in the shadowy rear of the shrine. It was not made of the same type of rock as the mountain, but was greenish and translucent, almost like jade. Carved upon it was the image of three interlocking circles of different sizes, and in their common center, a single round depression. Spiralling rays surrounded this hollow. In its center there was a hole. I put my longest finger in and it slid down to the depth of the last knuckle.

"Something was set in here."

"It's dangerous to stick your finger into strange holes," Altrus said.

"Who taught you that?" Martala asked.

"A girl in Alexandria. At least she said she was a girl."

Holding up my finger, I wiggled it. "Nothing chopped it off."

"Is this an image of Yog-Sothoth?" she asked.

I studied it more critically. "It could be."

"Alhazred, behind you by the path," Altrus murmured.

I checked to make certain the glamour over my face was holding, then turned and saw the young monk who the day before had escorted us to our chambers, and later to the dining hall.

He hobbled toward us, breathing heavily from his long climb. "I came ... to see whether ... you needed anything," he gasped between breaths.

"Rest a moment before you speak," I told him. "You are winded."

"There are so many steps."

"Why didn't you just fly up here?" Altrus asked him.

The monk smiled at the notion. "Only the most skilled of my brothers possess that ability. I am yet too young."

When he had rested for several minutes, Martala approached him.

"Do both of these shrines belong to your holy order?" she asked, smiling and blinking more than was necessary. She always was a clever girl.

The youth blushed, but his eyes were bright on her. I noted again, as I had earlier, that they were as blue as the eyes of the abbot. Indeed, there was a distinct resemblance between the face of the monk and that of the abbot.

Altrus gave me a look, and I discreetly backed away so that the monk could move nearer to Martala.

"The small shrine nearest the path is ours. The other was here when the founders of my order came lost and wandering across the barren plain. Nobody knows who built it, but they must have been the same people who carved the monastery into the side of the mountain."

"Didn't your order build the monastery?"

He shook his head. "Most of the rooms and passages were here when the first brothers came. That was two centuries ago. They found the mountain deserted and made it their home. They were starving and dying of thirst. They found the cisterns full of rainwater and the granaries full of grain. It was as though the inhabitants had only gone away a short while before their arrival. They interpreted this as a sign from God to remain here."

"What do you know of this carving?" she asked, pointing at the slab of green stone.

"Only what the elder monks tell us—that it is the image of some ancient pagan god of a lost people. Even its name has been forgotten."

She put her finger into the hole in the center of the depression.

"It almost looks as though something set here in the stone has been pried out."

His face paled. "I know nothing of that," he said with a slight stammer.

She smiled and put her hand on his. "Is it true there are no women in your monastery?"

"There are none. The nearest woman is in the village of Erda, and that is a full day's ride to the east."

"It must be strange, to live your whole life without a woman's touch."

He cleared his throat nervously, so that his Adam's apple bobbed. I saw small beads of sweat form on the top of his bald skull.

"We have all taken an oath to remain pure in body and spirit. We become accustomed to our celibacy."

She leaned nearer and spoke in a low voice. "We should talk more together, tonight while the other monks are asleep and no one will disturb us."

He glanced over at Altrus and I, who turned our heads and pretended not to pay attention.

"Don't worry about them," she said. "I am a free woman, and come and go where I please."

"Well, perhaps it would be good to learn more about Damascus."

"And in return, you can tell me more about your way of life here at the monastery."

They agreed to meet after midnight in the girl's sleeping chamber. I almost felt sorry for the monk. He stood trembling like a newly foaled colt, and did not want to release Martala's hand. Finally, she had to jerk her fingers out of his sweating grasp. After a few more words, he left us and began the long descent back down to the monastery.

"Do you think he can tell us anything of use?" Altrus asked her.

She shrugged. "He has lived here all his life. It may be that he knows more about its secrets than he realizes."

"He knew something about whatever was set in that hole in the stone," I said. "I saw him hesitate before denying it."

"After tonight, we will know it also," she said with confidence.

"Do you mean to actually take that trembling flower to bed with you?" Altrus asked in disbelief.

"That is a matter between the monk and me," she said with a smile.

He shook his head and turned away, muttering to himself.

"Don't tell me you're jealous? He's not much more than a child."

"Neither are you."

"Enough foolishness," I said. "Search the peak for caves or cavities in the rock, anywhere anything might have been hidden. We need to be certain nothing of value remains here."

We spent the next two hours searching the top of the mountain and down the slopes where they were of gentle enough incline to descend them. We found several openings but they were empty, and did not appear to ever have been used to hide anything.

"Useless," Altrus said in disgust. "We've wasted our time."

"Not at all," I said. "We now know that if the talisman

exists, it is almost certainly in the keeping of the monks of Saint John."

With this thought in mind, we descended to the monastery.

5.

Martala let herself into my chamber and eased the door shut behind her. A flame burning on a short wick in the stone lamp on the table cast only a dim glow. It was enough to show that I sat on the cot fully clothed, and Altrus dozed in a chair with his head resting back against the wall. He sat up when he heard the door, instantly alert, then relaxed when he saw it was her.

"How went your evening of pleasure?" he murmured.

We had already ascertained that the stone walls of the cells were so thick, minor sounds could not be heard from one to another. It was safe to speak in low voices with the door shut.

She shrugged. "Brother Manasseh became so excited, he could not contain his enthusiasm. It spilled out over his thigh."

"An excess of zeal. A common failing of the young."

"What have you learned?" I asked.

"In the folklore of the monastery there is a tale that when the first brothers came to this mountain, they found a jeweled talisman embedded in the pagan altar on its peak, and removed it so that it could be sanctified in the service of Jesus Christ."

"We were right," Altrus said, meeting my gaze.

"Did you discover the keeping place of the talisman?"

"There, we encounter a slight problem."

"Which is?"

"The talisman is in three parts. One part hangs around the neck of the abbot. The second is the ruby on the brow of the serpent in the statue that stands in the abbot's private chapel. You glimpsed it through the wooden screen."

"And the third part?"

"The folktale says it is in the form of a key, which, when inserted into the back of the jewel's gold setting, locks the jewel into the center of the golden medallion, so that all three parts become joined together."

"Very good. Where is the key?"

She spread her slender fingers. "Brother Manasseh did not know. He said that nobody knows apart from a few of the most senior monks."

"The Abbot will know," Altrus murmured.

I nodded. "I'm sure he will be happy to tell us, if we go to his private chambers and ask him."

"When?"

"What better time than now?"

"Good. This place bores me."

The monks placed no guards on the passageways at night. The monastery was well-nigh impregnable and had never come under attack, so they saw no reason for such precautions. It was good to have such trusting souls in the world, I thought. It made things easier for the rest of us.

We entered the long room that was the Abbot's audience chamber and private chapel of worship, and went directly to the wooden screen that divided the room. Its door was locked, but Martala opened it without great difficulty. She has a natural talent for locks.

"A simple antique design," she murmured as she swung the door wide.

The light was so poor, I could see only masses of shadow against shadow, even though by this time my eyes were fully adapted to darkness.

"We need light to work. Strike your tinder, Altrus, and look for a lamp or a candle."

The flint of his tinderbox sparked against its steel rod, and Martala gasped and stepped backward, banging into me. I held her arms to steady her.

The statue I had glimpsed through the screen towered above us, at least eight feet tall. It was an ambitious work. A naked man I took to represent Jesus stood with the long body of a scaled serpent coiled around his legs, hips, chest and arms. The head of the snake peered into his face, and his lips appeared about to touch the lips of the snake. In the forehead of the snake sparkled a ruby the size of an acorn, surrounded by a thick band of gold.

All this was revealed in the instantaneous flash of the flint against the steel. The tinder in the box ignited and a glow spread, revealing the lines of the statue, which, I saw, was not stone, but bronze. In the flickering flame it almost seemed to breathe and move its limbs.

I gave Martala my dagger and put my head through her legs to lift her onto my shoulders. "Take the setting around the jewel as well."

"Naturally. I'm not a fool."

She began to worry the soft gold setting from its harder bronze socket.

"Try not to damage it."

"I'm doing the best I can," she snapped. "Hold the light nearer."

The ruby flipped from the head of the snake, and the girl caught it from the air in her left hand and passed it down to me.

I lowered her to the floor and examined the jewel near the flame in the tinder box. "A fine stone."

"The eye of Yog-Sothoth," she said.

"Not the eye. Only the pupil of the eye. We must visit the Abbot for the rest of the talisman."

Altrus cursed and the flame went out.

"It got hot," he said.

"No matter. Follow after me."

Earlier, I had asked one of the monks in a casual way where the Abbot slept, so I knew in a general sense where to look. We returned to the audience chamber and I passed through a door into a side corridor. As we crept along it, I heard gentle snores. These led us directly to the old man's bedchamber.

6.

We entered silently. Altrus struck his tinder alight. By its flame I saw that the bed held two men, the elderly Abbot and a younger monk of about the same age as Manasseh. I was not shocked, but I was surprised. I would have sworn that Joram was too old to copulate with anything, whether woman, man, or goat. The evidence of my eyes said I was wrong.

The young monk opened his eyes first.

"Kill him," I told Martala.

She darted to the side of the bed and slit his throat with her dagger before he gathered enough of his wits to yell for help.

The gurgling of blood from the wound in his throat and his thrashing arms woke Joram. He blinked beneath his white, feathery eyebrows and stared about in confusion, then fixed his gaze on my face. "Demon," he croaked.

I had not troubled to put on my glamour for the night. Kneeling on the old man's side of the bed, I held my dagger to his throat. "Remain silent, or I will kill you."

He must have believed me, because he stopped croaking. By this time, his young sleeping companion had expired.

He looked down at the spreading blood soaking into the sheets and bolster cover. "Why are you doing this?" he whispered. "Are you fiends?"

"Not fiends, only thieves," Altrus said.

He transferred the fire in his tinderbox to the old man's oil lamp, and the room brightened. It was windowless, like so many rooms of the monastery.

"We are here to take the talisman of Yog-Sothoth," I told him.

He made no spoken response but his blue eyes betrayed him. They flicked toward a wall rack, where hung his monk's robe. Beside it from another peg dangled the golden medallion. I took it down and mated it with the ruby. The gold setting of the jewel fitted perfectly into the hole in the medallion. I saw that there was some mechanism concealed in the setting, and a slot in its back, presumably for the third piece of the talisman.

"Where is the key?"

The Abbot stared in horror at the red jewel. "What have you done? Heretic! Blasphemer! Demon."

"Where is the key?" I repeated.

"Christ will punish you for this night of blood. Murderers!"

Altrus grunted cynically. "I suppose you'll tell us the blood of sacrifice on the altar of the shrine at the top of the mountain came from the throats of animals."

Joram did not respond with words, but his eyes betrayed him.

"I thought not," Altrus said. "What do you do? Buy children from the village of Erda?"

"Christ will punish you," the old man repeated. "You are all going to hell." His voice was stronger and clearer. He seemed to be finding his courage.

"Tell me, Joram; I'm curious. Is Manasseh your son or your grandson?" I asked.

"That is none of your affair," he snapped.

"We're wasting time," Altrus muttered.

I sighed wearily. I hated torture. In my youth I had grown up in a king's household as his royal poet, and my soft early years had given me tender sensibilities in many respects. I was kind to animals, other than camels. For the most part I refrained from beating children or striking women. Nonetheless, my months as a ghoul of the Black Spring Clan had taught me the necessity for cruelty.

The old man withstood the torture well. I was inhibited by the need to keep him alive and able to speak. Toward the end he began to drift in and out of awareness, and I feared he was bleeding to death. He would not tell us where he had hidden the key.

"Where would you hide a key?" I mused to Martala, who was busy cleaning the blood from her dagger on the corner of the bed sheet.

"In the midst of other keys."

I stopped and thought. The Abbot had keys for every locked door and strongbox in the monastery. "Where does he keep his key ring?"

We searched his rooms, and found the ring in a drawer of his writing desk. It held at least half a hundred keys of various lengths and sizes, some brass, some iron, a few of silver, and one of gold. The gold key was strangely shaped. Its end was broad and flat, with the teeth projecting forward instead of to the side, as is the usual way with keys. I worked it off the ring and fitted the setting of the ruby into the center of the medallion, then inserted the key into its back. It slid in with a satisfying click.

"In the name of Christ, whatever you do, don't turn the key!"

The Abbot had managed to crawl out of bed and now stood in the doorway to the study, blood streaming down from his mutilated hands and from the cuts in his chest and thighs, so that his nightgown was saturated with red.

Something in his tone of voice made me hesitate. I removed the key, and the two other pieces of the talisman fell apart from one another in my hand. "Why not?"

The old man's blue eyes were wide and staring, but whatever he looked at, we three could not see it.

"What do you think happened to the people who built this monastery?" he mumbled. "Why did they all leave the mountain, with their storehouses filled with grain and their cisterns filled with water?"

"Ah, yes; I take your point," I said, sliding the ruby into one pocket of my thawb and the medallion into another pocket. I tossed the key to Altrus, who caught it. "Keep this safe."

"The three parts must never be joined," Joram moaned. His legs would no longer support him, and he slid slowly down the doorframe, leaving smears of blood behind.

"Should I kill him?" Altrus asked.

"There is no need. We have what we came for."

"I hid bags with food and water near the gate of the monastery," Martala said.

"Did you hide rope with them?" Altrus asked.

"Of course I hid rope."

"Then let's bind the old man and gag him. By the time morning comes, I want to be many miles away from this place."

ר.

The torrent slowed our progress. It was almost impassable. We tied the rope around Altrus's waist and anchored it while he crawled from submerged boulder to ledge, the white foam breaking over his back and shoulders. Several times I was sure he was about to be swept over the cliff, and that the girl and I would be forced to haul in his broken corpse, but somehow he held on against the weight of the water.

When at last he was safely on the other side, he tied his end of the rope to a boulder and I did the same on our side with our end, pulling the rope as tight as I could pull it in the process.

"You go first," I told Martala.

The girl bent her head nearer to mine—the roar of the surging water made it almost impossible to hear each other. I repeated myself, and she nodded.

I extended myself out from the bank, keeping one foot on dry rock, and supported her as she inched herself into the thundering stream. On the other side, Altrus imitated my posture and extended his hand for the girl to grab it. She almost lost her footing and had to catch herself on the rope, but at last she strained forward and caught the mercenary's strong hand. He drew her out of the water, wet and shivering.

The icy chill of the mountain torrent was worse than I had imagined it would be. Within seconds I was cold to the bone and shivering uncontrollably. I inched out on the rope, feeling in the foaming water for secure places to stand that I could not see. It closed around my waist and tried to lift me and fling me over the cliff. I fought it with all my strength for what seemed hours, and when I was sure my strength was about to fail, I felt hands pull me to dry rock.

"I hope we never need to do that again," Altrus said.

I tried to answer, but my teeth chattered together so loudly, I could not speak.

"We have to move quickly," Martala said, looking at the path behind us. "The sun has been up for over an hour. The monks must have found their abbot by this time."

We hurried as best we could single file along the narrow mountain path. It was impossible to go without caution or we would have fallen to our deaths. We were still in the open high places when a stone the size of a large melon fell from the sky, narrowly missing Altrus.

I looked up and saw a levitating monk some thirty feet above our heads. He balanced a second large stone in his left hand, preparing to drop it on us.

"Begone, you flying freak," Martala shouted.

She snatched up a piece of rock and threw it at him. The rock struck him in the leg near his knee. We heard him grunt with pain, and he dropped the large stone. It missed the path by several feet. Altrus and I looked at each other, then bent and gathered handfuls of rocks for throwing. The monk was forced to elevate himself above the range of our missiles. He drifted away from us back along the path.

"He is going to pick up more big rocks," Altrus said.

"Look, here comes one of his brothers," I said, pointing.

It was two monks, not one, who drifted through the air toward us, one behind the other. Each balanced stones on both palms that were large enough to split our skulls and dash out our brains. We stopped and threw rocks until they were compelled to rise higher. They released their cargo, but because they were so high, we had time to judge the paths of the stones and step out from under them before they struck.

It was a deadly game, and we played it all the rest of the morning and into the afternoon. The need to watch for the floating monks slowed our progress along the path. We still found ourselves in the open, with nothing to hide beneath.

"Thanks be to the Old Ones there are not more of them," I

said when we had a few moments to draw our breath. "They would surely overwhelm us."

"They may do so yet," Altrus said. "My arms are becoming weary."

I realized then how tired my arms had become. It was all I could do to throw the chips of rock upward, and they flew no more than twenty or thirty feet. It was becoming harder to dodge the falling stones dropped by the seemingly tireless monks.

"Sooner or later, one of them is going to hit one of us," Martala said.

I made no response because I knew the girl was right. It was only a matter of time until one of us made a mistake and stepped the wrong way, into the path of one of those cursed falling stones. It would be hours before we reached a sheltering ledge, and we could not continue this deadly dance for hours.

"Why hasn't one of them used his magic to pull us over the edge to our deaths?" Altrus asked. "They can move the torrent, why not us?"

"Who knows?" I said wearily. "Maybe they can move water, but not flesh. Or maybe they don't want to risk the loss of their talisman. It's powerless without its three parts, and they have no way to know who carries them."

"I wish I had a good hunting bow," the girl said. "I'd end this quick enough."

"Count your blessings the monks don't have bows," Altrus said.

Not long after this conversation, there came a time when I discovered that I could no longer lift my arms above my head. My muscles refused to obey me. I saw that Martala was in a similar state, and Altrus not much better.

He felt my gaze upon him. "I think we're finished," he said, too low for the girl to hear.

"Not yet," I said, my resolve firming itself. "There is one other thing we can do."

He realized what I was talking about. "The abbot said that would be a very bad thing to do."

"The abbot is not here on this path, having rocks dropped upon his head."

Another fell as I dodged aside. It missed me by mere inches and clattered its way down the mountainside. I glared up in fury at the impassive monks who circled high overhead. Soon they would realize we had ceased to throw our little stones, and they would come nearer. That would be the end for us.

"Give me the key," I told Altrus.

He did not argue, but passed me the golden key.

Martala watched me nervously. "If this thing ate an entire monastery full of people, how do we avoid being eaten by it?"

"I have an idea about that."

"An idea? A *good* idea?"

"We'll soon know."

I dropped the jewel into the medallion and fitted the golden key into the slot at the back of its setting. Holding it at arm's length and pointed away from myself, I turned the key. There was a click as the jewel locked into place on the golden disk. The key also locked into place. Using the key as a kind of handle, I pointed the talisman at the floating monks.

"Is something supposed to happen?" Altrus asked.

As if in response, a spiral vortex formed upon the air above our heads. It was composed of bands that resembled pale mist. With little cries of dismay the monks were drawn into its turning center and vanished one by one. A fifth monk who was further away from the others made haste to levitate himself out of danger, but I turned the eye upon him, and he also vanished into the turning vortex. The strange thing was, the device made no sound. After several seconds, the vortex vanished of its own accord.

I looked at Altrus and the girl.

"That was interesting," he said.

Out of nowhere, a kind of face formed in the sky. It was composed of turning spheres of different colors that were linked by rays of light, and in the center there was a vortex that had the appearance of an eye, or a mouth. It filled the entire heavens. Words thundered from the mountainside. The voice that spoke them was deeper than any I had ever heard. Altrus and Martala clapped their hands over their ears and fell to their knees. I would have done the same, but did not dare to drop the talisman. The words were in a guttural language I did not understand, but their tone was angry.

Frantically I tried to separate the pieces of the talisman, but the key would not turn. All the hairs on my head and arms lifted and prickled, as they do when lightning is about to strike nearby. There was a terrible sense of oppression in the very air itself, which suddenly became humid and warm.

The talisman was torn from my hands by an irresistible force and flew upward toward the turning eye or mouth of the face. A peal of thunder knocked me off my feet.

8.

I awoke with Martala leaning over me, concern on her face. She had my head on her lap and laved my forehead and cheeks with a damp cloth.

"What happened?"

"You were struck by lightning or something very like it."

"The talisman?"

"Gone," Altrus said. "It rose upward and never came down."

He sat on a jut of rock, watching me with his arms folded across his chest. I tried to sit up, and on the third attempt managed it with the girl's help.

"Did more monks come back?"

He shook his head. "Either we killed all those who could fly, or their disappearance frightened the rest so much, they decided to leave us alone."

"Even so, we should not linger on this mountain."

"Agreed."

Martala prevented me from rising with her hand. "First,

explain to me how you knew the talisman would not consume us."

I shrugged. "I didn't know; I guessed. It was shaped like an eye. An eye sees only what is in front of it, not what is behind. When it was set in the hole in the green stone in the pagan shrine, it faced outward across the open mountaintop. I reasoned that whatever it did, it would only affect those in front of it."

"That makes a kind of sense," she said. "How do you suppose it came to eat all the original residents of the monastery at once?"

"They must have gathered together on the mountaintop before their shrine for a sacrifice or some other ritual," Altrus said. "When the talisman was activated, they were all in front of it."

"That is my thinking on the matter," I agreed.

"But how could the Brothers of Saint John have removed it from the stone without meeting a similar fate?"

"You saw what happened when I held it. After a short time it ceased to function. It must deplete its occult virtue within seconds, and then lie dormant until deliberately activated. They removed it during its dormant phase."

Martala took my arm and helped me to my feet. I stood swaying until my dizziness began to diminish, and noticed a blackened hole burned through the side of my boot. I raised my hand to the top of my skull and winced. Whatever knocked me to the ground had left a scorched patch on my head as it entered my body, and a similar burn as it exited my foot.

"There's one last thing that puzzles me," the girl said as we continued along the path down the mountain. "Why did Yog-Sothoth allow the monks to keep the talisman?"

"You ask too many questions," I said with irritation. The roots of my teeth ached.

"I know you, Alhazred. Don't tell me you haven't already considered the matter."

"Will it make you happy if I tell you my idle speculation?"

"It will make me less unhappy."

"It may be that the monks learned of the existence of the talisman from written records left by the former inhabitants of the monastery, and were so afraid of its power that they did not dare to use it. If Yog-Sothoth was never summoned by them, he would have no reason to become wrathful."

She considered this for a time in silence.

"Then it isn't because Yog-Sothoth hates you?"

"On the contrary, I suspect he is fond of me."

"He has a strange way to show affection," Altrus said dryly.

"If Yog-Sothoth hated me, I would not be alive. Only one Old One hates me, and we do not speak his name."

Brazen Vessel

1.

It began when I awoke in the middle of the night with something tickling my lips. I brushed my fingers across my mouth and turned on my side to go back to sleep. Then I cursed softly, sat up, found my tinderbox by touch on the table next to the bed, and struck a spark to light the oil lamp.

Martala was sleeping on the other side of the bed but she did not wake. This should have alerted me—the girl is a light sleeper—but my mind was elsewhere.

I held the oil lamp close to the bed sheets and carefully turned the top sheet this way and that. For good measure I checked under the bolster. The tickle on my lips could have been a spider. It could even have been a scorpion. My many nights sleeping on the desert sands beneath the stars had taught me to pay attention to such warnings.

There was no spider in the bed, and no scorpion. Setting the lamp down in disgust, I started to slide my naked body beneath the sheet once again, then stopped. I was fully awake. On a sudden impulse I decided to take a stroll around my walled garden.

I threw on my boots and thawb, and did not neglect my belt with my sword and dagger and Gor's white skull. Another thing I had learned from my days alone in the Empty Space was never to go anywhere without weapons. As for the skull, it went with me everywhere to remind me that I was still a ghoul.

Brazen Vessel

I might wear the body of a man, or what was left of a man's body after King Huban of Sana'a had finished mutilating it, but in my heart I was a ghoul. The Black Spring Clan had adopted me and taught me ghoulish ways when I was alone on the sands, and the leader of the clan, Gor, had given me his friendship. It was not a bond that I would ever forget.

I left through the rear door of the house. All the servants were asleep, for the hour was late. The night was mild, with a cooling breeze, and the sliver of waning moon cast enough light to show me the white gravel along the paths and the dark shapes of my fruit trees. The air was laden with their scents.

At some point in my stroll along the paths I became aware of a dark shape sitting on the bench in my rose bower, near the wall at the rear of the garden. I pretended not to notice, and idly worked my way nearer while studying the flowers my gardener had spent so many hours pruning earlier in the week.

I turned my back to the bower and bent over a flowering shrub. As I did so, I put my hand on the hilt of my dagger. I felt the shadowy figure approach silently behind me. Without betraying my intention by any motion or sound, I suddenly whirled and raised the curved steel blade to strike.

The intruder clutched me close, so that I could not strike for the heart as I intended. I found myself wrapped in filmy layers of silk and spinning like a spindle. The night air, before so silent, began to roar all around me. I was lifted up bodily off my feet and could not breathe. I clutched the slender shoulders of my attacker and gasped in a futile effort to fill my lungs. All murderous intention left me in my panic. I began to suffocate.

How long this went on, I cannot judge. It seemed a long time but when you are gasping and cannot get air, time extends itself so that a minute becomes an hour. At last my assailant released me, and I batted the folds of dark silk away from my face and drew in a shuddering breath.

I turned a complete circle, my dagger raised defensively.

44

No longer was I on the gravel path of my back garden. Desert sands stretched away in all directions, undulating in dunes to the starry horizon.

"Fear not, Alhazred, for we intend you no harm."

The voice was that of a woman, deep and musical, a voice so lovely that my ears ached when it ceased.

She unwrapped her veil of black silk from her face, and I saw that she was as beautiful as her voice. She stood tall and proud, regarding me with impassive eyes that were like polished jet. Her skin was as white as ivory. I noticed that her feet were bare and decorated with geometric patterns of henna, and that she wore golden rings on her toes. The moon revealed the swell of her hips and breasts beneath the translucent black silk of her robes.

Have a care, my love. She is not human.

I did not take her for a woman, I said in my mind to Sashi, my familiar spirit. *Is she a djinn like you?*

Not like me. She is much more powerful.

"To whom do you speak?" the djinn asked. She stared at me intently for a moment then smiled. "Of course. You have a little creature of the desert within your flesh. A *chaklah*, isn't it?"

"She is of the *chaklah-i*," I admitted.

The djinn regarded me for several moments with an expression that might have been amusement, or delight.

"You are an unlikely coupling."

"We are content."

She nodded. "I see this is so. But it is not for this that I have carried you hundreds of leagues from Damascus, Alhazred of the Black Spring Clan."

"You know my name. May I know yours?"

She drew herself up still straighter. "I am Allesalasallah, a djinn of the Seventh Circle," she said with pride.

I nodded in acknowledgement. Now that I could breathe again, I was regaining some of my poise. "Why have you brought me to this desert waste, Allesalasallah?"

"Simply this, Alhazred. We have need of your skill as a necromancer."

"We?" I looked around at the empty sand dunes.

The night air wavered and swirled, and was empty no longer. Four great figures towered above me like the massive stone statues of Egypt. They were not stone, but alive. All four were male and of threatening aspect, with attributes not wholly human. Their faces glared and leered down at me, eyes blazing with fire. Strings of human skulls dangled around their necks. Their skin was black and gleamed in the moonlight like oil.

"My brothers and I have a task for you. If you accomplish it successfully, you will be well rewarded. If you fail ..."

"What is the nature of this task?"

"The task is simplicity itself. Others of our brethren are imprisoned near this place. We wish you to free them."

"What is the nature of this prison?"

She rolled her eyes, and even that was beautiful.

"It is a small thing, a tiny thing, a trifling thing that should not resist a necromancer of your reputation for more than an instant."

"If it is so trifling, why have you and your brothers not already done it?"

"The evil sorcerer who made the prison placed wards upon it that are fatal to my kind. We cannot touch it, or even go to the place it resides. These wards were made for djinn, not for humans. They will offer you no obstruction."

"That is good to hear. I ask again, Allesalasallah of the Seventh Circle, what is the nature of this prison?"

"It is a small thing, a weak thing, a poor thing, a vessel in the shape of an urn or cauldron cast in brass."

Something tickled in the depths of my memory. This was not the first time I had heard of such a vessel, but the memory refused to come to the front of my thoughts. It was probably just something I had read in an ancient text, I reflected.

"What was the name of this sorcerer who gave your brothers such an insult?"

"He was a king of ancient times. His name was Solomon, and his people surnamed him the Great."

46

2.

"Solomon the Great," I repeated, feeling a numbness in my head. "You want me to open the brazen vessel of Solomon the Great."

"That is your task, Alhazred."

I searched my memory for fragments of the legend. Solomon was a king of the Jews, and a great magician. With his magic he compelled the djinn of the desert to build his Temple at Jerusalem, and then, because they were of evil inclination and held hatred in their hearts toward him, he made a vessel of brass and forced the djinn to enter it before sealing it and casting it into a lake or, as another version of the tale said, into the sea.

"Isn't the brazen vessel lying somewhere deep beneath the water?"

"Such was the case many centuries ago when Solomon completed his wickedness against us, but the lake has dried and turned to desert."

"If it is just a matter of opening this vessel, why do you need me? Any laborer could do this with a hammer and a chisel."

"The seal upon the lid of the vessel is not a seal that can be broken by force alone," she said. "It was cunningly made by magic, and only by magic can it be unmade."

More of the story of Solomon was coming back to me. The djinn were called demons in the tales told by the Jews. They were reputed to be evil incarnate. Then again, many have said the same about me.

There was nothing to gain by hesitation. They would kill me if I refused this task. That was plain enough. It was also clear that I could not escape them, or fight them. They were too powerful. I wondered how I was to defeat the magic of an ancient king who had fought their brothers, and beaten them? I had no hesitation in assuming that Solomon's magic was greater than mine.

"Of course I accept your trifling task. It will be my pleasure to free your brothers from their long bondage."

"It is good. I will go with you as your guide and protector."

"I thought you said you could not approach the place?"

"In my true form I could not go there, but by wearing this human shape and simulating the flesh of a mortal woman I am able to approach quite near, although I cannot touch the vessel itself."

What she did not need to say was that she would accompany me to ensure I did not find a way to flee before completing my task. I could have told her I had no intention of trying to run. How do you escape from beings of such power?

"Solomon has been dead for a long time," I said to her. "It may be that the magic of his seal has weakened over the centuries."

"It has not weakened for us."

"I am not a djinn. Solomon would never have imagined it necessary to guard the vessel from human beings. No human in his right mind would even try to approach it, to say nothing of trying to open it."

"And for this reason you were chosen. You are human, yet not completely human. You are also a ghoul, and something more that cannot be defined."

"Something more?"

"There is in you an otherness."

"It was whispered in my village when I was a small child that a djinn had visited my mother in the night, and that I was the result of their union."

"That may be the source of your strangeness. In any event, you are unique, Alhazred. Human, yet more than human."

We walked side by side across the dunes. I had no way of knowing where I was, and it seemed pointless to ask. She had brought me here, and when the time came, if she wished she would carry me back. Or kill me. One or the other.

I wondered if my enemy Nyarlathotep walked the dunes this night. Such was his custom, although he usually preferred the vastness of the Arabian desert known as the Empty Space. How he would laugh to know of my predicament. Opening that vessel, even were it possible, would be like opening the door of a cage filled with starving leopards. After all these centuries there was a good chance that the djinn inside the vessel were completely insane.

It was some consolation that neither of the companions who shared my house in Damascus had been abducted along with me. Martala had a keen mind and probably knew more of necromancy than I did, but she was still a young girl. Altrus was the finest swordsman I had ever seen, but fighting skill was no use against the wrath of the djinn. I was alone, as I had been so often at critical moments in my life, and I would either solve this dilemma alone, or die alone.

You are never alone, my dearest.

Forgive me, Sashi. You are so much a part of me, I think of us as one being. If you find an opportunity, you must leave my body and escape to safety.

I would never leave you to die alone, my sweet love.

I had not expected her to accept my offer to release her, but it was one I had to make.

It comforts me that you will be with me, no matter what may happen.

It comforts me to be with you, my love.

Allesalasallah guided me to a small valley, the floor of which was covered by drifted sand. By the shape of the basin in which it lay, formed from the surrounding hills, I could see that in the distant past it might have been filled by a lake that was fed by some river or spring.

She stopped in the middle of the valley.

"You must dig here. I cannot help you. If I touch the bronze with my fingers, or even use magic to clear away the sand, it may rebound on me and strike me down."

There was something in her manner I could not place for several seconds, and then abruptly I knew what it was. Fear. This made me uneasy. Anything that frightened a djinn of such power was worth fearing.

I looked around at the barren sand, which was rippled by the wind.

"With what am I expected to dig? My hands?"

From the thin air she produced a shovel with a steel blade. One instant her hands were empty, and the next instant she passed me the shovel. It was solid steel and wood, as real as my own bones. Shrugging with the fatalism of ghouls, I began to dig.

The night paled to morning, and the sun rose to the zenith and began to decline in the west, and all the while I dug deeper into the sand, making my pit wide and throwing the sand as far away as I could so that it would not slide back into the hole. By late afternoon the hole was large enough to swallow an ox cart.

Periodically, Allesalasallah brought me water to drink. I needed it. The hot sun sweated it out of my body almost as fast as I could swallow it.

"Are you and your brothers certain this is the place?" I asked at one point.

"We are certain."

"But how can you be sure?"

"I can hear my brothers screaming."

I bowed my head and went back to my digging.

3.

The shovel struck something metallic with a sharp clink. Using great care, I scraped away the sand and exposed the rounded edge of a flat bronze plate. I began to dig around it, and saw that the vessel was like an urn with a fat belly, capped by a flat bronze lid. It was canted to one side in the sand. Upon the lid were the raised lines of a pentagram enclosed in a pentagon, both surrounded by a band with Hebrew writing on it.

During my youth as royal poet at Sana'a I had improved myself by the study of Hebrew and other languages. I have a natural gift for learning foreign tongues.

"*And it came between the camp of the Egyptians and the camp of Israel; and it was a cloud and darkness to them, but it* gave light by night to these: so that the one came not near the other all the night," I recited.

I turned to Allesalasallah and saw that the djinn had her hands pressed firmly over her ears. Distress marred her face.

"Speak not those words aloud, Alhazred."

"My apology, Allesalasallah. I did not realize the words would be painful to you."

"They are sacred words, and filled with holy might."

"It is a verse from one of the books of Moses," I murmured, studying the seal. "How many djinn are bound beneath this seal?"

"Seventy-two."

"It must be very crowded," I could not resist saying.

She did not realize it was an attempt at humor.

"We do not occupy space as your bodies do. When we subsist in our essential nature, a grain of sand becomes a palace, and a drop of water an ocean."

I continued to dig, and succeeded in exposing most of the enormous vessel. It was almost spherical, approximately four cubits tall, without any handles on its sides. The round opening that held the seal was two cubits in diameter. The entire surface of the vessel, which was a dull-brown bronze color, was covered with arcane symbols and lines of Hebrew text. These lines of Hebrew letters wrapped around the body of the vessel as though they were ropes tied around it. The flat seal , which resembled a war shield, was held in place with molten lead that had been poured around the edge and allowed to set in the crack.

"I will need a chisel and a hammer."

Before I could finish the words, these tools were in her hands. She extended them to me and I took them.

"Hurry, human. My brothers call out to me."

I was glad I could not hear them.When I set the blade of the steel chisel against the lead, Sashi cried out in my mind.

Stop, Alhazred, I cannot bear the pain.

"Of course," I murmured, annoyed with myself for my carelessness. "I should have realized. You are a djinn. Not as powerful as these others, but still a djinn. You must leave my body, Sashi, while I open this seal."

She did not argue. I knew she would have died with me, had such a thing been necessary, but a temporary separation was not fatal to our union. We had separated before in the past, and reunited. I stood with my arms at my sides and allowed her to pour herself out of my eyes and through the hole where my nose had been and past my parted lips. There was a kind of pulling on my skin, and then a sense of emptiness and aloneness that I did not like. I had grown accustomed to Sashi's presence within me and felt incomplete without her.

I looked around the valley but could not see her. She was invisible to normal sight. In my house at Damascus I possessed the dried bodies of certain white spiders that when ingested would have allowed me to see her true form, but I had none with me.

"I will enable you to see your companion," Allesalasallah said. She made a gesture in the air with her hand, and Sashi appeared, as though made of normal flesh

She hopped across the sand on her elongated legs, turning her round head with its bat-like ears to stare at me through enormous black eyes. When she saw me watching her, she smiled and revealed a wide and lipless mouth filled with needle-like teeth.

"This won't take long, my love." I told her aloud.

She nodded her head to show that she had heard me.

Setting the point of the chisel on the band of lead that surrounded the edge of the seal, I began to chip at it and lift it with taps of the hammer. The lead peeled up like the skin of an orange. I worked the chisel around the seal, shifting my position to keep the best possible angle, until at last I returned to my original place. The last of the lead dropped away from the brass lid of the vessel.

"Lift it out, Alhazred," Allesalasallah said, emotion filling her voice. The agony of her anticipation was painful to hear.

I hammered the corner of the chisel between the edge of the seal and the mouth of the vessel, then used it to pry the seal upward. A small crack formed and I heard air rush into the vessel. Hammering some more, I got the shaft of the chisel between the lid and the side. Some force seemed to hold it in place, but I could feel it weakening. I muttered a charm of opening that I knew. In the past, I had found it useful for opening locked doors or chests.

"Recite the charm again," Allesalasallah directed.

I did so with greater focus of mind, and felt the last of the resistance fall away.

The bronze seal flipped through the air as a great rush of wind blasted out of the vessel. Far more wind came out than could ever possibly have been contained within it. In my head, not with my ears, I heard a moaning and crying and groaning, as from a multitude released from torment.

All around me on the sand of the valley stood semi-human giants. Some were male and others female. Some faces were beautiful and others grotesque. They towered over me like the lotus pillars in the Egyptian temple at Karnack, which I had walked between on one of my travels.

A male djinn freed from the vessel, who may have been their leader, spoke to Allesalasallah in the language of the djinn, and she answered. A shout went up to the heavens from dozens of throats, and I saw joy on their countenances. Then they turned their attention to me, and a silence fell over the valley.

"You spoke of a reward," I said to Allesalasallah.

She smiled at me in a way I did not like.

"Doesn't it trouble you that you have unleashed beings who hate your race, and who will work untold suffering on countless humans in the coming centuries?"

"Not at all," I answered truly. "I stopped thinking of myself as human when I became a ghoul. I care nothing about what happens to humanity. You may revenge yourselves on it as you will."

"So we shall," she said, and again I did not like her look.

Sashi, come back into me, I thought.

The little djinn leapt forward and embraced my upper

body with all four of her long limbs. I felt her pressing herself into me through the openings in my head and the pores in my skin.

I am returned, my love.

Good, I told her. *We may need to move quickly.*

"For centuries my brothers and sisters have waited for the chance to inflict torment on mankind," Allesalasallah said. "Now a man stands before them."

"A man who set them free from their prison," I reminded her.

"They are aware of what you did. It is for this reason they will make your suffering brief."

I ran to the bronze seal and snatched it up from the sand. It was heavier than it looked. Without pausing, I returned to the brazen vessel and climbed into its opening, drawing the seal down over the mouth as quickly as possible without jamming my fingers in the crack.

٩.

"Are you in pain, Sashi?"

No, my dear one.

It was as I had hoped. Once the mouth of the vessel was opened, it was possible for a djinn to enter into it and abide within it without suffering in the body. Yet when resealed, the vessel was impenetrable to the djinn from without.

From the dark interior, I heard the giant djinn talking and arguing amongst themselves. They did not sound pleased with me. I had retreated to the one place on this terrestrial globe where they could not follow. The seal of Solomon, and the bands of holy texts that encircled the vessel, prevented them from entering it, or indeed from even touching the exterior surface.

"Alhazred, come out of there," Allesalasallah said in a commanding tone from near to the outside of the vessel.

"I don't believe that would be in my interests," I told her.

"We won't harm you. We never meant to harm you. We want to reward you for your great service."

54

"I don't believe you."

A great roaring shook the vessel like a bronze bell.

"Come out at once," a deep voice rumbled. "If you do not obey me, your torments will extend for years."

I realized it was still Allesalasallah talking to me, but her anger had caused her to use her true voice.

"It's really quite comfortable in here," I told her. "All it needs is a feather mattress, an oil lamp, perhaps a writing desk and a small rug."

Angry roaring from different quarters was the only response.

"You cannot stay in there for more than a day, or at most two days. The heat of the sun will roast you, and you have no water."

I looked up at the feather-thin crack of light around the seal, and wondered if enough air was getting through the crack to prevent me from suffocating to death. If not, the need for water was the least of my worries.

"We don't need to kill you ourselves," the djinn spoke in her newly harsh voice. "We will bury you alive beneath the sands."

"Wait," I told her. "I will come out, if you grant me one request."

"You ask for the granting of a wish?" She sounded intrigued in spite of herself.

"Yes, a wish. Grant me one wish. It is little enough for releasing seventy-two djinn from their bondage."

She spoke to the other djinn in their language, and I listened while they conversed for several minutes, but I understood not a word.

What are they saying, Sashi? Do you know their language?

One says they have no need to grant you a wish, that it is better to let you die beneath the sands. Another says that it would be amusing to turn your wish against you. Still another reminds the rest that it is a tradition to grant wishes to those who do the djinn services.

A shadow fell across the crack around the seal.

"Alhazred?" Allesalasallah said in her soft womanly voice. "We have decided to grant you a wish. You may choose anything your heart desires, but of course you must not ask us to harm ourselves or destroy ourselves, for that we will not do."

I considered the matter intensely for several seconds. It was vital that I did not ask for something which the djinn believed would actually thwart their intention to kill me. I knew they would never knowingly agree to anything that would rob them of my painful termination. Their lust for vengeance against humanity was too keen. If I asked for too much, they would simply deny it. I must ask for something plausible that yet still left them a way to kill me. Once they agreed to grant me my wish, I could be reasonably sure they would not betray their sworn word.

Will they keep their word once they give it? I asked Sashi.

Yes, my love. But they will try to twist your wish against you.

"Alhazred? Can you still hear me?"

"I ask only this, Allesalasallah of the Seventh Circle—that all of your brothers and sisters leave this place without harming me, and swear never to harm me or any member of my household in any way, direct or indirect, at any future time."

She spoke to the other djinn, and they conversed amongst themselves.

Alhazred, it is not my place to correct you, but there is a fatal flaw in your conditions.

I smiled but said nothing to Sashi.

"My brothers and sisters have all agreed to your terms, necromancer, and have sworn oaths not to violate them."

"Good. Let them go from this place, and trouble me and mine no more."

A great stirring of wind sent sand hissing against the sides of the brazen vessel. Some of it even found its way through the crack around the seal and made me cough and cover my mouth with the fabric of my thawb.

When the wind died away, I stood up and used my arms to

push the seal out of the neck of my temporary prison.

At least it will not become my tomb, I thought as I crawled out to the sand.

The valley was deserted, except for the slender, black-robed figure of Allesalasallah. She smiled at me with amusement, and watched me with bright interest, as a cat watches a mouse it has just caught.

"All my brothers and sisters have departed, as you wished, and none will harm you or your household from this time forward forevermore."

"It is good," I told her. "Now carry me back to Damascus."

She laughed. "Why should I carry your corpse to Damascus?"

"My corpse?" I said, feigning surprise.

"You fool. My brethren swore not to harm you, but I made no such oath."

I stared at her with an expression of scorn. "Do you really think I fear you, Allesalasallah of the Seventh Circle? I am a necromancer of vast occult knowledge. You are no more to me than a buzzing fly of the desert. Be gone. I grow weary of your company. Or if you believe you can contest against me, do your worst and witness your futility. Your presence bores me."

Her face darkened as though covered by a shadow and twisted into something less than human. I saw rage mount in waves within her. Her form expanded and lengthened upward, until she stood not less than thirty cubits, towering over me like a man who prepares to step on an insect.

"What arrogance. Everyone calls you mad, and I see they speak the truth. Do you imagine that your puny magic can stand against a djinn of the Seventh Circle? I am older than these hills, older even than your vile and verminous species. You dare to speak to me in such a tone? I will burn the flesh from your bones."

She raised her arm and began to gesture while intoning a barbarous word of power.

I did not hesitate, but dove backward and snatched up

the bronze seal in my hands, balancing it before me as I crouched behind and beneath it, while taking care not to let my fingers project beyond its edge.

The blue sky split with a blinding flash of white light. A bolt of crackling fire arched down upon me. It struck the seal of Solomon and rebounded upon Allesalasallah, whose towering body was immediately engulfed in blue flame. She screamed and became a turning vortex, but the fire did not go out. Instead, it blazed more intensely. The vortex lost its cohesion and the flames expanded outward.

When the last of the flames died away, and nothing remained on the sand where Allesalasallah had stood but black ashes, I cautiously emerged from under the bronze seal. The fire had melted its surface so that nothing remained of the pentagram within the pentagon, or the words of the Hebrew holy verse. I slowly approached the ashes, alert for any deception, but the valley was empty. If the other djinn watched, they watched from a distance. I hoped they would remember their oaths.

You are a wonder of duplicity, my love.

"Thank you, Sashi. That is high praise, coming from a djinn."

How did you know the trick would work?

"I remembered a story of the Greeks, about the hero Theseus and his confrontation with a terrible creature known as a Gorgon, whose very glance could turn a man to stone."

How did this Theseus defeat such a monster?

"He polished his shield so that it became a mirror, and used it to reflect the destructive ray of the Gorgon's glance back at her, turning her to stone with her own weapon."

Theseus was very clever, my beloved, yet not so clever, I think, as you.

"No more praise, Sashi, you will make me blush."

You are the first man ever to destroy a djinn of the Seventh Circle.

I stared around at the desert valley with disgust. "Were I

truly clever, I would have found a way to make the hag carry us home before destroying her. As it is, we must walk."

It is not the first time, my love.

Nor is it likely to be the last, I thought, but saved the moisture in my breath for the ordeal ahead.

Isle of the Dead

The rain was so heavy and hard-driven by the storm winds that it was difficult to separate the sea from the air. I felt sand under the toes of my flailing boots and pushed myself forward through the surging water to what I thought was a beach. Soon I was crawling on my hands and knees through the foaming surf, thunder crashing in my ears above the howl of the storm and flickers of lightning blinding my night vision. There were trees ahead and a hill, that much I saw by each flash of lightning. I pushed myself to my feet, but found that the days at sea had taken away my land legs. I sat down on the sand before I fell down.

Above the wind and rain I heard my name shouted.

"Alhazred!"

"Here!" I yelled through my cupped hands.

Altrus staggered into view, supported under one shoulder by the slight figure of Martala. Lightning flashed, and I saw that something was wrong with his right thigh. A patch of blood had seeped from a rent in his pants.

There was little point in trying to talk above the shriek of the wind. I picked myself up from the wreckage of what had once been our ship and now lay strewn all around me on the sand, and made my way with my companions toward the line of trees at the head of the beach.

The trees cut the force of the wind, so that the drops of rain no longer felt like pebbles. We sat beneath the best cover we could find and huddled with our heads together.

"What happened to the ship?" Altrus shouted. "One moment I was in my hammock, asleep, and the next I was in the water."

"I think we struck a sandbar," I told him. "It broke the hull open and brought down the mainmast."

"Are we on the coast of Arabia?" the girl shouted.

"We were too far from land. This must be an island."

"Curse the Caliph and his diplomacy," the mercenary said. "We should be home in Damascus, not castaways in the middle of the Red Sea."

"When Moawiya asked me to carry his letter to King Yanni at Sana'a, I could scarcely refuse. He knew that Yanni and I grew up together as brothers in the royal palace."

"You should have made up some excuse. No good ever comes from meddling in politics."

"The meeting went well enough. Better than I expected. My mistake was deciding to take a ship for our return instead of traveling overland."

"When you take ship you put your life in the hands of the gods."

"What happened to your leg?"

"I don't know. Something gashed it when I went over the side."

"It's not a deep wound, but it has a nasty look," Martala said.

"Don't worry, I won't slow you down," Altrus said.

"Just don't die on us. We don't want to have to bring you back to life a second time."

The mercenary shuddered. "Don't even say such a thing. It is not an experience I ever want to repeat."

I knew what he meant. I, too, had been returned to life from the dead by a necromantic reconstitution of my essential salts, and it was the second most unpleasant experience I had ever suffered.

The most unpleasant was when Yanni's father, the late King Huban of Yemen, had cut off my ears, nose, and private parts, roasted them on a brazier in front of my eyes, then forced me to eat them as punishment for defiling the purity of his daughter.

When I went about in public, I wore a spell of glamour to make my face appear normal. Yanni had been astonished to see his lost foster-brother, whom he assumed to be dead, miraculously returned not only to life, but to normal appearance. He had agreed to the terms set by the Caliph in the matter of a dispute over caravan travel rights, and I had been returning to Damascus with good news and a royal letter for the Caliph. Alas, the letter was at the bottom of the Red Sea, along with my ship and her crew, unless it chanced any had survived to reach this island.

"I looked at the captain's chart for this section of the coast before we wrecked," I told them. "There was no island on it."

"What does that mean?" Martala asked.

I shrugged. "The chart must have been faulty. It's not as though islands move from one place to another."

"Don't be too certain of that," Altrus said.

"Of what?"

"I once heard a seaman tell of a ghost island that moved from place to place and wrecked ships."

I laughed bitterly. "Seamen are old women when it comes to superstitions."

"He said the island was harvesting souls, whatever that means."

"Do we still have souls, after all the things we've done?" Martala asked.

"We still have souls," I assured her. "They are not so white as they once were, but we still have them."

I sounded so convincing, I almost believed it.

2.

The storm eased its fury toward morning. By the time the sun came up above the trees, the sky was blue and the breeze mild. There was nothing to show that the night had been ripped in two other than the fragments of wood and sail and rope on the beach.

I was surprised to find no corpses.

"The men of the ship may have been washed ashore further along the beach," I said to Altrus, who limped beside me.

"If so, we'll run into them sooner or later. There's nowhere to go except into the trees."

A kind of road ran from the beach through the forest toward the heart of the island. It did not look much traveled, but it indicated some sort of human habitation. We set off along it and left the beach behind.

"It's strange there are no birds," Martala said.

"I noticed that," Altrus said. "Not a single bird chirped at dawn."

Now that I thought of it, I noticed that no insects bit my flesh. This was strange indeed. A walk in the shadows beneath the trees usually brought clouds of hungry flies. I said nothing to the others.

"Look, a man," Martala said, pointing ahead on the road.

He did not hear her, but continued with a slow pace around a curve in the road and was lost from view.

"I think it was one of the seamen from the ship." she said.

We hastened our pace, and soon saw him again, nearer this time. I called out to him but he did not turn his head. His seaman's clothes were salt-stained and his head lacked a hat. He walked with an oddly disjointed motion as though supported by strings.

"He must have hit his head when we wrecked," Altrus said.

That was the obvious explanation, but I continued to feel uneasy. Something about the way he moved seemed wrong.

We reached the man and Altrus clapped a hand on his shoulder and turned him around.

A splinter of wood projected several inches from one of his eye sockets. The other eye stared at us dully. The man's mouth lolled open, and his tongue was swollen and black. He stood without moving for several heartbeats, then slowly turned as though pulled around on an invisible rope and continued his lurching walk along the road.

"The splinter must have pierced his brain," Martala said. "He's lost his reason."

"He's lost more than that," Altrus muttered.

"What do you mean?"

"When I laid my hand on him, he was cold. He felt like a dead fish."

"There is nothing we can do for him," I told the others. "Leave him and go on."

We passed the seaman and continued ahead of him. Soon he was lost behind the trees as the road curved and the forest pressed in from both sides. There was still no birdsong.

"Look, there are others," the girl said when we had walked another quarter of an hour.

Three men dressed in the rough clothing of common seamen lurched along the road ahead. They did not converse or turn when we called to them. We approached with caution but did not touch any of them, and they did not stop for us, or even seem to realize we were there.

"This one looks like he has a broken neck," Altrus said of one man, studying the twist and tilt of his head with a practiced eye. He had broken enough necks himself to recognize one when he saw it.

"These other two look drowned," Martala said in a small voice.

A shiver of dread ran along my spine. Even a necromancer is not immune to the weirdness of corpses that walk. Looking at their empty eyes and slack faces, I had no doubt that all three of them were as dead as the man we had already passed.

"Something must be drawing them along this road," Altrus mused.

"You don't suppose—" The girl abruptly stopped speaking.

"Suppose what?" the mercenary asked.

She looked at me, and I divined what was in her mind. Another chill ran along my spine, this one more personal than the last.

"Touch my skin," I told her.

She took the hand I extended.

"What does it feel like?"

"Warm," she said, relief evident in her voice.

Altrus looked from one to the other of us, then barked laughter. "I've been dead. This isn't what it feels like."

"It feels like nothing," I said, remembering my experience.

"Speak for yourself," he said. "I was in a wonderful golden palace surrounded by beautiful women. It was a hell of a lot more pleasant than this stinking island."

We came upon the main body of the crew from the ship, eleven of them. Some showed evidence of a violent death, but the others had merely drowned. They walked almost touching, those behind pressing up against those in front, but they were not together. None acknowledged the others, and none spoke. They ignored our words. When I touched one of those at the back of the group, he stopped, then after a moment continued onward. Since they filled the road from side to side, we fell into step behind them, and eventually the three we had passed caught up with us. We let them go ahead of us, and did the same when the lone straggler with the splinter in his eye finally reached us.

"It looks like the entire crew. There's the captain. The sea must have stripped off his fine coat and taken his hat."

"Why are we alive and the rest dead?" Martala asked.

Neither of us responded. Was it mere chance, I wondered, or was there more than coincidence to it?

"For that matter, why are we following this road?" she went on. "I suspect we won't like what we find at the end of it."

"Where else is there to go?" I said.

"I'm curious," Altrus said. "I want to meet whatever dwells on this island." He fingered the hilt of his sword.

"You cannot slay the already-dead," I reminded him.

"I can make the experiment. At the very least, I can dismember whatever wrecked us here."

"Do you think our wreck was unnatural?"

"You said it yourself, Alhazred. No island exists in this part of the Red Sea."

"Very well; we will seek the masters of this island, and demand an explanation for their rude behavior."

Altrus laughed and slapped me on the shoulder. "I'll make a freebooter of you yet."

"Sometimes I think you're both mad," the girl said, but she said it with a smile.

3.

We left the trees and came upon a circular lake of calm blue water. In the center of the lake was a walled citadel of considerable size. A causeway of bricks linked the gates of this citadel to the road. We followed the crew of our ill-fated ship onto the causeway.

Across the water there came the sounds of industrious activity from behind the walls—the fall of hammers on chisels, the chop of axes into wood, the rasp of saws, the clatter of cart wheels over cobblestones. Missing from this chorus of industry were the cries of human voices.

The massive gates stood open. The stench that came through them was the vileness of rotting meat. There were no guards on the entrance arch as we walked under it. Inside, we stopped and gazed around in wonder as the dead seamen continued down the street. The citadel was a beehive of activity. Men carried stones and timber, mixed mortar, built walls, roofed buildings with tiles, laid cobblestones, and fired bricks in kilns. It was all done without overseers, and with no word spoken between the workmen.

I studied those nearest us for some time to be certain before I spoke. "They are all dead."

Altrus gestured to a man climbing a ladder with a stack of red tiles on his shoulder. "What was your first clue?"

The man's flesh had rotted away from his head, leaving little more than a skull wrapped in pieces of dried and blackened skin. He had no eyes in his empty sockets. He was missing one arm below the elbow, and from the ragged sleeve of his shirt a bare bone projected.

"What makes them move?" Martala wondered. "How do they know what work to do?"

"We saw something like this above the Cataracts in Egypt, remember?" I said to the girl.

"How could I forget? It was the thing that killed you."

An animated corpse set against me by a shaman had taken my life. Only Martala's determination and her skill at necromancy had brought me back from the land of the dead. If not for the girl, I would have been nothing but bones and dust.

"Don't underestimate them," I cautioned Altrus. "Whatever animates them may give them greater than human reserves of vitality."

We continued along the main street, stepping out of the way of the walking corpses that crossed our path, pushing wagonloads of building materials. Of horses and donkeys there were none. There was not so much as a dog or a cat. However, there were children. They worked along with the others, silent and slack of face, their flesh in various stages of decomposition.

The smell was amazing. I am a ghoul, so it did not trouble me, but I could see my companions struggling to contain the contents of their stomachs. It was perhaps just as well that they had not eaten that day.

"Do you notice anything odd about the windows and doorways?" I murmured.

Martala squinted up at the unfinished buildings. "The doors are strangely tall and narrow. And the windows are too high to look through without standing on your toes."

"What does that mean?" Altrus asked.

I shrugged like a ghoul. How was I to know?

In the center of the citadel we came upon an open courtyard, and in the center of this circular courtyard rested a black sphere that was some dozen cubits in diameter. We stopped and stared at it in wonder. Its surface was perfectly smooth, like polished glass, but it was the color of jet. It did not reflect our images, as I would have expected were it made of some wholesome substance.

"Are we going to touch it?" the girl asked.

"I'm not going to touch it," I said.

"Altrus, you touch it."

"Are you mad, girl? I'm not touching that thing."

"We have a consensus," I said.

There were no workers in the courtyard. I looked around at the walls, which rose some four or five levels to the roofs. They were unbroken by windows or doors. The only access to the courtyard was the archway through which we had entered.

"Why doesn't it roll away?" Altrus asked.

I approached the sphere cautiously and peered beneath it. "It doesn't quite touch the cobblestones."

"You mean it's floating?"

"That is the way it looks."

"What keeps it up?"

I looked at him.

He shrugged. "You always seem to have an answer for everything."

"Not for this."

"We should get out of here, right now," Martala said, eyeing the black sphere as though it were a viper about to strike.

"I think she's right," Altrus said. "We can steal some tools, cut some trees, build a raft."

"I believe you are right," I agreed. "I don't like the feel of this place."

"Fuck the feel of it; it's the smell I want to get away from."

"Find some axes and a saw. And rope if there is any. Let's get out of here."

We gathered our tools and made our way to the front gate. It was shut, and locked by some hidden mechanism.

"No point in attempting to cut through it," Altrus said. "The planks are too thick, and they're bound with iron."

"We'll find a way to go over the wall," I said.

"We have no rope," the girl reminded me. We had not been able to find any.

"Get to the top of the wall, and see if we can climb down the outside."

The walking corpses that passed us on the stairs that led to the top of the wall ignored us as though we were invisible. We peered over the parapet. The wall was built with an overhang at the top and was sheer. A spider could have climbed down it, perhaps.

"There's no way to climb that," Altrus said with disgust. "We need rope, and lots of it."

Throwing our axes and saw over the edge of the wall to the causeway below, we descended back into the citadel of the dead. By this time it was late afternoon, and the shadows were lengthening.

"There's nothing for us to eat," Martala moaned.

"Don't be silly," I told her. "There is ample meat for us to eat."

The two stared at me. I had seen that stare before. It was the look they gave me when I said something so outrageous or repellent, it caused them to reassess my humanity.

"I have no intention of going hungry. You two may suit yourselves."

I eyed the shuffling corpses as they passed, looking for one that was not too ripe.

"Food is the least of our concerns," Altrus said.

"How so?" she asked.

"Look around. Do you see any water?"

He was right. The citadel contained no wells, no cisterns, no water of any kind. The walking dead needed no water.

"If we don't get out of here, we'll die of thirst in a matter of days."

"Look for rope," I said.

We split up and wandered in different directions, searching for something with which to lower ourselves from the top of the wall, but not a strand of rope was to be found anywhere. When we came together once again, it was growing dark as twilight drew on.

"We could strip the corpses and try tying their clothing together," the girl suggested.

Altrus shook his head. "Look at those rags. They are falling off their backs, they are so rotten. They'd never support our weight."

"Maybe the gate will open," I said. "It opened for us; maybe it will open again."

"It opened to admit the crew of the ship," Altrus said. "Unless there's another wreck, why would it open again?"

I could not fault his reasoning.

The deep toll of a bell rang through the citadel, rebounding from the stone walls and tile roofs. Four times it rang. On the final peal, all of the walking dead collapsed where they stood like dolls made of sticks and rags. One fell off a ladder and hit the stones of the road with a sickening crunch of broken bones, where it lay unmoving.

"Quickly, we must conceal ourselves," I hissed.

9.

We hid in a deep doorway, concealed under shadow, without knowing why we hid. Some sense of danger had compelled me to act quickly. Now we crouched and listened to the silence. There is no silence so deep as a city of the dead. The purple of the sky turned to black, and the stars brightened. The moon in her first quarter cast down enough light to see. It seemed very important to me that we make absolutely no sound. I held a hand of each of my companions in mine and waited.

A faint rustle, like the brush of a dry leaf blown along a street by a breeze, reached the holes where my ears had been. I tightened my grip on my companions' hands and held my breath.

Something tall and thin and very black slid along the street on long legs that folded beneath it as it moved. It was not even remotely human. It reminded me of that large insect that catches its prey in its forelegs and eats them, the one they call the praying mantis. Its head swiveled this way and that on its slender neck, and its enormous eyes seemed to look everywhere at once.

It stopped at one of the corpses and bent over it. By the moonlight I saw a long, narrow tube extend from what must has been its mouthparts. This worked its way into the mouth and down the throat of the corpse, so that its stomach bulged from the movement of the tube inside it. The abdomen of the black creature pulsed, and something flowed down the tube into the corpse. Then the tube was withdrawn, and the creature moved on to the next corpse.

Raising my companions' hands, I pointed with them down the street and drew their heads closer to mine. "There's another one," I whispered, so softly I was not sure they had heard.

It was actually two of the creatures that stalked the far end of the street on their rustling legs. As they came to the corpses, they bent and inserted their tubes into their mouths.

"Are they feeding them?" Martala asked.

"I think so. It's the only way such wretched corpses could continue to work."

"What are they?" Altrus said.

One of the creatures stopped and swiveled its head with a quick motion, its long feelers twitching this way and that.

"It heard you," I breathed into Altrus's ear. "Make no sound."

It approached alertly, moving with deceptive speed on its long, folded legs. The feelers on its head seemed to test the air. I wondered if it could smell us. Our flesh was not rotting. That set our scent apart from the stench of the corpses.

It continued to draw nearer, questing this way and that, pausing to listen, until it was only a few steps away. There it stood, shivering and twitching while it smelled the air. As it started to slide toward the shadowed doorway where we crouched, Altrus released my hand and straightened his back. He stepped out into the moonlight.

"Looking for me, you ugly brute?"

The thing drew itself up on its hind legs until it towered above him, its forelegs twitching and making rapid grasping movements in the air. From some part of its body it began to emit a high-pitched scream, like the sound of a whistle.

Altrus drew his sword and severed its round head from its body in a single motion. The head rolled away, but the body continued to stand, and the scream continued. It was answered from different parts of the citadel by similar sustained shrieks.

I stepped out, drew my own sword, and cut off one of the creature's hind legs. It fell to its side, kicking and flexing its long body. We began to hack at it, chopping off pieces until what was left stopped moving.

"We need to get away from here and find a place to hide," I said.

There was no time. I doubt we could have hidden from them in any event, once they were aware of our presence within the citadel. They closed in around us with caution, but left us no avenue of flight.

Altrus stepped toward the nearest monster. "Here I am," he said.

The girl and I closed in behind him and turned to face outward at the ring of creatures.

I heard Altrus cry out and felt him stagger. I turned to look and was struck by some kind of net that stuck to my skin and clothing and would not come off. Nor could I break it. Struggling against it only tightened it around me.

Martala turned to help me, and one of the creatures extruded a kind of sticky mass from its chest and dexterously stretched and worked it in its long arms into a net. This it did in a matter of a few seconds. Before I could warn the girl, the net was cast upon her, and she too was caught like a fly in a spider's web.

They took away our swords and daggers and carried us between them, four of them to each of us, so that we swung between them like trussed fowls. As they went, they made clicking noises. I realized they must be speaking a language of some kind. The sounds emanated not from their heads, but from their chests.

"Where are they carrying us?" the girl asked.

I twisted my head, the only part of my body I could still move, and looked past my shoulder.

"The black sphere."

One of the monsters stood before the sphere and made a series of whistling tones that almost sounded like the melody of a flute. The black sphere did not appear to change, but suddenly the thing stepped forward and vanished.

"They are taking us inside," I said for the benefit of my companions.

I was lifted toward the blackness, and suddenly I was elsewhere, being placed on a table and bound there with more of the sticky string the things seemed to extrude. Altrus and Martala were bound to similar tables, and then all three tables were rotated on their pivots so that they were upright. Everything around us was black and in shadows.

"We can't be inside the sphere," Martala said. "This room is too large."

"They carried us into it, but we must have passed through it to some other place."

One of the creatures put its head close to my face and studied me. Its huge protruding eyes rolled in their sockets as it looked me up and down the length of my body. I felt one of the feelers on its head brush against my cheek and shuddered involuntarily. It was like being touched by the leg of a spider.

The mouthparts of the creature opened from side to side and the long black tube I had seen earlier extended itself and forced its way into my mouth. I tried to keep my jaw clenched but the thing used the claws on the ends of its long forelegs to force my teeth apart.

I felt the tube slide down my throat and further, inside my chest, until it forced its way into my stomach. It hurt, but only for a moment. A cool liquid spurted from the end of the

74

tube into my stomach and numbed the pain.

"Alhazred, what's happening?" Martala cried out, and then began to choke.

Rolling my eyes, I saw two other creatures insert their black tubes into the mouths of my companions. The table I was bound to felt as though it were slowly spinning.

The three things that had violated us gathered in an open space on the floor and inclined their heads until they touched, then twined the twitching feelers on their heads together. They began to click rapidly. A blackness rolled over my vision and took my mind to a dark place.

5.

When I opened my eyes, Altrus and Martala were already awake. We were still attached to the upright tables by the strands of silvery web. My throat burned and my stomach rolled with nausea, but I did not vomit.

"What did they do to us?" I asked in a croak. My lips were dry.

"You mean other than fuck us in the mouths with their black cocks?"

"Yes, Altrus, other than that."

"Nothing, so far, unless it was while we were all unconscious."

"What did they put inside us?" Martala asked fearfully. It was one of the few times I had seen the girl express fear.

"Some kind of saliva that made us sleep."

"Nothing else?"

I rolled my abdominal muscles experimentally. My stomach felt empty.

"Nothing else."

She sagged visibly with relief.

"We have to get out of here," Altrus said.

"I agree. How?"

"My sword is the finest Damascus steel. It will cut anything, even this silver web, if I can only reach it."

Our naked swords and daggers had been placed on a round table on the other side of the room. I noticed for the first time that the room was also round. Roundness was important to these creatures. The citadel itself was round. From somewhere behind the black walls I heard the pulse and flow of liquids through pipes. That was good, it would help cover the sounds of our voices.

Beside the swords was a long table similar to the tables that held us, but it was not elevated vertically. On it lay a corpse that had no head. Its torso had been cut open and laid wide with steel pins and hooks to expose its organs.

"These things must be studying us to learn how our bodies work," I speculated aloud.

Neither the man nor the girl responded. They were accustomed to me talking to myself. Altrus began to thrash back and forth against his restrains so that the silver threads cut into his skin and drew droplets of blood.

"Stop it, you fool; you'll only injure yourself."

"We need to get out of here," he repeated with more force.

"Alhazred, there may be a way," Martala said abruptly.

"If you have an idea, don't keep it to yourself. Tell us."

"Look over there, on that table. It's a dead man."

"I'm inclined to agree, since it has no head."

"We're necromancers."

I started to speak, then held my tongue. In the cellar of my house at Damascus, the girl and I had spent many nights working rituals to summon back the spirits of the dead into their decaying flesh. Most were failures, but a few had achieved a partial success. There might be a chance.

"Can we work a ritual without being able to move?"

"I think so," she said.

Martala was more skilful than I was at the necromantic arts. She had a natural gift for them. This was something I never admitted to others. It would undermine my growing reputation as a great necromancer, and that reputation was useful to me. It opened doors—and purses. Even the Caliph had taken favorable notice of me. Altrus knew the true state of things, so there was nothing to hide from him.

"How do you wish to proceed?" I asked the girl.

She named a ritual of reanimation we had worked not ten days ago, with a measure of success.

"Do you remember the barbarous words?"

"I do," she said.

"Then I will visualize the ritual circle and project it in my mind, while you recite the words of power."

It was a strange feeling, to try to work magic while bound hand and foot to a table. Most of magic functions in the mind, not in the external world, but magicians use the things of the world to direct and strengthen the ritual patterns in the mind. The world anchors magic with its solidity and density. We were trying to work it without that anchor, to perform the ritual purely on the mental level of imagination and force of will. It is immensely more difficult to do magic in this way.

I concentrated on making the circle and its symbols and inscriptions so clear in my imagination that I could see them with my open eyes. Around the corpse on the table I projected mentally a triangle of manifestation while letting the ancient words of power Martala recited echo in my thoughts. These words were so old, their exact meaning had been forgotten, but they retained their potency in works of magic. Maybe they were the names of ancient and forgotten gods. No one knew their origins, only that they held power that could be released by uttering them aloud.

The girl stopped speaking. I looked across at her, and saw red trickle down her chin.

"We need blood, Alhazred," she said, then resumed the barbarous chant.

I understood. Of all forms of magic, necromancy is most in need of the vitalizing and animating spirit that is concentrated in blood. The spirit that returns to the corpse must be fed if it is to move the dead flesh. I bit the corner of my mouth with my teeth and let the salty blood that welled in my mouth dribble from my lips. It would have been much more effective if the blood had been set beside the corpse, or smeared over the corpse.

"Altrus, cut yourself," I said.

He grunted understanding. His hand lay near his wounded thigh. He worked his fingers toward the wound and dug them into it, opening it afresh so that it flowed red. The smell of blood reached my nose-hole. That was good. It would pervade the entire room.

The ritual reached its climax. The girl and I both concentrated our wills on the corpse, projecting our combined purpose into it. For several minutes, nothing happened. Then one of the hands of the corpse twitched and lifted to grasp feebly at the air.

"Concentrate, Alhazred," Martala said between her teeth.

"I am concentrating," I told her.

Then we had no energy for talk. All our awareness went into infusing our purpose into the flesh of the corpse. It began to tremble and shake until I feared it would fall to the floor, but instead, it abruptly sat up and slid its legs over the side of the table. In another moment it lurched to its feet and stood swaying. It was a ludicrous sight, to watch it stand there without its head, but the effort to send my will into it left me with no inclination to laugh.

The dead flesh fumbled over the round table that supported our weapons and grabbed at the curved blade of my dagger, which lay outside its ivory sheath. The sharp edge of the blade sank deep into the fingers of the corpse, but no blood flowed from the wounds. The corpse twisted around and staggered across the floor to where Altrus hung.

"Focus, Alhazred, focus," Martala said, her face covered with silver beads of sweat.

I realized my own face dripped as well. There was a dull ache between my eyebrows and the edges of my vision began to go dark as my sight narrowed upon the dagger. We both concentrated in making the corpse extend its arm toward the mercenary's hand, which was held down at the wrist by the silver web.

His clutching fingers brushed the hilt of the dagger twice, then closed around it. The headless corpse staggered as though invisible strings supporting it had been cut, and it fell to the floor.

Altrus ignored it. He concentrated on turning the dagger in his hand until the sharp edge of the blade slid under one of the strands of the web. He began to work it back and forth. A strand parted, then another. The more strands of the web he cut, the easier it was to cut them. Once he got his arm free, he was able to free the rest of his body in minutes, and then cut the girl loose, and finally, me.

I took my dagger and slid it into its sheath at my belt. We collected our other weapons and went to the door of the room. It opened on a corridor.

"Which way?" Altrus asked.

"When in doubt, go right."

Neither of them objected. I led them down the right side of the long passage, wondering where the black insect-things might be. We passed many doors, all of them locked shut. At the end of the passage was an arch made of the same shiny black substance as the walls and floor. I wondered where the light to see originated. It was not bright, but neither was it dark. I reached out my hand, and it passed through the shadow beneath the arch.

"I'll go first," I said.

"A wise plan," Altrus said.

"On second consideration, you will go first."

He shrugged and stepped through the shadow, vanishing from sight. Martala and I looked at each other. After several minutes, he came back.

"Is the way safe?" I demanded.

"In a manner of speaking."

"What does that mean?"

He shrugged and stepped aside. "See for yourself."

The girl and I stepped through the shadow together. I expected the courtyard in the citadel, but we found ourselves standing beside the black sphere on a high ledge that overlooked a valley. It was all rock and sand. Across the valley we saw citadels similar to the one on the island. There were dozens of them. All of them looked deserted, presumably because it was the time of sleep for the creatures. I looked up. A small red ball burned in a black sky that was filled with impossibly bright stars.

"This is not our world," I said.

6.

The air was strangely hot and dry in my lungs. It burned in a way that did not feel healthy.

"We should not stay here long," Martala said.

"Wait a while. Look at that construction."

I pointed at two bridges that spanned the gorge between where we stood and the hill on the other side that sloped down into the valley of citadels. One bridge was narrow and looked old and worn-out. The other was wider, newer, but only half finished. On the ledge not far from where we stood were various building materials and tools that had been left by the workmen after their period of labor.

"The monsters are building a new bridge to reach our world more easily," the girl said.

"But notice how the bridges are constructed. They are supported by ropes hung from either side of the gulf."

"I see what you intend. We can use such a rope to climb down the side of the citadel wall and escape."

I continued to study the building materials, and noticed a wooden spool wound around its waist with a silvery strand the thickness of my little finger. "This must be the rope used for the bridge. We can take it back with us."

"Let's get it and get out of here. I do not like this place. The sun burns my skin."

The spool was too heavy to lift. Fortunately, its ends were rounded, and the girl and I were able to tip it over and roll it back through the side of the black sphere.

Altrus waited for us with his arms folded on his chest.

"We should have turned left."

I did not lower my dignity by answering, but merely pointed at the spool. He understood its purpose immediately. I led the way back along the passage, he and Martala rolling the spool behind me. The passage was still empty, but I wondered how long it would remain so. The black creatures must all be asleep, I reasoned, but we had no way to know how long they slept or when they would awaken.

At the other end of the corridor we encountered a similar arch of shadow.

"If this leads to another strange land ..." Altrus said.

"This time, I'll go first." Before he could argue, I stepped through the shadow and stood looking around.

It was the courtyard of the citadel, and it was late afternoon to judge by the angle of the sun, which was yellow and familiar. The others did not wait for me to report back to them, but stepped out together and stood beside me.

"Let's get this strange rope to the top of the wall and get out of this place," Altrus said, his face red and sweating from his exertions with the spool.

"Wait awhile," I told him with my hand raised.

I stood staring at the blue sky, thinking, while Altrus scowled and fought to hold his temper.

"Alhazred, we need to leave *now*."

"These creatures have done great insult to us, would you agree?"

"Yes, I agree, and we need to get out of here."

"I am of a mind to leave in such a manner that will remind them of us after we are gone."

"What do you plan to do? We can't burn the citadel. It's made of brick and stone."

"We could cut all the walking dead into pieces and deprive the monsters of their workers," Martala suggested.

"An excellent idea, but I fear it would take too long," I told her.

"Then what, Alhazred?"

"Find a wagon, and load it full of stones or bricks."

They knew me well enough not to argue when I used that tone, but they looked at each other as they went to do as I directed.

By the time Altrus and Martala brought the loaded wagon back to the courtyard, I had finished my own task and stood waiting for them.

Altrus scowled at the silver rope that trailed off the spool and out through the entrance to the courtyard. "What is the purpose of all this?" he demanded.

"Patience, my friend; you will see in good time."

I unspooled more of the rope to the extent I thought necessary and began to wrap the rest around the wagon and its heavy load, passing the lightened spool over its top and under its belly. After a while, the others helped me. I used all that was left on the spool to wrap the wagon tightly and tied off the end of the rope.

"Now what?" Martala demanded.

"Now we push the wagon into the sphere."

She frowned in confusion but she said nothing. Even with the three of us, it was no easy task. We managed to get the wagon rolling, and Altrus guided it from the front while the girl and I pushed from the rear with the excess rope trailing behind us.

"Don't stop," I said as we passed through the black shadow and entered the long passage. I was gratified to find that the wagon fit in the passage. I would have looked like a fool had it not. We grunted and strained along.

As the wagon exited the shadow arch on the far end, I shouted in warning, "Altrus, jump to the side, quickly."

He needed no prompting. The edge of the cliff was only a dozen paces from the sphere and the wagon rolled directly toward it. The girl and I continued to push until the wagon went off the edge. I grabbed her arm and pulled her away from the rope, which made a hiss as it whipped along the ground and slid over the cliff after the falling wagon.

The rope jerked tight and held for only an instant, then continued to slide into the gulf. Half a dozen heartbeats later, a mass of splintered timber and bent iron strapping burst forth from the side of the black sphere with a deafening crash and hurtled over the cliff.

We approached the edge cautiously, and were in time to see the wagon strike the rocks at the bottom. It exploded in flying fragments of brick, wood and stone.

"It would have been easier just to climb over the wall," Altrus said.

"Easier, but not nearly so satisfying," I said.

Some kind of siren began to sound from the valley on the other side of the ravine.

"The noise must have alerted them," Martala said.

We wasted no time, but hurried through the black sphere into the courtyard and made our way along the street toward the front gate. The sight that met our eyes was gratifying in the extreme. Both sides of the gate had been torn from their hinges and shattered into splinters. Pieces lay scattered all down the street. Several of the walking corpses had been caught by the flying debris and lay twitching and broken on the cobblestones with great splinters of wood through their bodies.

"They are going to try to stop us," Altrus shouted.

We began to run toward the gate as the shambling corpses assembled before us with their tools raised in their hands like weapons. What saved us was speed. Before enough of the dead managed to assemble in front of the gateway, we cut down those that blocked our progress, and ran across their headless and mutilated bodies. We were on the far side of the causeway before I dared to look back. The walking dead had not yet left the citadel.

"What now, Alhazred?"

I grinned at the mercenary without mirth. "We leave this island. If we stay here, we will surely be hunted down and killed."

When we reached the beach, we selected a single large piece of the hull from our wrecked ship to use as a support, stripped off our boots and piled them along with our weapons on top of it, and pushed it into the waves. Extending our bodies on the warm water with our hands grasping the edge of the wreckage, we began a lazy kicking rhythm with our feet. We could see the mainland on the horizon, and I judged it would take us ten or twelve hours to reach it.

"If we had done this at once, we would have saved ourselves much trouble," Altrus said.

"True enough," I agreed. "But what man can know what the future holds? We roll the dice of fate and live or die by how they fall."

"Do you think the monsters will send their island after us?" Martala asked, casting a fearful glance behind her.

I remembered the sensation of the black tube sliding into my gullet.

"It is they who should be afraid. I know of their existence now, and they have wronged me. Sooner or later I'll find a way to destroy them."

Dance of Durga

The sandstorm hit us unprepared. I should have been ready for it, but my mind was distracted by philosophical matters. Our camels fled before we could hobble them. I managed to snatch one waterskin from the back of mine as it bolted into the blowing sand. Apart from this water, my two companions and I had only the clothes we wore and our weapons. Our loose trousers, cotton shirts, and felt vests were designed for sea travel and ill-suited to the desert. We had nothing to cover our heads but bits of rag.

Three days ago we had shipwrecked off the coast of Arabia in a storm while returning to Damascus from Yemen. Fortunately, I was able to buy camels and water from a tribe of nomads on the coast. None of us wanted to return to the Red Sea, so I decided our best course was to join a caravan traveling north. Before I could locate the caravan road, the sandstorm overtook us.

The young Egyptian girl, Martala, had grown up in a land where water was always plentiful, and Altrus, although he was a battle-hardened mercenary, had spent most of his life in the cities and on roads in large companies of men. I alone knew the degree of danger we faced, and how much our lives hung on the turning of fortune's wheel. We were one waterskin away from death, and in the desert a waterskin does not go far when shared three ways.

I showed them how to protect their faces from the sand with scraps of cloth torn from the hems of their shirts, and pressed them onward, searching for some shelter where we could huddle and wait out the storm, but I found nothing. When the sand blows, there is no horizon, no sky, not even ground. We may have walked in circles, for I soon lost all sense of our direction.

At last I accepted that we would not find shelter in time to do any good, and I huddled with my companions on the open sand. We sat with our backs bent and our faces turned inward to shield them. Even though our foreheads touched, we could not talk above the howl of the wind. The sand slowly covered our feet, our legs, our hips, our backs, our shoulders, but before it rose above our necks the wind stopped blowing and it returned to the earth where it belonged. The storm had lasted almost two full days.

We stood on stiffened legs, helping each other up, and shook the sand from our bodies like dogs. It was early morning and the heat of the sun had not yet reached its peak, but already the air I drew into my lungs felt hot. It dried my mouth when I opened it to spit out sand.

All around us dunes mounted upon dunes to the horizon. There was not a blade of grass, not a bush, not a patch of shade. High above, two vultures wheeled in slow circles.

"Which way?" Altrus asked.

It was a measure of his awareness of our danger that he did not complain or speak sardonically, as was his usual custom.

I pointed toward the sun rising in the east. "The caravan road runs north and south in this region, although it winds to the east and west to reach various deep wells. If we walk east we are certain to cross it, sooner or later."

"Let's hope it is sooner," Martala said. She shook the sand from her long hair and replaced her makeshift head scarf.

I did not like the trousers I wore. The drawstrings at their cuffs made them confining and hot. I longed for my usual loose desert thawb. I had made the mistake of buying new travel clothes for our sea voyage home after the successful completion of my diplomatic mission to Yemen, and all of my garments had been lost in the wreck, apart from what hung on my limbs. At least my boots were sturdy.

We walked east at a moderate pace as the sun rose on our right shoulders. I taught the others how to step without fighting the sand. A man who does not know how to walk on sand can exhaust himself in a few hours. All my half-forgotten desert skills were returning to me. I had paid a heavy price to learn them, surviving alone in the Empty Space, which is the mother of all deserts.

Each time we stopped to rest, I let them drink from what remained in the waterskin. It was never enough for them, never what their bodies demanded, but it was enough to keep them alive and on their feet, for a while at least. I did not drink.

There was a time, I reflected, when Altrus would have cut my throat, killed the girl, and taken the water all for himself. Since coming to live at my house in Damascus, he had developed what might almost be called an affection for me. Even so, I did not hazard my life on his tender feelings, but relied on his awareness of my desert skills. Altrus knew that he had a better chance of surviving in this desolation with me than he had alone, regardless of how much water the skin contained. As for Martala, I felt confident that she could not move fast enough in the loose sand to kill me before I could defend myself.

Have I mentioned that I am not by nature a trusting man? Trust is for fools, and for the dead.

The skin was empty before we found the traces of the caravan road. I did not throw it away, for I hoped there might come an opportunity to refill it. A road meant wells, and while they were few and far apart in this place, they must exist, or the caravans could never survive their journeys north.

As it chanced, before we came upon a well, we saw the walls of a city shimmering in the rising waves of heat on the horizon. It took us four or five hours to reach it, which we did shortly before sunset. As we drew close, I made the gestures and spoke the arcane words that masked my disfigured face beneath a spell of glamour. I always do this when I approach strangers. My face tends to give them nightmares when I neglect the spell.

It was not a large city, but its brick walls had an ancient look about them that only centuries of weathering can produce. Part of the wall straddled a small oasis formed by the upwelling waters of a subterranean spring. There was no open water, but the date palms grew tall.

Before we reached the gates we heard the sounding of brass trumpets. The gates opened, and a column of armed men came forth with a splendidly robed nobleman in their van carried aloft in a sedan chair on the shoulders of four slaves. Other slaves bore three empty chairs behind the soldiers.

"Welcome, weary travelers," the nobleman said in heavily accented Arabic from his high seat, his soft white rolls of fat moving under his chin as he talked. "Welcome to the fair city of Xandakar. I am the Satrap of the city, Amjad El-Amin, and I offer you our hospitality."

I glanced at Altrus and saw his eyes already fixed on me. He raised a cynical eyebrow. It was not common practice for city rulers to greet vagrants from the open desert with the ceremony usually accorded only to visiting dignitaries.

"The hospitality of Xandakar is famed near and far," I said, stepping forward with a polite bow. "We accept it with gratitude."

In truth, I had never heard of the city of Xandakar, but when dying of thirst it is prudent to be polite.

The slaves, who appeared to be Nubian, to judge by the darkness of their skins, all with shaved heads and naked torsos, set down their empty chairs, and we sat in them. They lifted us and carried us through the open gates of the city to the welcoming cheers and applause of the gathered throng that lined both sides of the street.

2.

"This is like a dream. Am I awake, Alhazred?"

"If I am awake, you are awake," I said dryly, watching Martala.

She had just stepped out of a warm and scented copper bathtub, and now was clothing her slender, naked body in the silk garments Amjad El-Amin had ordered the mistress of his household to provide for her. They were brightly colored in blue and red and of a fashionable Persian cut. The soft slippers she put on her feet were of a similar style.

"Those clothes are completely unsuited to the desert," I told her.

"We are not in the desert."

It was a statement I could not very well deny. Even so, I was unconvinced.

Thus far, while the sun set over the western wall of the city and the stars blazed forth, we had been bathed, treated to a feast, given new clothing, and assigned rooms in the Satrap's own palace. Amjad El-Amin had informed me that a caravan traveling north was due to stop at the city in a week or so, and that he would place us upon it at his own expense. In the meanwhile, we were to enjoy ourselves as his personal guests. Anything we wanted, we had only to ask for and it would be provided.

"Your generosity to lost travelers overwhelms me," I admitted to him when he said this.

"It is an ancient custom of our city. We are far from other habitations, and those who come to us from the desert are always in dire need. It was decided centuries ago that a watch must always be kept from the wall for such wanderers, and that any who found their way to our gates should be treated with kindness, regardless of their poverty or their social standing."

As I remembered this conversation, I watched the silent departure of the two serving maids who had attended Martala while she bathed and dressed. When the door closed behind them, I turned to the girl. "Something is amiss. I do not trust this unnatural charity. Even for Christians it would be excessive."

"You never trust anything," she said, which was true enough.

"Where is Altrus?"

"He got bored and decided to find a tavern where he could throw dice."

"Did you notice how the people of the city lined up inside the gates to applaud our arrival?"

"It was thoughtful of them."

"Did you notice the expressions on their faces?"

She looked at me with mild disfavor. "No. What should I have noticed?"

"Their eyes were wide and bright, and their smiles fixed. They had the look of fanatics. I've seen religious sects with that look."

She turned away with a dismissive toss of her damp hair. "I think you worry for nothing. We're only going to be here a week. What can happen in a week?"

"It only takes an instant to die."

"Listen to yourself, Alhazred. You've been sour and suspicious for so long, you can't recognize charity when it is given. I don't want you to insult our host."

I gave up the effort to talk to her. She was not listening. The clothes and perfumes and wine had turned her head. I touched the polished white skull that hung from my belt. It was the skull of Gor, leader of the Black Spring Clan of ghouls, and my friend before his death. A merchant in a passing caravan had poisoned him and his entire clan. My clan. I was a ghoul, and no ghoul would trust a man of the city. I might wear the body of a man, but my heart and soul were those of a ghoul.

You are right to be wary, my love, said a female voice inside my head.

Sashi? What do you know?

The beautiful face of my familiar spirit, a djinn of the

desert that had chosen to share my flesh, arose before my sight. It was not her true appearance, but the one she used when she chose to show herself inwardly to me as a woman.

The Satrap of the city was not honest with you.

"Are you talking to Sashi?" Martala asked.

The girl was familiar with the one-sided conversations I held with the djinn. I was irritated by what she had said and ignored her.

Did the Satrap lie to me?

He did not tell you the entire truth. His heartbeat and breathing betrayed him.

I knew it. Something is not right about this place.

With a sudden resolve, I left the girl's room and crossed the hallway to my own accommodation. My sea-going clothes had been washed and mended, and my boots oiled. I took off the Persian silks I wore and put back on the rough garments, transferring my belt with my sword, dagger and Gor's skull. At once I felt better.

Martala followed me across the hall. "What are you going to do?"

"Nothing insulting to our host," I assured her. "I want to learn more about the history of this city. I noticed that this palace has a good library."

"Excellent," she said, turning on her heel. "Spend the night in reading and stay out of trouble."

For the next few hours I rummaged through the library while most of the palace slept. The custom of hospitality to strangers on the desert was indeed an ancient one, almost as old as the city itself, and the beginnings of Xandakar were lost in folklore. None of the chroniclers pretended to know the date the city was founded.

It retained pagan customs that the rule of the Prophet had not yet succeeded in suppressing, but that was true of many cities in Arabia. Chief among them appeared to be a ritual of expiation that took place on nights of the blood moon, when the full moon turns the color of blood. As every astrologer knows, this happens at irregular intervals during the year, but the cause of the redness on the moon's face is a matter of debate. It is said that at these times the gods are angry and lust for slaughter. Some astrologers claim to be able to predict when the blood moon will come.

I learned little about this occasional lunar festival from the scant references in the chronicles, other than its name. It was called the Dance of Durga. I gathered that Durga was the name of a pagan god or demon local to the city. The name meant nothing to me. Rites of propitiation were common in the more ancient cities of the empire. Before the coming of the Prophet, every city possessed its own gods with their wooden or stone images and sacred places. Even the Ka'aba at Mecca had been such a shrine until Mohammad had cast out all its idols. The law of the Prophet was a late-comer to the desert, and the old gods were not yet gone long enough to be forgotten.

I closed the book on the table before me with frustration and blinked my eyes to relieve their redness. Reading by oil lamp was always fatiguing. I had learned nothing to confirm my suspicions. *Perhaps the girl was right*, I thought. Maybe I had forgotten how to accept an act of kindness with good grace. But the little worm of doubt that gnawed at the back of my brain remained hungry.

I was leaving the library when Martala came hurrying down the hall. "Alhazred, you have to come at once."

"Why, what's wrong?" I said, my hand going instinctively to the hilt of my sword.

"Altrus got into a tavern brawl and killed a man. He's been arrested and put into confinement."

3.

"I'm sure it's only a misunderstanding," the Satrap said the following morning when I went to his audience chamber to speak to him.

He sat eating with obvious enjoyment, the grease dripping down his chins and glistening in the light from the windows.

He had offered me food, but I had no appetite.

"I can probably get your friend released in a day or two. Until then, I'm afraid the formalities of city law must be observed."

"May I at least speak to Altrus to ask him what happened?"

Amjad El-Amin wiped his short, thick fingers on a napkin." Of course, Alhazred. We are not barbarians. I will personally see to it that your friend ... what is his name...?"

"Altrus."

"I will personally see that Altrus is given every consideration, even though I cannot in good conscience order him released."

Martala was waiting outside the door to the city jail when I arrived with the Satrap's written order that I be allowed to speak with the prisoner. She had changed back into her traveler's clothes and once again wore her boots instead of those ridiculous Persian slippers. Lines of worry creased her young face.

"What did he say? Is he going to release Altrus?"

I shook my head and showed her the paper. "The most I could get from the fat fool is permission to talk to him."

The warder of the jail took the Satrap's seal and admitted us without comment. We were led down to the basement level where the cells were. Only a few of them were occupied. The doors of the rest stood open, as though waiting. Through the barred window on the door of Altrus's cell I saw the mercenary pacing back and forth. The guard unlocked the door and ushered us into the cell, then locked it behind us. I listened to his footsteps recede before speaking.

"How could you get yourself into such a situation?" I demanded.

"The man I killed was a cheat. The dice were weighted."

"Did you need to kill him?"

"He left me no choice. When I objected to his cheating, he came at me across the table with a knife. I acted on instinct to defend myself, and stabbed him through the heart with my dagger."

"If that's how it was, there must be others who will testify and support your account."

He smiled without mirth and shook his head. "No one has come forward. They all claim that I stabbed him in a fit of rage because I was losing money."

"And that's a lie?"

"I was losing money, that's true enough, but I don't get angry when I gamble."

For a time, I turned my back to him and studied the scratchings previous prisoners in the cell had made on the wall, while I considered what to do. The name "Durga" appeared more than once, and the words "blood moon" and "dance of death." There was an odd little drawing of a stick-figure of a man racing away from something large and poorly delineated.

"All we need to do is find two witnesses to support your story," I told Altrus. "If they are reluctant to come forward, a bribe of gold should make them more inclined to do their duty as honest citizens of the city."

"Find them quickly. I go before a judge in the afternoon."

"So soon? The Satrap did not mention that."

"There may be other things the Satrap is not saying."

"What do you mean?"

"When I went to the tavern, it was to get a sense of the tone of the city. Something is going to happen soon, Alhazred. They were keeping it secret from me with sly winks and knowing glances, but when I pretended to be drunk I heard two talking about the festival of the moon."

This quickened my interest. "Did they talk about the moon of blood?"

He nodded.

"What about the Dance of Durga? Does that mean anything to you?"

Altrus shook his head.

"What do you think they are really up to?"

"I don't know, but a city that keeps secrets is a dangerous place for the uninitiated."

The girl and I spent the rest of the morning going from tavern to whorehouse, seeking anyone who had witnessed Altrus kill the gambler. No one admitted to being in the tavern when the fight occurred, but I saw many sly sidelong glances cast from one man to another when they thought my attention was elsewhere. It was clear to me that something was being hidden.

When we returned to the jail, we discovered that Altrus had already been taken from his cell for trial. The proceedings were in progress when we arrived at the courthouse. There was no jury. A single nobleman sat in judgment, an elderly lean man with dark shadows beneath his eyes. As we entered at the rear of the chamber, an officer of the city guard was giving an account of the incident. Altrus sat upon a bench, flanked by two armed guards, a cynical smile on his scarred lips, the sear on his cheek he had received in childhood as red as a flame.

"This stranger to our city struck down the merchant Abd Al-Burza without warning as he was reaching to pick up the dice cup. He had no time to defend himself."

"That's a lie," Altrus said quietly. "He attacked me and tried to kill me."

"Silence!" the judge roared. "This is a court of law. The accused shall not speak."

Altrus shrugged.

"Have you witnesses that will support your account of the crime?" the judge asked the officer.

"There they are," the officer said, pointing at three poorly dressed men who stood together nervously blinking and staring around.

"Do you concur with this account of events?" the judge asked them.

One of them stepped forward and cleared his throat self-consciously. "We do."

"Then there is no need to waste further time on this affair. I find the accused, who gives his name as Altrus, guilty of murder. The punishment is execution by beheading, to be carried out in seven days."

He stood and left the chamber through a side door. The guards jerked Altrus to his feet and began to guide him toward the rear door.

Martala and I looked at each other.

"Swift justice," I said.

"Swift, but not just."

As Altrus was led past I pretended to stumble against him. "Be ready," I murmured in his ear.

He caught my glance and nodded as a guard shoved me out of the way.

5.

"We must prepare," Martala said. "They watch him day and night, and even if we get him away from the city there is still the desert."

"We'll need water and food, at a minimum. Camels would be useful."

"What did the Satrap say?"

"He refused to see me. I called on his chambers yesterday morning and again in the evening, but was turned away at the door by his servants."

"Did you manage to talk to Altrus this morning?"

"Only for a few minutes while I argued with the warder. He had been given orders not to let me close to his prisoner, but I managed to whisper a few words through the grille on his cell door. He had his ear pressed against it."

"What did you say?"

"I told him not to act in haste, but to wait for us to prepare our provisions."

"We only have three more days before the execution. I saw them setting up the block in the marketplace."

"It will have to be enough."

The door of my sitting room burst open, and to my surprise the Satrap entered, followed by his scribe and his bodyguard. His broad smile made his fat face beam like the sun at noon.

"Friend Alhazred, good news for you, excellent news. Your unfortunate servant is not to be executed after all."

"Good news indeed," I said. "How comes this about?"

I did not bother checking the spell of glamour that still covered my face. Had it not been there, his emotions would have been quite different.

"Well, I did not want to raise your hope falsely, but over the last few days I have been working with the city counsel on a way to save your friend." He stopped and cocked his head to the side. "Do you know any of the customs of our good city?"

"Some of them. I have been reading at night in your library."

"Splendid. Then you probably know that on irregular occasions we hold a festival in the streets. This celebration only takes place on the rare nights when the full moon is partially occluded by shadow, and turns a blood-red color."

"You speak of the night of the blood moon."

"Indeed I do. The astrologers of the city can predict when this momentous event is to occur in advance, and it seems that we are to have a blood moon tomorrow night. It is the custom of the city to conduct a rite of expiation on these nights by which the accumulated sins of the people are washed clean."

"The Dance of Durga," I said.

"Exactly. You have read of it?"

"What role would Altrus play in this festival?"

Amjad El-Amin put his fat finger to his lips in thought. "The most important actor in the festival is the one we call the Bearer of Sins. This is a man or a woman who has been judged by the council the most sinful in the city. Upon this actor's head are heaped the sins of the entire city and he carries them in the procession. By participating in the Dance of Durga, all these sins are washed away by the blood of the moon, including the actor's own sins, and he is made clean and innocent."

Martala came forward. "Are you saying that if Altrus takes part in this procession through the streets that he will not be executed?"

He laughed and the scribe tittered along with him. The bodyguard did not smile.

"My dear woman, after the festival your friend will be innocent of all sins. How could we execute an innocent man?"

The girl looked at me for guidance. I hesitated. Something about the plan troubled me. It was too easy, and the timing of the arrest and sentencing so soon before the festival seemed more than coincidental. On the other hand, it offered an alternative to a prison break and a reckless flight through the desert, pursued by the city guard.

"You must put this matter before Altrus." I told him. "It is his decision."

The Satrap laughed with good humor. "So I did, friend Alhazred, but he told me that he could not agree until you had given your opinion on the matter, so highly does he hold your judgement."

"He said that he would agree to it if I allowed it?"

"He did."

I glanced again at the girl, but what choice did I have?

"Very well, release him. I agree that he shall serve as the Bearer of Sins."

The Satrap threw up his fat white hands. "Alas, that I cannot do. Until after the festival, your Altrus is still a convicted murderer. We can hardly have him wandering freely around the streets of the city, can we?"

"But you will release him after he takes part in the festival?"

"Of course, it will all be quite different then. His sins will be washed clean and he will become an innocent."

After the Satrap said his closing pleasantries and left my rooms, Martala turned to me.

"This makes no sense. Why would they release a convicted murderer?"

"If you expect to extract reason from religious customs and city folklore, you will be forever disappointed. The Dance of Durga has been conducted in this city for centuries."

"What exactly will Altrus have to do?"

"That, I am not certain about. I will do more research in the library, but I fear I have exhausted our host's reference books on the topic."

"You could simply ask him."

"And he could simply lie to me, if he wished."

"We need to be near Altrus during the festival, so that he will have help should he need it."

I rubbed Gor's skull thoughtfully with my thumb. "Agreed. Whatever happens on the blood moon, the three of us are leaving this city together."

I did not tell the girl where the Satrap's talk of expiation of sins had led my mind. It reminded me of the ancient legend of the Hebrews concerning what they called a scapegoat, a beast that was selected to carry the sins of the city beyond its walls and into the desert. The fate of the scapegoat was not certain—by one account the goat was released into the wasteland to be prey to a demon, but by another account it was driven off a cliff to its death. Perhaps the Dance of Durga was a more innocent festival, but my heart felt heavy with my misgivings.

5.

All the day of the blood moon there was singing and dancing in the streets to the sounds of drums and flutes. The women bared their breasts and the men gashed themselves on their forearms with knives and held up their arms to let the blood trickle down into their armpits, all the while chanting the name "Durga" in a kind of building frenzy that became wilder as the afternoon wore on.

I had learned from Amjad El-Amin that the procession was to start on the hour the moon was predicted to darken and redden. It began at the steps of an ancient and disused temple of Durga and wound through the streets to the central square of the city, where a great open fire was to be lighted beside the city well as the moon regained her normal brightness. It all sounded innocent enough. I was not reassured.

The Satrap had readily given me the weapons and clothing of Altrus, who was to be dressed in a white undershirt to represent purity, covered by a black robe, which stood for his sins. Martala and I had already tied his sword, dagger and travel clothes on the back of one of the camels that were being held at the ready for us in a stable behind an alehouse, not far from the city gates. If we needed to make a hasty departure from fair Xandakar I wanted us to be prepared.

As twilight darkened into night, torches were lit all along the route of the procession. The people of the city had dressed themselves in black robes. I presumed they had white garments beneath, and would tear off the black robes at the dramatically appropriate moment of renewed moral purity. They danced and chanted in the streets in a kind of mindless ecstasy and seemed not to notice me as I made my way toward the old temple of Durga.

It was a squat structure out of keeping with the rest of the city architecture. Whereas most of the city was built of small red stones or clay bricks, the gray stones of the temple were massive. They almost looked Egyptian, they were so large. Another anomaly was the entrance. It appeared much wider and taller than the proportions of the temple would justify. The doors of the temple stood wide, but I could not see within it from my place in the street.

All the leaders of the city and representatives of its most prominent merchants were gathered on the temple steps. Young girls in revealing black dresses danced suggestively at the foot of the steps to the lilting of flutes and the tapping of drums. I counted them and found they were nine in number. Each seemed to express a different kind of sin by her stylized dance gestures. The dance had an ancient look to it, as ancient as the temple itself.

Altrus stood alone, midway down the steps. My heart fell when I saw what he was wearing. In addition to the white shirt and black robe the Satrap had told me about, he was weighed down by plum-shaped pieces of what looked like tarnished silver, each tied to a different part of his body by a silken cord. There were at least several dozen of them. Those on the longer cords dragged on the steps behind him as he moved back and forth like a chained wolf.

His restless, darting eyes fixed on me as I drew nearer. The city guard would not let me go up the temple steps. Above the noise of the music and the crowd he mouthed words, "Where is Martala?"

"She is safe," I mouthed back.

He nodded and seemed satisfied.

The music ceased and the dancers drew aside as Amjad El-Amin came forward at the top of the steps in his splendid ritual robes. He did not wear the white and black garments of the people. Perhaps he was too exalted a personage to carry sin. He raised his fat hands for attention, and the street became silent.

"This good man, a stranger to our city, has agreed to carry our sins in the Dance of Durga. The silver weights tied upon him are twenty-eight in number after the days in the lunar cycle, and each is tied with nine knots. It is at his discretion whether he chooses to run with the weights trailing behind him, or pause and untie the knots that will release each weight. If he wishes, he need not leave these steps."

The gathered crowd laughed as though the Satrap had made a particularly fine joke.

He smiled broadly and raised his hands for silence once again. "He has been well informed that when he reaches the city square, he has only to leap across the fire that burns there, and all his sins will be forgiven him."

Again, the crowd laughed. I wondered how many Bearers of Sins had ever reached the city square.

"Let us all take a moment to thank this brave and civic-minded stranger for his contribution to the well-being of our fair city."

The crowd applauded and shouted its approval. They were keyed up to an emotional frenzy and actually jumped up and down with excitement. Some of the men smeared the blood from their gashed arms on the exposed breasts of the women.

The Satrap consulted a priest, who looked at the moon and nodded. I glanced up and saw that the lunar disk had gone dark on its edge. It was beginning.

"Uncover the well," he shouted through the open doors of the temple.

From the darkness within I heard the grate of stone against stone and the clang of heavy iron bars. Four men came running out of the doorway as though their lives depended on it. Brass horns sounded. Drums resumed their tap and flutes began to trill. The nine young dancers executed elaborate dance movements in the street as the council men and nobles hastily followed the waddling Satrap off the steps, leaving Altrus standing there alone.

I looked around the street and saw that the entire population of the city, including the older children, danced to the music, but also pulled away from the ancient temple. Altrus had his head down as he studied the knots that bound one of the silver weights to his body. I forced my way forward toward the steps and was not hindered. Even the city guard was moving back.

"Altrus, get off those steps," I shouted.

He heard my voice but not my words. He tilted his head. I motioned him toward me with my arm.

He took a step, and the weights dragged him back. I realized they were filled with lead. With a more determined set of his shoulders he strode forward, and succeeded in dragging the weights off the temple stairs and onto the cobblestones of the street. Each leaden drop must have weighed at least a dozen pounds. It was like having two dead men dragging on the ground behind him. He could move, but not quickly.

Something shifted in the shadows of the old temple. I heard a kind of sliding sound, the rasp of wet leather on stone. As Altrus shuffled forward along the street, a rounded white mass emerged from the temple entrance. It seemed to scent the night air as it waggled this way and that, before working itself forward onto the steps with a kind of humping motion of its elongated, hairless body. With mounting horror I realized that it was a kind of maggot, but a thousand times larger than any I had ever seen.

6.

Altrus glanced over his shoulder and redoubled his efforts. The crowd of the city that lurked and watched some distance further down the street laughed at him, and the nine dancers resumed their sinuous and sensual mocking dance.

I wanted to rush forward to help the mercenary, but knew that any breaking of the rules of the festival would result in the crowd tearing us both to bits with their teeth and fingernails. This was the ancient faith of their city and not a thing for outsiders to violate with impunity. I was not even confident my sword would hurt the hulking monster that humped and wriggled itself blindly after him—for I saw that the white worm was blind.

An elderly man, his face twisted with maniacal glee, limped behind Altrus and began to leap and caper before the worm as if to taunt the monster. As it extended its gaping mouth forward, he darted back and dodged away from it, and all the while the worm continued to advance at a walking pace along the cobblestones.

The inevitable happened, and the bearded old man's bad leg collapsed beneath him. At once the worm was on him with its gelatinous bulk. I heard the crunch of breaking bones. It lifted its mouth in time for me to see the old man's bare feet slide into the round hole and disappear from view.

Apparently one corpse was not enough to satisfy the monster. It continued to advance with even greater avidity, its appetite awakened.

A metallic clank on the street drew my attention back to Altrus, who had paused as the old man was devoured to untie the knots on one of the weights. The watching crowd cheered as it rolled away.

Mindful of the approaching threat, he bent his shoulders and took short quick steps to open some distance between himself and the worm, which seemed unable to move itself at more than a slow walking pace. However, at no time did that forward motion of its great white body cease, or even pause. It was as relentless as the creep of sand in the wind, or as the moon across the stars. Glancing up, I saw that the greater portion of the lunar circle was stained a deep red.

So it went on, like some endless nightmare, as we progressed along the streets on the winding course laid out for the festival. The more bold or foolish of the city dwellers amused themselves by dancing between Altrus and the worm. They were younger and quicker than the old man and did not get caught, but it was a dangerous sport. Every so often Altrus would succeed in untying a set of nine knots with his fingers and his teeth, and another silver weight would fall away. He could not untie them while they were pulled tight against the weights—he had to stop to work at the knots. That was the fiendish cleverness of what the city dwellers called the Dance of Durga.

He fought valiantly to free himself, but I saw that he was losing the battle. As the weights fell off, his burden became lighter, but the effort of dragging himself through the streets exhausted him. His face dripped with sweat, and his black robe was as wet as if it had been dipped in the sea. He gasped for breath at each dragging step. When the worm drew near, it became harder for him to summon the burst of vitality needed to pull himself away from it.

The people of the city cheered him on even as they watched his strength fail. The further he progressed, the more excited they became, and I realized that wagers had been made as to how far he could drag the weights before the great worm finally killed him. To judge by their growing frenzy, Altrus was surprising them.

I resolved not to let him be taken by the worm. If it came

to that, I would rush forward and put my sword through his heart. This I came quite near to doing when he stumbled over an uneven paving block on the street and fell. The worm seemed to sense that he was vulnerable. It reared up over him.

"Altrus, get up. Get *up*, damn you!"

He heard my voice and grinned, then pushed himself off the stones with both hands and managed to drag himself forward before the white mass fell on him, but it was a close thing.

The street opened into the central square of the city, and I saw the fire burning beside the old well, the stone cover of which had been removed. I had wondered when passing the well why its cover, so heavy in itself, was bolted into place with iron bolts and straps. The well in the square and in the old temple must be access portals to the surface for the creature, I realized, one to let it out and the other to return it beneath the city.

The fire was arrayed curiously in a crescent with the well at its center. It was designed to direct the blind creature into the open well when it reached the middle of the square. Men stood ready near the well with long iron levers to lift the stone lid back into place after the worm entered it.

Altrus had done as well as any man could do, but his strength was gone. He crawled along the stones of the square toward the curved line of the fire, but could no longer stand on his feet. I saw that he had managed to untie half a dozen of the silver plums, but it was not enough. The people dancing in the square around the worm cheered wildly, sensing the end was near.

I looked at the roof of one of the buildings that lined the square, where a small fire burned, and raised my hand. A flame separated itself from the fire, and suddenly arced through the air to bury itself in the back of the worm.

The sound the creature emitted was extraordinary and quite unlike anything I had ever heard. It was a roar of outrage mingled with pain, but at the same time a deep tone similar to the deepest note of a flute, but many times lower in its pitch.

The joy of the city faltered in confusion. As another flaming arrow embedded itself in the back of the cringing worm, and another, and yet another, their discontent became outrage, then fear as the massive worm writhed upon itself and rolled to the side directly into the crowd. Several of the young female dancers were killed outright beneath its bulk, along with a dozen others. Martala continued to send burning arrows into its body with her powerful recurved bow.

In the chaos I ran forward with my dagger drawn and began to cut the weights off Altrus.

"Give me your sword," he gasped.

I did not argue but handed him my sword, and he used its straight blade to cut more of the silver plums away from his shoulders and waist.

Now the worm was rolling through the fire and bellowing its oddly musical cry of pain. All pretext of formality had been lost. The city guard used their poleaxes to push the blind creature toward the well. Its hide was incredibly tough. The blades of the poleaxes were not able to penetrate it. But the arrows continued to bury themselves in its flesh to halfway down their length, where their fletching burned like torches.

From deep in the well there sounded an answering note that was so low, it made the ground beneath my feet vibrate. For an instant the entire square fell silent and stopped moving. Then the worm thrashed its tail and the chaos resumed.

"Get me to my feet," Altrus said between his teeth.

"Can you walk?"

"I can walk. Just get me up."

Helping him up, I supported him beneath his left arm. From the corner of my eye I saw the corpulent figure of Amjad El-Amin behind the line of fire. He gestured at us and screamed something to the city guard, but his voice was lost in the general din. Most of the people of the city had fled from the square, leaving the soldiers and the dead, who lay scattered all across its expanse.

Two guards leapt over the fire and advanced on us with their swords drawn. I turned Altrus to face them. He wasted no time but killed the first with a thrust through his eye and slashed the other across the face, almost in the same motion of my blade. I left him long enough to set my dagger between the second man's ribs. When I returned, he was still standing, although he swayed with weariness and muscle strain.

We wasted no more time watching the fate of the great worm, but hurried from the square into the darkened side streets of the city that had not been illuminated for the festival, and were completely deserted. The people of the city had sought refuge behind walls wherever they could find it, and had no inclination to wander the streets.

At the stable behind the alehouse, Martala waited with our camels. She held the bow in her hand and wore a leather quiver of arrows across her back.

"You did well," I told her.

"Why didn't you shoot that fat parasite when you had the chance?" Altrus said.

"You're welcome."

"We can't kill all our enemies," I said philosophically. "At least, not all at once. When we get back to Damascus, I will see what can be done about Amjad El-Amin, the Satrap of Xandakar."

There was no guard on the small side gate in the city wall. We rode through unchallenged and turned the noses of our camels to the north.

The Caliph's Necromancer

"I am willing to do what you ask of me, but I wish something from you in return," I told the Caliph.

"Naturally," he said. "What is it?"

"Have you ever heard of the city of Xandakar?"

The young man narrowed his eyes in thought. "I believe so. It's a strange place in the middle of the desert."

"The Satrap there, a man named Amjad El-Amin, recently did me a disservice. I want him punished for it."

"It is possible that may be arranged. How severely punished?"

"Severely."

"Ah, that way. I will need to send an agent. I have little real authority over such cities, which function as autonomous city states in practice if not in name."

"It is perhaps time Xandakar were made aware of the length of the Caliphate's arm."

"I will grant your request."

He called over a senior counselor and the two talked with their heads close together for several minutes. The elderly man glanced at me with no evidence of affection and left to do his master's bidding.

"Now tell me, Moawiya, who do you think is trying to kill you by necromancy?"

I called the young ruler by his familiar name rather than by his formal title, because that is how he had asked me to address him, but it felt strange on my lips. He put the fingertips of both hands together and stared between them with a moody expression.

"It can only be one of three people who seeks my life, and all are staying with me here at the Eagle's Nest. I invited the three to my dining table this evening so that you may evaluate them. As to which sorcerer or necromancer my enemy may have hired to do the work, that you must discover for yourself."

"Is it wise to invite to dinner someone who wants to kill you?"

"I would rather have my enemy close and under watch here in this mountain fortress than plotting against me in some back room in Damascus. Besides, I do not wish to alert them of my suspicions, and they would know something was wrong if I failed to invite them to dine with me."

I sipped from my silver wine cup. The vintage was excellent. On the other side of a low table laden with delicacies and sweetmeats, the Caliph lounged on a padded couch that was covered in tasselled cushions of delicate pink and blue.

"I confess, Moawiya, I am surprised that you have chosen to place your trust in a newcomer to Damascus and a native of Yemen."

"When you rule, you quickly learn that you must trust other men. Sometimes you trust unwisely, but trust must be given, for no ruler can do everything by himself. I have watched you at your work in the Lane of Scholars since the recent death of my father, Yazid ibn Muawya, and have been impressed both by your code of honor and your abilities."

"Is that why you chose me to carry a diplomatic letter to King Yanni in Sana'a?"

"Your intimate connection with the royal family in Yemen gave me an excuse to use you."

"But I failed you."

"Not at all. You succeeded in securing the agreement. It was hardly your fault that your ship was wrecked on the return voyage and the paper lost. A paper is only a paper. It has since been replaced." He drank from his cup, and eyed me over the brim. "Why do you look surprised?"

"You are not the kind of man I expected when I learned that you had replaced your late father as Caliph."

"You expected a fop and a fool, and probably a degenerate as well." He waved his hand to stop my protest. "It's all right, everyone expected it. I took care to create that false personality."

"You played the fool so that your family would not think you a potential threat and order you murdered."

"You strike to the heart of it, Alhazred. That is one reason I like you."

To my immense astonishment, I found myself starting to like this young Caliph. He was refreshingly free from affectations, and although he put on a display of wealth and luxury for the people of Damascus, it was obvious that these things meant nothing to him. Sometimes I think of myself as an old man because of all I have seen and done, but in actual years the Caliph and I were the same age, and I felt the beginning of an understanding between us.

"Tell me more about these three you suspect."

Moawiya sat back on the cushions and stared at the intricate geometric tile work on the ceiling. "One of them is my mistress, a woman named Alyssia who has shared my bed for almost two years. She is Persian by blood, and grew up in my father's palace where she learned to dance, sing, compose poetry, play the dulcimer, use cosmetics, and become expert in all the arts of love. She was my father's lover before she was mine, but he was not fond of her, which was fortunate, given his blood lust. Recently she learned that I was contemplating a marriage alliance with a royal family in Mecca and she became more distant."

"Does she practice the arts of magic?"

"Not to my knowledge."

"And the second suspect?"

"Al-Burni ibn Mowabi, my mullah and principal advisor in affairs of state. He also served my father and now serves me. He is an elderly and learned gentleman of considerable acumen in matters of political intrigue. Lately he has been irate at my failure to more strictly enforce the code of religious law handed down by the Prophet."

"And the third?"

"Wanassah, a companion of my youth who shared my period of exile with me here in this mountain keep and at other retreats. He is of high birth and has an estate and independent wealth. There is a rumor that he was approached by a faction of noble families concerning my possible overthrow, but he is said to have rejected this treasonous plot."

I spread my hands. "They may have minor differences with you, but why would you suspect one of them of trying to murder you?"

He sat upright on his couch and set down his wine cup to lean toward me over the table. "Last week an attempt was made on my life at my palace in Damascus."

I leaned forward also and lowered my voice. "What happened?"

"It was in the private wing of the palace where I have my own rooms. Only my most trusted companions and advisors are permitted to sleep there, and it is within that part of the palace that all three of those I have named have their sleeping chambers. I awoke in my bed, aware that something had drawn me from sleep but not knowing what it might be. I was alone at the time. Listening, I heard my name called softly through my chamber door and got up from my pillow to investigate. When I opened the door I found both my personal chamber guards collapsed on the floor of the corridor, dead."

He stopped his story, and I perceived that the memory disquieted him.

"What else did you find?" I prompted.

"There was a kind of black dust on the floor just beyond the threshold. I did not notice it until after I walked through it. Quite by chance my feet were not bare, for I had taken a moment after getting up from bed to put on my slippers."

"They saved your life," I said with understanding.

"Indeed. One of the palace guards who responded to my alarm chanced to touch a black smudge on the face of one of the dead door guards, and fell instantly dead himself. A servant touched the powder on the floor to see what it might be and also dropped dead."

"The pollen of the black lotus," I said. "Its properties are well known to sorcerers who deal in poisons."

The Caliph nodded, his youthful face bleak at the memory. "Usually I do not bother putting on my slippers. Whoever tried to kill me must have known this."

"Why are there three suspects for this crime?"

"My guards made an immediate search of the corridors and rooms of the private wing, which as I said is sealed from the rest of the palace. All three of them were found awake even though the hour was after midnight. When questioned, they offered different reasons for not being in bed at that late hour. All sounded plausible."

"What were the reasons?"

"The holy man said he had sat up late to compose a letter to a friend at Medina. There were no ink stains on his fingers but parchment, ink and a pen were on his writing desk. My courtesan said she awoke from a nightmare and rose from bed to walk off her night fears. My friend claimed to be reading a book of poetry, and was able to produce the book."

"If one of them tried to kill you, wouldn't it have been wiser of that person to feign sleep?"

"There was no time. My guards began to search the rooms almost immediately after I found the two dead men outside my door."

I sat back and thought about all this for a time while the Caliph watched me and waited in silence.

"Poison is not necromancy. Why do you assume they are using magic against you?"

He took from a pocket of his robes a folded sheet of

parchment and passed it to me. It bore an occult pentacle of the most malicious kind drawn in black and red ink, but it was incomplete. Something had interrupted its maker before it could be finished.

"This was found just outside the door of Al-Burni's private study."

"Someone else may have dropped it there to cast suspicion on the old man," I suggested.

"The same thought occurred to me as well."

"Why not simply execute all three of them, and have done with it?"

Moawiya smiled sadly and shook his head. "I don't want my reign known for such capricious acts of murder. That was my father's way, but it is not my way."

"You make it harder for yourself, and more dangerous," I pointed out.

"So be it. I put my trust in you, Alhazred. Use your arts to expose the one who plots to murder me, so that the evidence of guilt is certain. When you have done this so there can be no possible doubt in anyone's mind, I will have the traitor publicly executed."

2.

The old mountain fortress called the Eagle's Nest stands at the approach to the Anari Pass and has done so for centuries. The Caliph sometimes referred to it as his hunting lodge. He spent more than a year living here in exile during a period in his life when he was out of favor with his father. It had never been designed as a pleasure palace. The purpose of the fortress was to guard the pass. The wall hangings were few and crudely woven, the floors no more than rough boards covered with well-worn carpets, and the fireplace in the great hall built of unsquared stones mortared together with a lack of sophistication.

In keeping with the utilitarian nature of the fortress itself, the cloth chosen to cover the low dining table in the hall was the simplest white linen, and the dishes of food upon it were made from pewter or wood. The fire that crackled and sparked on the hearth behind my cushion gave an agreeable warmth to my back, for the air grew chill after sunset this high in the mountains. In one corner of the hall, four musicians made a pleasant music on stringed instruments that did not hinder the table conversation.

The number seated at the table was less then twenty. Moawiya occupied its head. An elderly and somewhat corpulent man wrapped in a black robe, with gray hair peeking out beneath his turban and a long white beard that trailed down his chest, sat at the Caliph's right hand. From the description I had been given, I knew this must be the holy man, Al-Burni ibn Mowabi. He seemed in a bad mood this night. He picked at his food with a scowl on his face and barely replied when spoken to, unless it was by the Caliph himself.

Beside the sour old mullah sat an animated, cheerful man of about twenty summers with a scant black beard on his pointed chin and laughing gray eyes. This I knew from his description to be the Caliph's noble friend, Wanassah, who had shared his exile. I could see why he would make good company in this wild mountain keep. He had a free and easy wit that he managed to use without offending anyone, and a pleasant smile.

The only woman at the table was on the cushion at the Caliph's left hand. Not even an expert application of face powder could disguise that she had seen more than thirty summers. Alyssia sat with her back perfectly vertical, as though balancing an invisible water jar on her head. Her glossy black hair was done up in an elaborate and impressive structure, and haunting dark eyes beneath thick, black eyebrows lent her an air of intrigue. Her silk dress was of Persian design and shimmered with iridescent colors in the firelight. When she glanced around the table, it was as though she were throwing black darts at the other guests. Whoever she looked at immediately turned toward her. It was an impressive display of personal power, and I was not immune to it. I found it difficult to take my eyes from her.

Most of the other men at the table were young nobles or older military officers. The first group was in attendance to keep the Caliph entertained when he went riding or hunting in the mountains, and the second group to ensure his security while he was away from Damascus. None of them paid much attention to me.

They knew who I was, of course. Gossip travels through a palace faster than a bad smell. Some of them may have been afraid of my reputation. If so, they did a good job concealing it. I was left undistracted to study those present in the hall, when I could turn my eyes away from the Persian woman. It was very likely that one of them had attempted the assassination with the pollen of the black lotus.

The military men seemed interested in a tall, lean figure in black garments who stood quietly behind the Caliph, his dark gray eyes scanning the hall. They resented that a mercenary had been chosen over them to occupy this honored position as the Caliph's personal bodyguard. That was my doing. I wanted someone I could trust close to Moawiya at all times. Altrus had agreed to the task with reluctance. He would have much preferred to remain in Damascus. The foppery and empty chatter of the royal court repelled him. But he was the most deadly man with a blade I had ever met, and, inasmuch as I trusted any living human being, I trusted him.

Martala caught my eye as she leaned over an officer of the guard to refill his wine cup from her pitcher. I had caused the Caliph to place her among the female servants so that she could get close to the courtesans who were living at the fortress and sound them out for any gossip about the assassination attempt. An Egyptian by birth, from a family of tomb robbers who had pursued this profession for many generations, she was clever at this sort of game but hated playing the part of a servant.

She jerked her head back toward the door that led to the

kitchens. This conveyed nothing to me, so I merely raised my eyebrows. Frowning, she began to work her way around the table toward me.

"The table of men is no place for a woman," I heard Al-Burni say sourly to Wanassah, who laughed and made some joking remark I did not catch. With one eye on the girl, I watched the reaction of Alyssia and saw her painted lips quirk into the merest shadow of a smile.

Martala bent over my shoulder as I held up my pewter cup. "Something is not right in the kitchen," she whispered in my ear.

Before I could speak, a young nobleman called to her for more wine and she was forced to move on.

As I tried to think of some excuse to leave the table so that I might investigate the kitchen, Moawiya raised his hand for attention. The table became silent.

"Only those who are my dearest friends or most trusted servants are ever asked to share the hunt with me at the Eagle's Nest, this ancient keep that served me so well during my exile from Damascus." He raised his wine cup. "I say to you all now, eat well, drink deep, and let us enjoy our time together, for none of us knows the hour of his passing."

The entire table drank with him, even the scowling holy man. He clapped his hands and gestured toward an attendant, who nodded and went into the kitchens.

An older bald man I recognized as the senior cook at the palace at Damascus came forth bearing a round silver tray, on which rested an enormous pastry still steaming from the oven. There was genial applause from the table as he came across the hall with it held before him.

The vague smile on my own lips slipped away. His eyes had a strange lack of focus, as though he stared off at the horizon, and his complexion was unnaturally pale in the firelight.

I glanced at Martala, who watched me, not the cook. She nodded with a frown. Turning to the head of the table, I caught the roving eye of Altrus and inclined my head at the cook as he bent to deposit the tray before the Caliph.

"You have outdone yourself tonight, Hazani," Moawiya said with a smile.

The cook did not respond. There was something unnatural in his crouched posture. I opened my lips to shout a warning just as he grabbed up the carving knife from the tray and stabbed at the young ruler's heart.

He was halted in mid-thrust by the point of Altrus's sword. Its straight blade entered the cook's neck at the pit of his throat and lodged against his spine, where it held him supported. Despite the gush of blood that spurted over the steaming crust of the pastry, the cook continued to try to push forward against the sword, and it took all of the considerable strength of the mercenary's arm to hold him away from the cringing young Caliph.

The table erupted into madness, with everyone leaping up to either flee or rush to their ruler's aid. Through the milling bodies I saw Martala lean behind the cook and stab him in the kidney five or six times with her little dagger. Then some of the officers of the royal guard climbed onto the table and blocked my view. One stepped into the blood-covered pastry, slipped, and fell on it.

As I stood up on my stiff legs, I noted Alyssia was well away from the table, her expression surprisingly composed. On the other side of the hall, Wanassah supported the aged holy man, Al-Burni, by the elbow. Both wore expressions of surprise mingled with horror.

The cook was already dead when I reached the Caliph's seat. I looked down at his bloody corpse with disappointment. Had he lived, he might have told me much.

"It seems we have our assassin," Moawiya said to me. He was trembling, and there was relief in his voice.

"I don't think we do."

"What do you mean, Alhazred? He's right here."

I drew the Caliph aside so that the rest of the dinner guests would not hear my words. "That man was under a spell."

"How do you know that?"

"His eyes. He was following the will of a mind not his own."

"Do you mean he was possessed?"

"In a manner of speaking. It was not a demon who controlled him, but a man or a woman who planted the command to kill you in his mind at some time before the dinner began."

"But you can't know this for certain," he protested.

I shrugged. "You asked for my help because of my expertise in matters of magic. You would be wise not to disregard what I say."

He thought for several minutes as the hall gradually returned to some semblance of order, and the blood-soaked corpse of the cook was carried away.

"If you are correct, any of the three could have placed a spell on Hazani."

"A second attempt on your life has been made in less than a week," I told him. "Whoever is behind them must be desperate to kill you."

He looked at me, and I saw fear in his eyes. "They are going to try again, aren't they?"

"They are going to keep trying until you are dead, unless we kill them first."

3.

"Take this charm." I pressed the folded square of parchment into Altrus's hand.

He unfolded it and looked at the design drawn upon it. "What does it do?"

"Not much," I admitted. "It should prevent you from being possessed as the cook was, and may ward off attacks by magic of a minor kind."

Altrus laughed and tucked the charm away in his black shirt. "You really are becoming a necromancer."

"My reputation is still far in excess of my abilities, but I have managed to learn a few tricks over the past year."

"Martala knows more than you do."

"Yes. She probably always will. She has a gift for necromancy."

He lounged in a padded chair in my sitting room, one leg thrown up over its arm and his fingers laced behind his head. "The cook's strength was unnatural."

"You were lucky to stop him. The girl cut open his kidney and the loss of blood weakened him."

"Which of the three do you suspect?"

"The woman."

"Why the woman?"

"Moawiya is drifting away from her. She is ten years older than he. All her arts of lovemaking and her cosmetics can't conceal the lines in her face. He's ready to move on to someone else, and she knows it."

"But what would she gain by killing him?"

"Revenge. It's a potent motivator."

He thought about it and shook his head. "She is too cool, too calculating. She's not going to allow his indifference to injure her feelings. If he does move on, she will ensure that she gets everything she can get for her years of service."

I shrugged. Maybe Altrus was right. Not all women were motivated only by emotions. "You should get back to the Caliph's bedroom."

"Do you really expect something to happen tonight, only hours after the attempt in the dining hall?"

"We can't take the chance that his enemy will not strike. Another attempt so soon after the last would catch the royal guard off balance."

"I left six of the oafs watching over him while he slept. They are unimaginative but skilled at their job, and loyal enough as far as I can determine."

"Even so, I want you with him tonight."

I took out the parchment with the partially completed pentacle drawn on it and showed it to him. As he examined it, I told him how it had been found outside the door of the old mullah.

"I was able to identify it, after I mulled over it for a few hours. It's a summoning charm."

"What does it summon, or do I even want to know?"

"It calls forth a kind of wraith that is partly in this world and partly in the next. It is a thing of shadow and darkness. As a consequence, it can move through walls and is not troubled by swords. One touch can freeze the blood in a man's body and kill him without leaving so much as a bruise on his skin."

"Nasty."

"Whatever you do, you must not let it touch you. Its touch is death."

"How do I fight it?"

"You don't. You run from it, and you find the pentacle that summoned it and destroy it with fire."

"If I could find the pentacle before the wraith comes, it would save everyone a lot of screaming and dying."

"Yes, it would. Which is why I want you to return to the Caliph's private rooms and make a quiet search of his personal things—his clothing, his bed, his writing desk, his wardrobe. If a completed successor to this partly finished pentacle exists, it can only do its evil work when placed near to him, or on his person."

"How near?"

"It will have to be in his bedroom. When activated from a distance, the pentacle calls the wraith, and the creature then recognizes the man it is to kill by his appearance."

"I can't very well search the royal bed while the Caliph is sleeping in it."

"Just do your best."

Altrus chose not to argue, but pushed himself to his feet. He did not share my budding admiration for Moawiya. To him it was just a job, but I knew he would do it well.

Martala entered as he was leaving. He murmured her name in passing and went out the door.

"How are the women's quarters?" I asked her.

"Asleep, for the most part."

Something in her eyes made me smile.

"What have you discovered?"

"The Caliph's Persian mistress has taken a young lover."

"You saw them together?"

"When she left her rooms, I followed her. She met him in an alcove off the passageway, and they went to an empty storeroom to fuck."

"Don't keep me in suspense. Who is he?"

"Wanassah, the Caliph's young friend."

"She must like them young and innocent," I murmured, thinking about this information.

"Do you think they plot together?"

I shook my head. "Who can say? Alyssia may be using this foolish young nobleman as an instrument against the Caliph. Or he may merely be insurance against her expulsion from the palace."

"Either way, Wanassah is not showing great loyalty to his boyhood friend," she said.

Martala placed a great store in the virtue of loyalty. I found this an admirable quality in her nature but did not share it. In my experience, men were loyal when it suited their own purposes.

I gave her the protective charm I had prepared for her, and told her to hide it somewhere in her clothing. She did not argue but did as I directed. Then I showed her the uncompleted pentacle and explained what I conjectured to be its purpose.

She examined it with curiosity, turning it this way and that, and wrinkled her nose. "It has a funny smell."

I took it and sniffed it. Even though King Huban of Yemen had my nose and other important body parts cut off for violating the virginity of his daughter, I can still smell almost as well as the average person. By holding the parchment near my face, I was able to detect a faint sweetness. It was vaguely familiar, but at that moment with everything else that was on my mind I could not place it.

"I don't see why anyone would be in haste to kill the

Caliph," she murmured. "What has he done to warrant such frantic hatred?"

"Nothing that I know about," I admitted. "Moawiya himself can think of no reason why any of the three we suspect would seek his death."

"Can we be sure the assassin is not someone else entirely?"

"I am sure of nothing. It must be one who has close access to his chambers, and who knows his habits. Other than that, it could be anyone."

A woman's high-pitched shriek sounded faintly through the closed door of my room. I stared at Martala, and she stared back at me with wide gray eyes. After a moment, another scream came, but this time it was cut off in the middle.

There was no need to speak. I checked that my sword and dagger were still hanging on my belt, and we ran together out of the room and down the passage toward the Caliph's private rooms.

9.

Even had we not known where to go, the irregular screams and cries of alarm would have drawn us. We came upon a servant woman lying lifeless in the middle of the corridor, her arms outstretched and fingers spread, as though she had been trying to ward something off when she fell forward onto her face. We did not pause but ran past her. My heart sickened at the thought that we would be too late. I had not really believed another attempt would be made this night, so soon after the failure at dinner. It was clear that the assassin did not know the meaning of patience.

The initial screams had roused other servants and guests and brought the soldiers of the royal guard running. This was unfortunate for all of them. We began to find their bodies in increasing numbers as we drew nearer to the Caliph's chambers. They lay across each other where they had fallen like sticks of firewood.

Rounding a corner, we almost stumbled into the wraith.

I put out my arm and pushed Martala back and behind me.

It was an uncanny thing, a flickering, floating black shadow of irregular shape that somewhat resembled a monk in a cloak and hood. This was an illusion, for the shape of it was not human at all, but the mind seeks to find the human form in rocks and in the twisted stumps of trees. So did my mind suggest that the changing shadow that faded and blurred was the shape of a man, even though I knew it was not. It did not move in the usual way by a continuous progress, but periodically it dimmed and seemed to leap forward several paces and reform its nebulous void on the empty air. It sent forth slender filaments that were like long black threads, and these floated on the air in front of it. When it dimmed and danced forward, it was along these threads of darkness.

The progress it made was slow, but inexorable. As we watched from behind, a royal guard stepped forward to slash at it with his sword. The blade passed through it without effect, but the man dropped dead with an expression of surprise on his frozen gaping mouth and staring eyes. Another guard wavered, then backed away from it making a whimpering noise in his throat. The wraith, in contrast, was utterly silent.

"We have to stop it," Martala said. "It will kill Altrus."

She was right. The mercenary would not be able to resist the impulse to fight the thing, and when his sword touched it, he would die an instant death, his blood frozen in his veins.

"We can't stop it. Nothing can. But maybe—" I turned to the girl and grasped her by her shoulders. "Keep your distance. Whatever happens, don't come close to it. When you get the chance, run into the Caliph's bedroom and lead him away. Cover his face and lead him away."

"What are you going to do?"

There was no time to explain to her. The wraith was nearly at the Caliph's sitting room door. His bedroom lay just beyond it.

The door burst open and two soldiers came into the corridor. When they saw the flickering, changing mass of shadow with its array of wire-thin tendrils expanding and questing forth on all sides, their faces turned grim and went white. Through the open doorway I glimpsed the Caliph in his sleeping gown, surrounded by the four remaining guards, with Altrus at their front.

Crouching with their swords raised, the two royal guards approached the wraith with caution. It abruptly blinked forward and enveloped them with its shadow body. They dropped like statues, and their swords clattered across the floor.

Taking my chance, I darted past the thing a few paces down the corridor, and as I turned to face it, I spoke the spell of glamour that I use to conceal my disfigured features from other men. This time I made subtle changes in the words, and held in my mind the image of the Caliph. I filled my awareness with the sound of Moawiya's voice, the remembrance of his habitual posture and gestures, even the memory of his smell.

"Here I am, you mindless piece of filth," I cried out in Moawiya's voice.

I had never attempted to simulate the countenance of another man, but saw no reason why it would not work.

To my disappointment, the wraith ignored my attempt to lure it past the doorway, and instead entered the sitting room. I ran after it, holding up my arm to caution Martala not to get too near.

"Cover his face," I shouted.

Altrus stared at me, then looked at the Caliph. They were all staring at me open-mouthed past the black shadow that approached them with a gliding blur.

"Cover the Caliph's face, you fool," I shouted again.

Altrus looked around, saw a cloak on a peg on the wall, and grabbed it as the four remaining guards pulled the Caliph back toward the open door of the bedroom. He threw it over the Caliph's head and drew him to the side, away from the doorway.

"Keep him still," I said.

Dancing around the wraith and into the bedroom, I waved my arms to attract its attention. "I'm here, you mindless monster. Come and kill me."

It noticed me for the first time, and began to flow toward me. In the midst of its dark mass I saw points of brightness, like faint stars in the night sky, and realized they were its eyes. *The pentacle must be somewhere nearby*, I thought. But where?

"Alhazred, get out of the way!" Martala cried with alarm.

The wraith had backed me into a corner of the bedroom. Its tendrils expanded on either side of its body, cutting off my possible escape. I drew my sword even though I knew it would be useless. *At least the Caliph will live for this night*, I thought. The wraith would stay in the general vicinity of the pentacle until first light of morning, and then would vanish. It was occultly drawn to the pentacle, but could only identify its intended victim by sight. My altered countenance had confused it long enough for the Caliph to be led beyond the range of its senses. Or so I assumed.

The corner of the room pressed against my shoulders. I made a gesture in front of my face and dropped the false features of the Caliph, letting the thing see my true face. It continued to advance with murderous intentions. Then it hesitated. It hovered in place for several seconds as though testing the air, its black threads rippling. It began to move away from me toward the door.

I followed it cautiously with the girl at my side. It was not behaving as I had anticipated. It seemed to follow an unseen beacon. I did not believe it could recognize the Caliph when he was beyond its range of sight, so what was drawing it?

The fools had stopped to wait at the end of the corridor. I saw that it was the Caliph's doing. He stood with his head and face bare, and held a sword from one of the guards in his hand. When the thing began to glide down the corridor, the remaining guards dropped their swords and ran, leaving Altrus alone with Moawiya.

126

"I won't run like a coward from my own rooms," Moawiya said. His voice shook as he said it, but he stood his ground.

"Idiot!" I yelled from behind the wraith. "This isn't about courage, it's survival. Keep running."

"No. I'll face it here and now."

What had drawn it out of the bedroom? With the Caliph beyond the limit of its senses, the hidden pentacle should have held it in the bedchamber until morning. And then the answer came to me.

"Altrus, the cloak."

"What about it?" he said.

"The pentacle must be sewn into the lining of the cloak. We need to burn it."

He pushed the stubborn Caliph back as far as the corridor would allow and snatched up the cloak. With frantic fingers he felt around its hem, his eyes darting from the cloth to the wraith.

"Something's here, I feel it," he said.

"Rip it out. Hurry."

He tried to tear the lining of the cloak, but it resisted. Using his teeth, he made a small hole and was able to rend the lining away from the outer layer of wool. A piece of parchment fluttered to the floor.

"There it is. Quick, burn it."

He snatched the pentacle almost from under the black skirts of the wraith and conveyed it quickly to the oil lamp that burned in its bracket on the wall. For a second, the parchment refused to ignite. Then it burst into a ball of yellow flame, burned fiercely, and fell to ash. At the same instant, the wraith vanished. It happened silently and without drama. It was there one moment and not there the next.

"Is it gone?" the Caliph asked, voice shaking like that of a small child.

"It's gone," I assured him. "But there's nothing to stop whoever called it forth from drawing up another pentacle."

"Then I'll never be safe," he said with sudden realization.

"Not until the assassin is dead."

"You were right from the first, Alhazred." He turned to look directly at me and blinked. "By the Prophet, what's wrong with your face?"

I turned away as though looking down the corridor behind me and made the gesture of the spell that concealed my true features, uttering the accompanying words silently in my mind as I did so. I have applied this spell so many times that it takes me no more than a moment.

When I turned back, I smiled. "What was that you said?"

He stared at me, then wiped the sweat from his forehead with a trembling hand. "Nothing. It does not matter."

"What did you mean when you said that I was right from the first?"

He took a deep breath and released it slowly, sadness in his eyes. "I must have all three of them killed. It's the only way to be certain that the assassin won't strike again."

I put my hand on his shoulder to reassure him. "It need not come to that. I know who the assassin is."

5.

The door to the private chambers of Al-Burni ibn Mowabi was locked. I hammered on it for several minutes with my fist, and was just about to tell Altrus to break it down when the old man unlatched and opened it, blinking bleary-eyed at the light from the lamp in the corridor. He wore a sleeping gown, slippers and a sleeping cap.

"Your Highness, this is an honor," he said. "What is it you wish of me?"

"We were hoping you could help us determine the identity of the man who is trying to kill me," Moawiya told him.

He blinked in surprise. "Certainly, if it is within my abilities, I will help you any way I can."

We entered his outer room and waited while he lit several lamps. The room brightened. In addition to the sitting room that opened on the corridor, there was a bedchamber and a library with a writing desk and shelves of books and manuscripts. Picking up one of the lamps, I led the way into the library and the others followed.

"You are a scholar," I said, gesturing toward his books.

The old man looked at the Caliph and realized he was expected to answer me.

"I read the sacred texts," he said. "I ponder what has been written concerning the correct interpretation of the teachings of the Prophet."

"An admirable study." I gestured at the writing desk, which contained a stack of parchment sheets, a steel-tipped pen in a holder, an inkwell, and a small silver casket. "You also do a lot of writing?"

"I write letters to others of my kind in different cities of the Caliphate." He frowned. "May I ask what is the purpose of these questions?"

I took the unfinished pentacle from my shirt pocket and showed it to him. His face betrayed no recognition.

"This was found outside the door of your chambers in the palace at Damascus."

"What is it?"

"A work of magic. It summons a wraith from the outer spheres."

"I know nothing of such matters, or how such a thing came to my door. An enemy must have laid it there to incriminate me."

"So I at first assumed," I told him. "That you would simply drop it from carelessness seemed so unlikely."

"I know nothing about such things," he repeated indignantly, and turned to Moawiya. "Your Highness, am I to be slandered by this lying necromancer?"

I raised the pentacle to my face and smelled it. The sweet scent was still there.

I held it out to the mullah. "Smell it."

"Are you mad?"

"Do it, old friend," the Caliph ordered.

Reluctantly, the old man took the parchment and sniffed

it. Realization flashed across his face like summer lightning.

He handed the parchment back to me. "I smell nothing."

"You made a mistake at the palace in Damascus," I told him. "You didn't give yourself enough time after poisoning the Caliph's door guards and laying down the pollen of the black lotus on the floor in front of his door. The search was made too quickly. You had only minutes to dispose of the remainder of the deadly black powder. When the guards burst into your rooms to search them, they found you sitting at your writing desk with a pen in your hand, but there was nothing on your parchment."

The old man's eyes narrowed and darted to the writing desk.

"I wonder where you concealed the rest of the black dust?" I picked up the small silver casket, which was chased all over its surface with interlocking arabesques. "What is this?"

"That is my ink," he said, staring hard at my face.

I opened the casket. In it was a fine black powder.

"You mix a small portion of it with water when you are about to use it, don't you?"

"Of course. How else would you make ink?"

I raised the casket to my face and smelled its contents. The sweet odor from the unfinished pentacle was strong. I extended it for Moawiya, Altrus and Martala to sniff.

"You had only a minute to dispose of the unused portion of the black pollen. You dumped it into this casket where it mixed with your powdered black ink and went unnoticed. After the search was over, you carefully scooped out the pollen and discarded it. But enough remained that when you later started to draw up this pentacle, a trace of the pollen was mingled with your ink, and left its distinctive and unmistakeable odor."

The mask fell away from his face, leaving naked hatred. "Yes, I confess it. I tried to kill the Caliph."

"But why?" Moawiya asked. "I've known you all my life. I thought you were my friend, or at least a faithful servant. Why would you betray me?"

The old man glared at him sidelong. "You are going to rewrite the laws of the Prophet," he said bitterly. "Such arrogance, such impiety, such outrageous wickedness. I could not allow it."

"What is he talking about?" I asked.

"Next month I plan to introduce three changes to the laws of the Caliphate," Moawiya said.

"What are they?"

"Yes, tell him," the old man sneered. "Tell the necromancer the extent of your impiety."

"It is my intention to make the laws of our empire more humane by enacting three changes. First, I will decree that the rights of all women shall be protected. Second, that no man shall be put to death for any crime. Third, that all must be compelled to give up a portion of their earnings to charity."

I looked at Martala and Altrus. "That's all?"

The white-haired mullah pointed at Moawiya and almost danced up and down in his extremity of hatred. "You see? You see? We are ruled by the devil himself. Such impiety must never be allowed. It spits in the very face of the Prophet."

Without any warning, he snatched a dagger from beneath the folds of his sleeping gown and raised it toward the Caliph. I flipped the contents of the silver casket I still held in my hands into his face. He staggered back, digging at his eyes, his entire face and beard covered with black powder, and in another moment fell down dead. The dagger clattered across the floor from his lax hand.

"I thought there might be enough pollen remaining in the ink to make it fatal," I murmured, snapping shut the lid of the silver box.

Moawiya stood looking down at the blackened face of the mullah in silence. After a while he turned to me. "Is there any chance that Alyssia or Wanassah are involved in this plot?"

I glanced at Martala. "In this plot? No, they are not involved."

"Good. I would not have liked to execute them."

"But you would have done it," I said.

"Yes, I would have done it. I need to be able to sleep at night."

"Have the old man's library searched," I suggested. "You will find forbidden texts on magic. He was a hypocrite. He condemned you for transgressing the laws of the Prophet, yet he himself was a scholar of the black arts. Only a well-practiced necromancer could have summoned the wraith."

"Those additions you intend to make to the law," Altrus said. "They won't be popular with the people."

Moawiya met his eyes and nodded solemnly. "I know. A ruler can't always do what is popular. Sometimes he must do what he knows to be right."

At these words my heart was saddened, for I realized the Caliphate had at last found a wise and enlightened ruler—and I also understood that his reign would be brief.

Revenge of the Djinn

I.

I was in the alcove off my bedroom, shaving my chin, when I heard Martala yell out for me. Her cry was cut off before she could finish my name, and then I heard a kind of snap, like the crack of a whip, or hands clapped together sharply.

With my soap-covered straight razor in my hand as a weapon, I hurried from the alcove into the room, where the girl had been dressing herself before a large oval mirror of polished brass. Various articles of her clothing lay on the bed, but she was nowhere to be seen. I went to the door and opened it. The corridor was empty. There was no sound. This was hardly surprising, given the early hour. Most of the household still lay asleep. The girl and I have always been early risers. I tried the window, but the carved satinwood screens that covered it were still latched shut.

A faint odor of sulfur hung on the air, and I noticed a wisp of blue smoke. I sniffed it with alarm. It carried the stench of recent magic. The realization came to me that the girl had been abducted by unnatural means. The protective wards placed over my house to prevent just such an attack had failed.

Something approaches, my love.

Where, Sashi? The djinn that lived within my body as my familiar spirit was often able to sense things that were beyond my perceptions.

133

The window.

One moment the bedchamber was empty, and the next, a man stood before the window with his arms folded across his chest, glaring at me with an expression of malice. I hesitated for a moment, then raised the razor to my throat and continued shaving by touch.

He was an impressive figure, although I gave no indication of that. Taller than the average height, with broad shoulders and a deep chest, he wore his beard close-trimmed to a point, and his hair, which was a black as a raven's wing, straight to his shoulders. His large eyes were as dark as his hair, but his skin was uncommonly pale, even as my own skin is. I do not tan, no matter how many hours I spend in the sun, nor does my skin redden and burn. It is a peculiarity of my nature. He was dressed for the desert in a black thawb and matching black turban.

"Give me a moment; I'm almost finished," I murmured.

My eyes sought out my belt where it hung over the back of a chair, my sword and dagger still attached to it. I wondered how quickly Altrus would come if I called out to him. At this time in the morning, the mercenary was usually sleeping off the effects of the wine he had drunk the night before.

This one is not wholly human, my love.

How do you mean, Sashi? I asked silently in my own mind.

He is like you.

"You are indeed as grotesque of face as they say you are."

It was not the first time I had heard this. When King Huban of Yemen cut off my ears and nose and slashed my cheeks, he made me a monster.

"Who are you and what do you want?"

"I am Xhalarhinni."

"The name means nothing to me."

"Of course not," he said. "We have never met."

"Then why by the Old Ones did you intrude into my house and abduct my servant?"

"Perhaps the name Allesalasallah will mean something to you."

134

The sound of her name brought back the memory of her face—not her nice face, her angry face.

"She was a djinn who compelled me to open the brazen vessel of King Solomon and release her brothers and sisters who were held prisoner there."

"You killed her," he said in a tone of accusation, his dark eyes smoldering with hatred.

"It was not quite that way. She tried to kill me and I defended myself."

"Lies," he said. "You are renowned as a liar and a deceiver."

"Why should that concern you?"

"Because I have come to bring justice to Allesalasallah and avenge her murder. I am of her blood, and I challenge you to single combat."

"That is not possible," I said, edging closer to my sword. "Before her death, Allesalasallah bound herself by oath that none of her brothers and sisters should ever harm me or any of my household in any way."

He nodded, regarding me the way a man looks upon something that has become stuck to the sole of his boot. "I know of her oath. All djinn of her blood know of it."

"Then why are we talking? Bring the girl back to me and I will overlook your rudeness."

"You have affection for the woman," he said.

"No. But she is a useful servant."

"You lie. Across the length and breadth of the Empty Space you are known as a liar."

"You said it yourself, Xhalarhinni, you are of Allesalasallah's blood. You are sworn not to harm me or any of my house. Bring the girl back."

He smiled, and there was something terrible in it. "I am neither her brother nor her sister. I am her son."

I studied him. There was indeed something otherworldly about his face, his body, even the way he held himself. He was inhumanly handsome. His voice was more melodic than any man's voice had any right to be. He radiated an aura of physical strength and dominance.

"Do you mean that you are half djinn and half human?"

"Even as you are. But this is not my natural form. I have adopted it so that I may offer you fair combat as an equal."

In my village in Yemen there had been a persistent rumor that my mother had lain one night with a djinn of the desert, and that I was the result. As a boy I had always discounted the rumor, believing it based on nothing more than my pale complexion and gray-green eye color. But sometimes I wondered whether there might be truth in it.

"What do you mean, even as I am?"

"Can it be you do not know the name of your real father?"

I answered him with silence.

He laughed with delight. "I see it is so. Before I kill you I will reveal this secret to you, so that it may torment you for eternity."

"I'm not like you."

"Your mother was human and your father djinn," he said. "My mother was djinn and my father human. We are both half-breeds."

"Xhalarhinni, you have my sworn word, I never wished to harm your mother. She attacked me and compelled me to defend myself."

"Even were that true, it makes no difference. You killed her, and for that you must die."

Setting my razor down on the table by my bed, I took another gliding step toward the chair that held my sword.

"Enough delay. You will come with me now of your own free will, or I will depart and kill your woman."

"Come where?"

"I have taken her to another reality where we can conduct our duel without concern over interference."

"Another reality? Do you mean another world?"

"I inherited my mother's ability to walk the worlds," he said with a trace of pride.

"I am surprised Yog-Sothoth permits it."

His eyes widened at the utterance of the name of the Great Old One, which so few men know. He looked at me almost with a grudging respect. "The Gatekeeper would not dare oppose a djinn of the Seventh Circle."

This was an idle boast and we both knew it, but I let it pass. I kept my features impassive so that my concern for Martala would not reveal itself. "If I consent to go with you to fight this ridiculous duel, it is only just that I am permitted the choice of weapons."

He considered this, trying to think of some way such a concession could be turned against him, but at last he nodded. "I agree. Come with me, face me in single combat with your life as the prize, and I will allow you to choose the weapons."

"If I win, swear to me you will return both me and the girl to this house unharmed, and never trouble us thereafter."

"Agreed." He smiled again that terrifying smile. "And if I win, I will rip out your liver and eat it while you watch."

"If you win, swear that you will return the girl unharmed. She had no part in your mother's death."

He hesitated, his bloodlust warring with his sense of honor. At last he nodded. "Agreed."

I spread wide my arms and stepped toward him. "Then let us do this thing, so that I can be back in time for breakfast."

2.

He spread his arms, holding the folds of his black thawb wide, and wrapped it around me. My face was hidden in his shoulder. I felt the immense power of his body and realized that he could snap my spine like a twig. He said he had chosen this body so that the fight would be fair, but he had not been completely honest. He was much stronger than I was, and probably quicker as well.

The room began to spin around me and I heard a whirring sound. There was a crack upon the air. He released me, and I stumbled backward, reeling from dizziness. My stomach rolled and threatened to spill its contents, but fortunately it was empty.

It was a place of shadows, but light came from somewhere because I could see in a dim way the feet and legs of the djinn who stood in a ring around us like great Egyptian pillars, silent and motionless. Their faces high above were cloaked in darkness, but I felt their eyes watch me with malicious satisfaction. They were bound by oath not to harm me or anyone of my house. That did not mean they couldn't take pleasure in my death.

"Alhazred, I'm over here."

Martala stood inside a spinning column of air. She did not appear to be hurt, but she was terrified.

"Have they done anything to you?"

"Not yet."

"Can you walk over here?"

"I can't move."

Xhalarhinni watched me with satisfaction. So far, everything had gone as planned, and he was enjoying every moment.

"Why not just kill me?" I asked him. "You're strong enough. You must be, to have walked through the wards on my house as if they weren't there."

"That would not be honorable. You killed a djinn of the Seventh Circle. You must be accorded respect."

"You mean I get to fight a fair and equal duel before an audience of my peers?"

"We are not their equals."

"This duel is not fair," I countered. "You are much more powerful than I am."

He shrugged. "In any contest, those who fight bring their own skills. When are warriors ever equal? It is the ground on which they fight that must be the same for both."

I could not argue. In any battle, one side was stronger than the other. The concept of a fair fight meant only that the more powerful warrior was free from manipulations or deceits to use his superior skill and strength to pummel his weaker foe into submission. But there was always the element of chance, and sometimes it produced an unexpected result.

"I'm ready to choose our weapons," I told him.

"Good. Then choose."

"It is my choice that we contest against each other with dice."

He stared at me for a time. "That is a poor jest."

"It is my choice, and you have agreed to abide by my choice of weapons."

"Dice are not weapons."

"Those who use them contest against each other. There is a winner and a loser. Why should they not serve our purpose?"

He looked up into the darkness at the hidden faces of the giants who surrounded us, and seemed to speak to them silently in his mind. When he returned his dark gaze to me, it blazed with impotent frustration. Extending his hand, he made a gesture in the air and turned his palm up. A pair of dice rested there.

"Do these meet with your satisfaction?"

I took the dice and examined them closely. They were made from elephant ivory, as all of the best dice are, and appeared perfect.

Sashi, can you see any weights inside the spots? I asked in my mind.

No, my darling.

Are the corners shaved?

I do not know what this means.

Are the corners all the same? Are they straight and square?

They are the same, my love.

"These will serve our purpose," I said, tossing the dice back to Xhalarhinni, who caught them deftly out of the air.

"How are we to use them?"

"We will play a game called Over and Under. The rules are simple. We each cast the dice to establish our points. Then we cast again. Whoever has the high point must cast a lower number. Whoever has the low point must cast a higher number. If we both succeed in this, we go on to the next cast, and the numbers of our last cast become our base points. If we both fail, we go on to the next cast, and the numbers of our last cast become our base points. But if one of us fails and the other succeeds, the one with the successful throw wins the contest."

He pondered my words, looking for some deceit. "Is this a game played in Damascus?"

"I doubt it. I just invented it."

"When did you invent it?"

"While you were carrying me through the air."

He regarded me with less arrogance and more wariness. "What is the trick to it? I don't trust you."

"There is no trick, Xhalarhinni. I've explained the rules. They are perfectly fair and equal."

Again, he seemed to consult with the silent statues standing around us. "Which of us shall throw the first cast?" he asked, his suspicion undiminished.

"I give you the selection of who shall throw first."

"Then I will throw first," he said quickly.

"That is good. You throw first."

"You try to trick me. There is an advantage to throwing second."

"You may throw second if you wish. It is your choice."

His indecision might have been amusing to watch, were he not so intent on eating my liver.

"I will throw second," he said firmly.

"Good. Give me the dice."

3.

He handed the dice to me and we sat down on the ground facing each other with our legs crossed. It was hard-packed clay, and cold.

I cupped my hands together, shook them so that the dice rattled, and extended them between us to drop the dice. We watched them bounce and roll.

"A three and a two. Your number is five," he said.

He shook the dice in his cupped palms and released them. They rolled to a four and a three.

"My number is seven," he said.

"I have the lower base point, so I can only win by throwing a number higher than five. You have the higher base point, and must cast a number lower than seven."

"The odds favor you," he said with anger, glaring at me as though I had deceived him.

"Do they?" I pretended to consider them. "Yes, I suppose they are in my favor."

I cast the dice a second time and rolled a nine. "I succeed in surpassing my number. Now it is your turn."

He took the dice with reluctance. Emotions played over his face. Shaking the dice, he dropped them with anger and glared at them, then visibly relaxed. "Four. I also succeed. I have the low number, and you the high. Therefore you must cast a number lower than nine, and I must cast higher than four. Is that not correct?"

"You are correct, Xhalarhinni."

Life is always a gamble, I told myself as I accepted the dice. *Whatever happens, I am with you, my dearest love.*

I know you are, Sashi, I told her in my thoughts. It was a comfort.

Since accepting the djinn into my flesh more than a year ago, I had come to depend on her not merely for her lovemaking, which was the only act of love possible for me since King Huban had made me a eunuch, but for her wise advice. When she left my skin for brief periods, I felt empty.

I cast the dice.

"Ten," the half-djinn said with vindictive delight. "You fail to cast below your point."

"You have still to make your cast," I reminded him quickly.

"I must roll a number higher than four. The odds favor me greatly."

"You haven't gambled much, have you, Xhalarhinni?"

"Why would I gamble? I have everything I need or want."

"A gambler knows that even when the odds are greatly in his favor, it is still possible to lose."

He cupped his hands and shook them as though trying to

shatter the ivory cubes within by knocking them together, then released them, his eyes never leaving mine. "Now I take your liver."

I dropped my gaze, and let out my breath. "Three."

He slammed his clenched fists into the clay, and I felt the vibration of the ground through the bones of my buttocks.

"You are cheating. I know you, Alhazred of the Black Spring Clan. You are a liar and a deceiver. Everything you do is a tissue of lies. You have found a way to cheat."

"They are your dice, Xhalarhinni, not mine," I reminded him calmly.

"This is an idiot's duel. Take up a sword and fight me like a man."

"If you wish to forfeit the duel, say so."

He calmed himself with an effort of will. Only his eyes continued to blaze. "You must cast below ten, I must cast above three. Is that correct?"

"That is correct," I told him.

For some reason, I had a bad feeling when I picked up the dice. Call it a foreshadowing. I rolled them between my fingers and tried to calm myself. There was nothing to be gained by hesitation. I cupped my hands and dropped the dice.

"A five and a six. Eleven. You fail," he said.

With an eager hand he snatched up the dice and shook them, then released them. I knew the outcome before the dice stopped rolling.

"Seven. I cast a seven. I have won the duel. Your flesh is mine."

Snatching up the dice, I leaped to my feet and held them high above my head. "Djinn of the Seventh Circle," I shouted upward into the darkness. "I demand justice. Xhalarhinni has cheated. These dice have been tampered with."

"You lie, false dog."

"Where is the honor of the Seventh Circle? Examine these dice and tell me they are not weighted."

"Do not listen to Alhazred. He is a deceiver. He deceived your sister, Allesalasallah, to her death."

I did not turn to face him, but I expected his sword to cut me down from behind at any moment. The sword-stroke never came. Instead, one of the giants extended a hand, and I placed the pair of dice on the vast expanse of its palm. The hand rose upward and vanished into the shadows.

Were the dice weighted, Sashi? I asked in my mind.

I do not know, Alhazred.

Martala's gaze was upon me. All during the dicing she had not uttered a single word. Her face was calm and resolute. Whatever the outcome, I knew she would face it better than I. Her courage was far greater than mine.

The outcome would depend on whether I had interpreted Xhalarhinni's nature rightly, and whether the djinn of the Seventh Circle truly did have a code of honor. It was another gamble, like a throw of the dice, but this time the odds were long indeed.

"You and the woman will be returned to Damascus," a deep voice rolled down like thunder from the heavens.

"No!" Xhalarhinni screamed. "You swore to me that I would have my vengeance."

"The half-blood sought to deceive you," the voice continued, ignoring Xhalarhinni as though he were a petulant child. "The dice are indeed weighted, as you said they were."

Xhalarhinni drew his sword and tried to rush upon me, but some invisible force held him back.

"I have not done with you, necromancer," he said venomously.

"Be true to your word, and trouble me and my house no more," I told him.

"You will never learn who your father is," he said, and vanished.

The column of light that held Martala prisoner faded away, and she ran to embrace me. The air around us began to spin and roar.

"How did you know?" she shouted into my ear-hole, holding me tight.

"Xhalarhinni could not believe I would contest with him

fairly," I said with lips close to the side of her head. "He was certain I would try to cheat, so I decided to choose a weapon that would ensure complete fairness. Since he was so convinced I would cheat, I judged that he would not be able to resist cheating himself, to avoid being cheated."

"Then you weren't certain the last cast of the dice would be loaded?"

"It was a gamble," I admitted. "What are the days of our lives, but one throw of the dice after another?"

Her answer was lost in the roar of the wind. I felt the ground fall away beneath my feet.

Hand of Nilus

I.

The audience chamber of Abbot John Climacus, leader of the Holy Monastery of Sinai, was surprisingly well furnished. Colorful tapestries hung on the walls and an excellent Persian rug covered the floorboards. Shelves of books stood behind his intricately carved writing desk. Above them hung a painted wooden panel of Christ as a babe, sitting in the lap of the Virgin Mary.

The abbot was a spry little bearded man well past middle age, but the twinkle in his blue eyes made him appear much younger. He wore robes of white silk, embroidered at the hem in a discreet way with gold thread. His eyes strayed to the polished skull that hung at my belt, but he made no comment. I wondered how he would react to my grotesquely disfigured face, which at present was concealed behind a spell of glamour.

Indicating that I should sit in a chair padded with red velvet, he went to a table against the wall and poured pale wine into two silver cups that were adorned on their sides with crosses. He handed me a cup and pulled a chair around to face mine.

I sampled the wine. It was excellent, much better than would be expected in such a rocky and barren wasteland. It took the utmost care and constant tending to make anything grow here. The only green lay just beyond the high monastery walls where the monks watered their orchard

145

and garden daily. The steep slopes of the gorge at the base of Mount Sinai had not a single blade of grass. I could see one of them out the window, rising like the wall of a prison to block half the blue sky.

"The arrival of your camels caused quite a stir among the brothers," he said in Greek with a smile. "We get few visitors here, and most of them are Christians."

"I hope we are not an inconvenience," I said, sipping from my cup.

"Not at all. You are a novelty. You may stay as long as you wish. But tell me, Abdul Alhazred, what brings you to Sinai?"

From the side pocket of my dusty white thawb, I took a parchment and passed it to him.

He unfolded it and studied it for a moment, then laughed. "I haven't seen one of these in years. I thought they had all perished."

"Is it genuine?"

He studied the parchment more closely and nodded. "That is my predecessor's seal at the bottom. It was before my time, but I'm told he had a hundred of these penned and sent out to all corners of Christendom and the Caliphate. Where did you happen across this one?"

"In Damascus. I keep a house in Damascus. My serving girl bought it from a traveling merchant in the marketplace."

"I hope she didn't pay very much."

"Why do you say that?"

He shrugged with a smile. "Well, it's a fool's errand. When I say that, I cast no aspersion on you, of course."

"The parchment offers to pay the sum of one thousand pieces of silver to anyone who can locate the lost relic it mentions. Is the offer not genuine?"

"Indeed it is genuine. We keep a store of silver coins set aside just for this purpose, as instructed by my late predecessor, Abbot Cyril Junius. But you should be aware that since this letter was sent out some twenty years ago, at least three dozen treasure seekers have tried and failed to find the relic."

"Even so, I wish to make the attempt. I have a natural gift for finding lost articles."

"By all means, you may try your hand ... try your hand, that's rather good, isn't it?"

He laughed at his own wit, and I forced a smile.

"The parchment says little about the relic. I was hoping you could describe it more precisely."

"Well, it's a hand, isn't it? The severed left hand of Saint Nilus the Elder, who used to live in a cave near here with his son, Theodulus. That was before the followers of the Prophet Mohammed drove all the solitary Christian hermits out of the mountains."

I looked around the chamber. "I'm surprised this monastery wasn't looted and swept away with them."

"Thank our strong, high walls for that, and the wisdom of your Prophet, who signed a decree that this monastery and its monks should never be molested."

"About the hand: how shall I know it when I find it?"

He finished his wine and leaned over to set his empty cup on the table. "All we have is monastery folklore to guide us. My predecessor was a bit of a fanatic about the subject, but I know far less than he did. Let me think. It was said to be a left hand intact down to the middle of the forearm, mounted in a base of silver and ringed with seven rings of gold from the base up to the wrist. Each of the fingernails is set with a different gemstone. The hand is mummified, you see, and if it exists, is probably as hard as wood."

"The left hand? Are you sure?"

"So the chronicle says. The rest of the relics of Saint Nilus were transferred to Constantinople under the order of Emperor Justin the Younger and placed in the Church of the Holy Apostles, but for some reason the left hand was overlooked. That was over a century ago."

He paused frowning and seemed to hesitate, undecided whether to go on.

"Why would it be overlooked?" I asked to prompt him.

"It's a silly story, really. I don't know if I should even tell it, especially not to a … non-Christian."

"It would be quite helpful to have as much information as is available, if I am to search for this relic."

"There is a story—a fable, if you will—that the left hand is cursed. It is said that Saint Nilus would bless with his right hand and curse with his left hand. It's a silly story the younger monks sometimes tell each other at bedtime, to give themselves the shivers. I'm sure that such a holy monk as Nilus would never curse anyone."

"Yet it is possible that if the agents of the Emperor Justin heard this story, they may have deliberately left behind this relic."

"Or even destroyed it," Climacus agreed. "Although, given the veneration heaped on relics during that period, it's doubtful anyone would dare to do such a thing. Abbot Cyril became convinced that it was hidden somewhere in or near the monastery, and that its malefic influence was blighting our crops and sickening our livestock. He was an old man and his mind was not quite sound near the end of his years. He had these horrible nightmares that would cause him to wake up screaming, 'The hand! The hand!' Poor man."

I shook my head and lowered my gaze in mock sympathy. "But the offer is genuine and current?"

"Yes, indeed. If you find the hand of Nilus, I will personally present you with a thousand pieces of silver that were minted at Constantinople. We must honor the contract sent forth across the world by Abbot Cyril."

I stood, and he rose from his chair as well.

"If you will give us the freedom of the monastery and its grounds, my companions and I will begin our search immediately."

"You have it. You may go anywhere you like, with the exception of the private cells of the monks, who cannot be interrupted while at prayer."

"Naturally, we will strive to avoid any disruption in the

routine of the brothers."

He put his hand on my arm. "There is one other thing. It's foolish for me to even mention it, but I feel I must if you are to know all the folklore about the relic."

I waited for him to continue.

"When you do find the hand, don't touch it. Nothing more than superstitious nonsense, I'm sure, but the stories say that the touch of the hand is death."

2.

"The way I see it, we have three roads before us," Altrus said.

"What would those be?" I asked as I adjusted the wick of my brass oil lamp to give a larger flame.

"One, we make a genuine effort to find this relic. Two, we substitute another mummified hand in its place."

"That won't work," I cut in. "The Abbot's description was depressingly detailed."

"In any case, where would we get a mummified hand?" Martala asked from her seat atop one of the sepulchres. "It would need to be prepared in Memphis."

"I don't think Abbot John meant that the hand of Nilus was mummified in a formal way, with natron and spices. I think he just meant dried out."

"Well, we may be able to find one of those here."

"But not one banded with gold and set on the fingernails with five different precious gemstones."

"And the third road," Altrus said, annoyed that he had been interrupted, "is that we forget about this relic and simply steal the silver coins."

"I've thought about that," I told him. "I'd rather not alienate yet another Christian monastery. If we cannot locate the hand of Nilus, we will steal the silver, but I intend to make an honest attempt to find the hand."

"It wasn't our fault those monks died on the Mountain of Shadows," Martala said. "They were trying to kill us. We had to defend ourselves."

"Indeed. But I'm hoping we can avoid killing any monks while we are at Sinai."

"We can try," Altrus agreed. "I'm not promising anything."

"Why are we in this dark hole?" the girl asked.

"This is how Christian monks bury their dead. They put them in little holes in the walls under their monasteries and churches. I presume they do it so that ghouls can't tunnel through the ground to reach them."

"Wouldn't the other treasure hunters have searched here first?"

"Probably. That's not why we're here."

We were in a long hall lined on both sides with burial cavities that held piles of bones. The skulls of the dead had been arranged with a kind of macabre sense of humor to face outward, so that they seemed to be watching us from their holes. The center of the hall was lined with stone sepulchres.

Holding the lamp at the level of my waist, I began to walk from one sepulchre to another, reading the Greek names cut into their sides.

"What are you looking for?" Martala asked. She moved her legs aside as I bent to read the inscription of the stone box on which she sat.

"The resting place of the previous abbot, Cyril Junius."

She didn't ask why, but slid down and used the flame of my lamp to ignite her own. Going to the far end of the hall, she began to study the inscriptions.

"I'd help, but I can't read Greek," Altrus said. "I learned how to speak a little of it while I was in Egypt, but not how to read it."

"It shouldn't be hard to find him," I murmured. "Where else could he be?"

"Do you think the arm of Nilus is buried with him?"

I didn't bother answering. The inscriptions were crudely cut into the sides of the stone boxes and hard to decipher. I had to concentrate.

"Here he is," Martala called from the far end of the hall.

I hurried over to her with Altrus trailing languidly behind me.

"Help me open the lid," I said, setting down my lamp.

The stone lid was heavy but smooth on its bottom. It slid to the side when all three of us put the strength of our backs into the task.

"Don't push it off, turn it to the side so that it lies across the box. I want to be able to return the late abbot to his resting place when we are done with him, and leave no sign that he was ever disturbed."

Martala stared at me with delight.

"You're going to use the raising ritual of Dass, aren't you?" she said.

"That is the plan."

"Must I always be the one asking what is going on?" Altrus said.

"As you know, Martala and I study necromancy."

"I've heard the screams from the cellar."

"Lately we've been working on a ritual to raise the dead in their flesh. That's more difficult than just raising a spirit of the dead. The ritual comes from a land to the east they call India. It's very powerful but precise. I mean to use it on Cyril here."

"Why Cyril?"

I shrugged like a ghoul. "Who better to locate a relic of the dead than one of the dead? Abbot Cyril was obsessed with the hand of Nilus during his life. If any of the dead can find it, he will find it."

"How many times have you worked this ritual?"

"This will be the first time."

"But we were close to success on two occasions," the girl said with excitement. She loved necromancy with a passion that was almost disturbing, and of the two of us, she was the better necromancer.

Altrus sighed and crossed his arms on his chest. "How long is this likely to take?"

"Not long; a few hours. Why don't you stand watch at

the door to the stairwell, so that you can warn us if anyone approaches."

"No one is going to approach; the monks are all asleep," he grumbled, but he went to do as I suggested.

"Did you prepare the powder before we left Damascus?" Martala asked.

"I have it here." From my pocket I took a glass vial and held it up to the lamp light. It contained a few ounces of a yellow mixture.

"The powder of Dass," she said.

"We only get one chance, so we must be accurate."

"I'm ready," she said, and I knew she spoke the truth.

From another pocket of my thawb I took a leather packet and unrolled it across the stone lid of the sepulchre. It was my traveling necromancy kit, where I kept those items I thought might be of use on my journeys away from Damascus. From one of its pouches I extracted a piece of white chalk and drew a circle on the stone floor around the abbot's sepulchre with the girl and me standing inside it.

"You remember your parts of the incantation?"

"I have them memorized," she said.

"Good girl. Follow my direction."

We began to chant the long and uncommonly difficult incantation in the language of Dass's distant homeland, all of it wholly incomprehensible to us. The unknown mage who had translated Dharam Dass's *Black Basilisk* into Latin had rendered the incantation phonetically, and it was essential to pronounce the words exactly as he indicated with his little accent marks and vowel symbols. We had both memorized the text. It is almost impossible to work necromancy by reading from a book. The incantations have to be held in the memory. One tiny error and all our effort would be for nothing.

At the critical moment I sprinkled the yellow powder over the corpse, taking care to cover it from the crown of its head to the toes of its feet. Martala and I took out our daggers simultaneously and cut ourselves on our forearms, then let our blood drip over the powder. I made sure to dribble a few drops into the parted lips of the abbot, who, considering he had lain there dead for over two decades, was in an excellent state of preservation.

We completed the final part of the incantation, which was the string of barbarous names of the demons called upon to fulfill the ritual and open the gates of the underworld. The Christians say their good men go to heaven when they die, yet pagan necromancy works as well on Christians as it does on pagans or the followers of the Prophet.

For a moment I was sure we had failed. Then the chest of the corpse heaved and drew in a noisy rush of air, and the eyelids flickered open. The eyes rolled in terror and the arms of the corpse twitched as though he were trapped in some evil nightmare.

"Look at me," I commanded in Greek.

His penetrating eyes fixed on my face, and his fear became an awareness that slowly transformed into malice.

"I am the master who called you forth from the grave. You will do my bidding for as long as you remain animate. Do you understand?"

Reluctantly, the corpse nodded.

"Then arise and stand forth."

The dried flesh and joints creaked and cracked as the dead abbot pushed himself from his sepulchre with the unnatural strength that is given to all the risen dead when they are fed on fresh blood. It would not last more than one night, unless renewed by the spilling of more blood.

He stood swaying, his face gray and black and sunk down close to his bones, his eyes dried in their sockets but burning with a fever of bright awareness. In life he had been a big man. He was as tall as I but much broader in the shoulders.

"Your task is a simple one," I told him. "Take me to the hand of Nilus."

He slowly shook his head, straining to make his dried neck muscles work. I did not like this show of defiance. It was unusual in one of the dead.

"You will do it. I am your master and I command you. In life you may not have known the location of the hand, but in death you surely know it."

He did not resist further, but turned and shuffled to the edge of the circle, where he stopped.

"Break the circle," I told Martala.

She scuffed away a section of the chalk circle with the toe of her boot. The corpse shambled through the gap, arms partway extended to keep his balance.

"Take us to the hand of Nilus," I ordered.

The dead thing turned in a circle as though questing through the darkness, then set off at a slow pace deeper into the catacombs.

3.

The extent of the passages and chambers beneath the monastery surprised me. I reflected that this walled compound had been here for centuries, giving the successive generations of monks ample time to dig. And who knew what was here before the monastery was built? It might be that some of these passages were older than the monastery itself.

We followed the dead abbot deeper into the darkness, and eventually came upon a small room with an open shaft descending in the floor. The mouth of the shaft was no more than two cubits across. The corpse stopped beside the opening and pointed downward.

"The hand lies there?" I asked in Greek.

The corpse nodded, his neck cracking audibly with the effort.

I leaned over the hole and peered doubtfully into the darkness. Taking a coin from my purse, I dropped it and listened. Several seconds passed before I heard the plink of the coin falling into open water.

"Is this a well?" Martala asked.

"At one time, perhaps. It doesn't look as though it has been used for a very long time."

"The water may be poisoned," she said.

"Something may have poisoned it."

Neither of us needed to speak; we each knew what the other was thinking.

"We'll need a rope to get down there," she observed.

"Go back and help Altrus find a rope. I'll wait here with the abbot."

I was pacing back and forth with frustration when they finally returned with a thick coil of hemp rope.

"Where did you get it?"

"One of the bells won't be ringing tomorrow," Altrus said with a grin.

We three looked at each other in silence.

"I can't go down. I need to stay here to control the abbot," I said at last.

"Well, I'm not going down into that poisonous hole," the girl said emphatically.

"We don't know for certain it's poison," I pointed out.

"I'll go, since there are no other volunteers," Altrus said.

"No, I have a better plan. Tie the rope around the feet of the corpse."

They secured the end of the rope around the feet of the abbot, who stood unresisting, his eyes rolling back and forth in their sockets as though lost in a dream.

"Pick him up and lower him head first into the shaft."

The abbot was surprisingly light for a man of his stature. I reflected that all the water in his body had evaporated and his blood had turned to dust. We slid him head first into the dark opening and began to lower him on the rope.

"How deep does this go?" Altrus asked. "We're running out of rope."

The tension on the rope eased.

"I think he's in the water," I said.

We continued to lower him for some time longer. At last the rope went slack.

"This must be the bottom," Martala said.

We waited in silence. Not the slightest sound broke the stillness of the chamber.

"How are we to know when he has the arm?" Altrus asked.

As if in response, there came a tapping from inside the shaft. It sounded as though the corpse was beating with something hard against the stones.

"Pull him in and let us see what we've caught," I said in a good humor. I felt reason to hope the abbot had not failed us.

We raised him with no great difficulty and stood him upright. The rags that wrapped his body dripped with water. In his hands he clutched the relic. He held it extended out before him the way a man might hold a sword.

"Don't touch it," I said with sudden caution. I remembered the warning of Abbot John Climacus.

"How are we to get it out of here?" Altrus demanded.

"We'll let the corpse carry it."

He used his dagger to cut the rope from around the late abbot's feet and wound it over his shoulder.

"Follow your master," I told the dead man and turned without waiting for his response.

We made our way back toward the hall of the dead.

"There must be some way to carry it safely," Martala mused. "Maybe if we wrap it in cloth. Or we could tie a length of rope around its wrist."

"We'll soon find out," I murmured. "I can't very well have the corpse carry it up to the Abbot. Christians take a dim view of necromancy."

I held up my hand to halt the shambling thing beside his former resting place. He glared at me with hatred from his dried and shrivelled eyes.

"Lay the arm down over there, on the lid of that sepulchre, and return to your resting place."

The corpse did not move. I repeated my command more forcefully. The abbot merely glared at me.

"Something's wrong," Martala whispered.

"He shouldn't be able to defy me."

"Well, he is defying you," Altrus pointed out.

I repeated my commands yet a third time. The dead abbot took a step forward, and then another, and another. He passed the open sepulchre without seeming to notice it.

"Stand where you are. Your master commands it. I am the one who raised you and I tell you to stand."

He continued to go forward, sliding his feet over the stone floor. I had to back away from him.

"Alhazred, the arm. Don't touch the arm," Martala said from behind the corpse.

"We have to stop him. I think he's going to try to leave the catacomb. We can't have him shambling through the monastery halls."

"First things first. We need to make him drop the arm," Altrus said, drawing his sword.

He extended the blade on its side and slapped down forcefully against the mummified relic. The sword clattered to the floor and he stumbled backward, clutching his right wrist in his left hand.

"My arm's gone dead," he gasped through his pain. "I can't move it."

"Stay out of the way. Martala, help him."

The abbot did not hesitate or turn, but continued toward the arch that led to the stairwell out of the catacomb. Backing up as he advanced, I held up both my hands and cried out in the most commanding voice I could muster, "Stop!"

The corpse ignored me. At the last moment, I jumped aside. He passed me without turning to look and began to mount the stairs.

"What are we going to do now?" the girl demanded.

"We need to stop it before it wakes the entire monastery."

"I have no feeling in my arm up to the shoulder," Altrus said. "I won't be much help to you."

"Let us worry about that," I told him. Picking up his sword, I slid it into its sheath.

He caught my wrist with his other hand. "Do you think this injury is permanent?"

"Let's think about that later. We need to stop that walking corpse."

٩.

The dead abbot walked slowly but never paused. By the time we got up the stair, he had already traversed the lower gallery and mounted another staircase to the second level.

"He seems to know where he's going," Altrus said. His face was white and covered with cold sweat, but he did not slow us down. He would rather have died than admit weakness.

"I think I know his destination," I muttered, and I quickened my pace.

A monk walking along the corridor almost bumped into the corpse before he raised his gaze from the floor. When he saw what came toward him, he stumbled backward and fell onto his buttocks. He continued to crawl away, screaming in a thin, high voice.

In moments the corridor was filled with sleepy monks. They cringed away from the corpse, and the dead abbot ignored those around him.

"He's heading for the Abbot's private chambers," I said.

There could be little doubt of it. The Abbot John Climacus's rooms occupied the end of the corridor.

Two of the larger monks found their courage and came forward.

"Don't touch the hand," I shouted in Greek.

They didn't hear me. There was too much babbling in the corridor. The dead abbot did not break his stride, but only flicked this way and that with the hand of Nilus, and the monks fell to the floorboards, dead with their eyes still open and staring.

"Alhazred, speak the formula of oblivion," Martala said.

I needed no second urging. Things were getting completely out of our control. Striding close behind the corpse, I made the ritual gesture of termination and in a loud voice recited the formula that would deprive the corpse of his animation.

The dead abbot stumbled and stopped, then slowly turned to face me, his eyes blazing with malice. In the sudden silence of the corridor, there came a cracking, popping noise, and with a grotesque distortion of his sunken cheeks the thing grinned at me. He turned back and continued toward the door at the end of the corridor, the monks edging around him with their backs to the walls like frightened children.

The door opened. In its frame stood Climacus, dressed in his nightshirt and sleeping cap, a burning oil lamp in his hand. "What is going on out here?"

When he blinked the sleep from his eyes and saw what came toward him, his face blanched and he stepped back. The corpse continued with its gliding step through the door.

"He has the hand," I shouted to the abbot. "Don't let it touch you."

If Climacus heard, he gave no sign, but continued to back up through the audience chamber where I had talked to him the previous afternoon and through another doorway into what appeared to be a private study. We followed as closely as we dared. Climacus continued through the study and into yet a third chamber, which I took to be his bedroom. This time he slammed the door, and I heard something being hastily jammed against it.

The corpse stopped at the door and stared at it for a time as though undecided how to open it. Awkwardly, he transferred the hand of Nilus to the crook of his left arm, and began to pound and press against the door with his right arm and shoulder.

"What's happening?" Climacus shouted through the door in terror.

"We found the hand of Nilus," I said loudly so that my voice would carry through the wooden planks. "We're here to collect our reward."

"What? Are you mad? What is that thing?"

"That is your predecessor, Abbot Cyril Junius. It seems he does not like you."

"What are you babbling about? Abbot Cyril is dead."

"Not at present."

There was silence save for the pounding of the dead thing on the door.

"Do you mean to say that you raised Brother Junius's corpse from its tomb?"

"It seemed the easiest way to locate the hand."

"You're necromancers."

As entertaining as this conversation showed promise of becoming, I was growing bored with it. "Tell us where you keep the thousand pieces of silver, and we'll take them and leave the monastery."

"Will you take his corpse with you?"

I hesitated and looked at my companions. "That may prove difficult. First, give us our silver, and then we will see what can be done about the corpse."

The silence extended for so long, I thought he had not heard me.

"I cannot," he said at length, in a smaller voice.

"What? What did you say?"

"Alhazred, you must realize, I never dreamed anyone would find the hand of Nilus. Repairs were needed for the monastery. We ran short of grain. I began to take small portions of the silver to buy what was needed to keep my brothers fed."

I glanced around the study at the costly wall hangings and shelves of many books, at the velvet seat on the chair behind the reading desk, and at the thick carpets on the floor.

"You took the silver for your brothers, you say?"

"Not all of it. There is still some silver left."

"How much?"

Again he paused.

"Eighty-three pieces."

I stared at Altrus and Martala. The girl's face was shocked, but Altrus had a slight smile on his lips. I don't know how I looked, but I felt like committing a murder.

"Eighty-three pieces? Out of a *thousand*?"

"That is correct."

"Let's go and leave him to the corpse," Altrus said.

"First things first," I told him, and said in a louder voice, "Where is the money?"

The abbot told me where to find what was left of the silver prize. It was in a trunk in the corner of the room. I scooped the coins into my purse and drew the drawstring tight. Then I stood, watching the corpse single-mindedly pound away at the door. The latch was weakening. Each time his wooden fist struck it, the door rattled and bounced on its hinges. It was only a matter of time before he broke it down, and he showed no signs of losing his unnatural vitality, which he must have been drawing in some way from the hand.

"We should leave," Altrus urged.

"We can't just leave him to die," Martala objected.

"Girl, you have too much sentiment," he told her.

"We can't leave him, not when it was we who raised the corpse."

"You and your scruples," he said, shaking his head. "I've said it before, one day they will get you killed."

They both looked at me.

To be honest about the matter, I wanted to stay and watch the dead abbot batter down the door so that I could see Climacus killed by the hand. I was furious at having spent so much to come so far for only eighty-three silver pieces. Still, the girl had a point. We had raised the corpse, and due to our incompetence we had failed to put it back into its sepulchre. Who knew how many more monks it might kill before its vital forces expended themselves?

"I will help you on one condition: that you tell me the truth."

"Yes, anything! What do you wish to know?"

"Did you murder Cyril Junius?"

As I spoke these words, the corpse stopped pounding on the door and stood with its head cocked to the side, listening.

"Yes, I poisoned him." The abbot's voice held an old bitterness. "The fool was destroying the monastery with his mishandling of its finances, and he would not die. I did what

I thought was right for my brothers, and I make no apology for it."

Even as he uttered this, the corpse gave a powerful thrust of his shoulder against the door and splintered it inward. He lurched into the bedroom.

Climacus had set his oil lamp down on a table, and now stood on top of his bed with his back to the wall, hugging his sides with his hands, his blue eyes wide with terror. He was a pathetic and somewhat comical figure.

Abbot Cyril did not pause to admire him but came swiftly forward on his gliding steps and extended the hand of Nilus across the bed with his long arm.

"Stay away, thing of death. Don't touch me!"

His words became a strangled scream that cut short the instant the fingers of the hand brushed his leg. He fell forward on the bed, lifeless before he reached the sheets.

The dead abbot straightened his back and stood contemplating what he had done. I would swear there was satisfaction in his posture.

5.

There was no time to hesitate. I grabbed the coil of rope from Altrus and threw one end to the girl, then leapt up on the bed and jumped across the body of Climacus. The corpse of Abbot Cyril seemed to regain its awareness and began to turn to pursue me, but I quickly ran around it while the girl pulled the rope taut.

The corpse took the hand of Nilus and brushed it against the rope. There was a slight tingling in my fingers, but nothing more hurtful. As I had hoped, the length of the rope attenuated the poison and rendered it ineffectual.

"What now?" Martala asked.

"Pull him out the doorway," I told her.

The dead abbot resisted us, but was not strong enough to prevent us from dragging him out of the bedroom and across the floor of the study into the audience chamber. He decided to change his tactics, and instead of resisting he came toward us with the hand extended before him.

"Get to the side of him and keep the rope taut," I told the girl. "Pull him toward the window."

We were able to draw him against the wall in front of the window and hold him there, pulling on the ropes on either side of him, but there my plan would have ended had not Altrus divined what I intended and grabbed up a wooden clothing rack that stood in the corner of the room. With only his left arm he used it like a lance and ran it against the back of the corpse near the shoulders.

The sill of the window was at the level of his waist. The dead abbot fell forward and tumbled slowly out the window, smashing the wooden screen out as he fell.

"Hold tight to the rope!" I shouted to Martala.

We came together and I looked around for something to anchor the rope. Altrus held up the clothing rack and I nodded. He turned it sideways and pressed it to the wall across the open window, pinning it there while the girl and I tied our ends of the rope to its middle.

Outside in the darkness, we heard the corpse twist and bang itself against the side of the wall. I looked out and downward. The light was poor, but I was able to make out the dim shape. Cyril still clung to the hand of Nilus, supported by the rope around his waist. The weight of his upper body and the hand caused him to tilt down with his head, and made his legs rise into the air. He was completely helpless.

"What now?" Altrus said. His injury had sapped his strength. He looked exhausted.

"We could wait until morning and let the sun destroy him," Martala suggested.

"An admirable plan, but do we know that the sun will harm him? The longer he hangs there, thrashing his limbs about, the more chance there is of him somehow working himself loose."

Altrus looked around the room. He strolled back into the study, and after a time emerged with the oil lamp.

"What do you intend?" I asked.

He did not speak, but went to the window and carefully poured the oil in the lamp down the rope without allowing the burning wick to go out. The girl and I went to the window on either side of him and leaned out, watching the operation with interest.

"A clever solution," I admitted.

He chuckled and touched the burning wick to the rope. A tongue of flame burst forth and began to descend the hemp like a living thing. When it reached the swinging corpse, fire spread itself over his body and limbs, so that after a few minutes the entire dried body was covered in yellow flame. The rising heat washed over our faces. The corpse began to scream, but even then he did not release his grasp on the jeweled hand of the saint. The hand burned along with him. When the body finally broke into two parts and fell to the paving stones far below, there was no movement left in it. The flaming limbs shattered like dry sticks, scattering burning clumps over a wide area.

"Now we go home with our great treasure," I said, jiggling my purse to make the silver coins clink together.

"It wasn't a complete waste of time," Altrus said. "We managed to turn another Christian monastery against us."

"One can never have too many enemies," I agreed.

"The five jewels that were on the fingers of the hand may still be below," Martala pointed out.

I shook my head. "Even if we could find them before the monks gathered enough courage to try to kill us, they may well still be cursed. It is too great a risk. We will leave them for the monks."

Red Claws

I.

The vultures wheeling in the sky alerted us to death on the road ahead, but it took us an hour to reach the place. I smelled the blood before I saw it upon the rocks and the sand. As we rode our camels nearer, the birds lifted off the corpses, revealing the slashed and mangled bodies of a camel and a man. Both had their throats torn out.

Great chunks of hair and flesh had been ripped from the camel's back and its belly lay open, entrails spilled on the ground. A swarm of flies rose from them as I dismounted to examine the slaughter. The man's back was slashed through his thawb and cloak with long, vertical cuts that laid bare the white bones of his spine. I bent to grasp his arm and rolled him over to find that he also had been disembowelled.

Altrus swung down from his camel with difficulty, using only one arm. The other was still paralyzed from the injury he had received at Sinai Monastery. In the days we had been on the road, making our way up the peninsula toward Damascus, some tingling had returned to his fingers, but the arm still lacked strength. He walked around the corpses with his head bent low, then motioned for me to come to him. "Look there," he said, pointing at the sand.

It was the track of some beast.

"I don't recognize it," I admitted.

"It's a leopard. The Sinai is filled with them."

"It must be quite large." I held my hand over it. The track was wider than my palm.

"It's bigger than any leopard track I've ever seen."

"It must be a formidable creature to do this to a camel and a man at the same time."

"I've never heard of a Sinai leopard killing a mature camel."

Straightening my back, I scanned the rocky horizon with my hands over my brow to shield my eyes from the sun. Nothing moved on the earth or sky save for the vultures that hovered high above us, waiting. Even so, I had a sense of being watched.

"Alhazred, Altrus. Over here!"

Martala's shout brought us running with swords drawn. She stood beside a low hill with a projecting ledge of rock that cast a deep shadow on the sand below it. As I got nearer, I stopped running and sheathed my sword.

"Is she still alive?"

"I think so."

In the shadow beneath the overhang lay a naked young woman. She sprawled unconscious on her belly with one knee drawn up and her arms spread. I saw scratches on her back and shoulders. Beside her on the sand was a wet mass that appeared to be vomit.

Altrus put his sword away awkwardly with his left hand and bent to touch the woman on the neck. He held his hand there for some time. "She lives," he said.

"Pull her out from under the rock so that we can see if she is badly hurt."

He helped Martala pull her into the sunlight. I saw that her face was uncommonly white—almost as pale as my own. That usually meant wealth and a high birth, since only the rich high-born could keep out of the sun and avoid being tanned. In my own case, it was the result of my father, a djinn of the great desert, or so I have been told. The villagers in Yemen where I grew up liked to say that my mother had gone into the desert and opened her legs to a djinn, and this was why I had such pale skin and pale eyes. But this young woman had avoided a brown complexion in the more conventional manner.

They turned her gently onto her back. Aside from a scrape across her belly, she appeared unhurt. She was surprisingly beautiful. Her breasts were small but shaped like bells, their nipples erect and dark. Between her white thighs, her mons had been plucked free of hair.

"She must be from some palace or noble house," Altrus said.

"What is she doing here in the middle of Sinai?" Martala wondered.

She brushed a few strands of long, dark hair away from the woman's eyelids, who moaned softly. Her long eyelashes fluttered, but her eyes did not open.

"She was traveling along the caravan road with the man. They were attacked by a leopard who killed the man and their camel. She managed to flee and hide beneath this ledge, and the beast ignored her because it had more than enough food."

"So it appears," Altrus said.

"You sound doubtful."

"Where are her clothes?"

I looked around but could see no sign of the woman's clothing. "The leopard tore them off her body. Look at the scratches."

"But where are they?"

"It must have carried them off," I said, with a ghoul's shrug that meant I wanted no more argument.

I walked back to the camel. The packs on its back did not appear to have been disturbed. I began to untie them. They could go behind Altrus, and when the woman was fit to ride she could sit behind Martala.

"Sling her over my camel and lead it far enough ahead that she won't smell the blood and the shit when she wakes up. We'll make an early camp and tend to her cuts."

"A little help would be useful," Martala said.

I saw that Altrus was struggling to help her pick up the woman using only one hand.

"Sometimes I forget that you were injured," I told him, taking the arm of the unconscious woman from him and helping the girl push her over the back of my camel.

"I wish it had not been my sword arm," he said, flexing his fingers. "I can fight with my left hand, but not as well as I can with my right."

"It will come back," I told him with confidence. "Look, already you can bend your fingers."

Privately, I wondered how long the recovery would take, and whether he would be a cripple for the rest of his days. Well, if it came to that, there were things the girl and I could do. Necromancy was a twisted root, but it usually found water.

2.

The sun was setting behind the western hills when she woke. Martala had already washed off the blood, wasting some of our precious water in the process, and dressed her in a blue dress she found in the woman's travel pack. There was nothing for her feet. None of us carried much in the way of extra clothing.

I had put on the spell of glamour that hides my disfigured face in preparation for her awakening. I find it easier to conceal my features from strangers than to try to explain what turned me into a monster. King Huban of Yemen, whom I sincerely hoped was burning in hell, had punished me for deflowering his daughter by having my ears and nose cut off, and my cheeks slashed. He had also severed my manhood and fed these body parts to me after roasting them in front of me on a charcoal grill. It was not a story I was fond of repeating. Fortunately, I had learned a simple spell that restored my face for a time to its former prettiness.

She sat up suddenly with a stifled cry and stared all around her at things only she could see. After a few moments her mind cleared and she became aware of us watching her. Raising her hand, she touched its back to her lips.

"Where is Hassan?"

I looked at Martala and nodded toward the woman. Martala went to her and sat beside her. Smiling, she took the woman's hand in hers. The woman did not resist.

"Is that the name of the man you traveled with?"

She nodded, eyes round with fear.

"He is dead. He was killed by the beast that attacked you."

The agony of this news bent her over. She began to sob and moan, rocking back and forth. Martala stayed with her. I did not try to talk to her while she was like that, but went to water the camels. We had less water than I would have liked, given our progress up the peninsula. The rocky hills were many and steep, and the road poor.

Later, after she had cried herself dry of tears, I returned to her. All this while Altrus said nothing, but merely watched her from the rock on which he sat.

"What is your name and who are you?" I asked. I have little patience for coddling the weak.

"My name is Thylissa. My father is—my father was Kazim ibn Hajjar, a merchant. We were coming north from the Feiran Oasis with his caravan when we began to be attacked night after night by a beast that came slinking out of the darkness and took us, one by one. It took the camels as well, and the horses, until only Hassan Alfarsi, my husband-to-be, and I were left. Last night it came for Hassan."

I looked at Altrus to see if he thought she was telling the truth. He raised his eyebrows and shrugged.

"You are saying that a single beast killed your father's entire caravan?"

She nodded.

"We saw no signs of slaughter on the road."

"The beast dragged its prey from our campsites before it killed them. We could hear their dying screams in the darkness."

"Can you tell us what this beast looks like?" Martala asked.

She stared at each of us in turn, her eyes wild with the memory. "I never saw it clearly. It came silently and moved swiftly. I only glimpsed the flash of its bloody claws in the moonlight and heard the screams of the men and the camels. When it attacked, Hassan hid me under our supply cart. In the end we had to leave the cart behind, since there was nothing left alive to pull it. We hid it in the hills in case we were able to come back for it."

Her father must have been a man of wealth. She was obviously well educated, and ill-prepared to face the harsh realities life had so recently pressed upon her.

"Hassan's body ..." she began.

"We can't bring it with us," I told her. "We have no way to prepare it, and not enough water to sustain us as it is without the added burden of a rotting corpse."

"I understand. Was the body terribly mutilated?"

She waited with apprehension as I framed my words.

"The beast damaged his body, but it did not harm his face."

She sagged in upon herself. "That is some comfort, at least. Thank you."

"You have nothing to fear now," Altrus told her. "We will take you to a place where you will be safe."

"You don't understand," she said, shaking her head so that her long hair fell over her eyes and gave her a mad look. "The beast is still out there, watching and waiting. It will come for me next—and for you."

"If so, we will be waiting for it."

We carried no oil for a cooking stove. I gave Thylissa some of our dried and salted beef to gnaw at. The meat was as hard as strips of raw leather, but softened enough to swallow when chewed. She ate a small portion but did not seem hungry. The horror of her ordeal had obviously taken away her appetite.

As twilight grayed the sky and filled the hollow in which we had made camp with shadow, Martala prepared to light an oil lamp. I stopped her. It was scarcely needed since the moon rising in the east was nearly full, and it would have dulled our night vision. I wanted to be able to see when the beast attacked, if it attacked us.

We unrolled our sleeping rolls.

"I'll take the early watch," Altrus said.

"Very well," I agreed. "Wake me at midnight."

I lay down on my bedroll and pulled my blanket over me, wondering if any scorpions lurked nearby. Directly overhead, the planet Mars glared down with his unwinking red eye. The rising moon frosted the rocky hills all around us with whiteness, giving the hollow a dreamlike appearance. There was no wind. Only the grunts and shuffling feet of the camels broke the silence. At some point I fell asleep.

3.

A scream woke me. I threw off my blanket and leapt to my feet, my sword in my hand before I realized I had drawn it. The moon was descending in the west but still cast enough light to see. Martala stood blinking sleep from her eyes, her dagger in her hand. She stared at me.

"Where's Altrus?"

I looked around. The camels were restlessly shifting and pulling against their stakes. They smelled something that made them afraid.

"Thylissa's gone."

We stood close together and listened. There was little else we could do. For a while we heard nothing but the camels. Then the night air was rent with a scream that was not human, but was unlike any I had ever heard. It chilled my blood and sent an icy shiver along my spine.

"A big cat," the girl said.

"I think it came from the west. You stay here and protect the camels. I'll try to find Altrus."

She was not happy to remain, but she did not argue with me.

The skin between my shoulders crawled as I crept through the hills, trying to walk without a sound. This I could do better than most men. My time as a ghoul among the Black Spring Clan had taught me how to move silently in darkness when on a hunting party. Tonight I did not know if I was hunting something, or if something was hunting me.

A shadow moved at the corner of my eye. I crouched and brought my sword point up. It approached nearer, and I saw that it was Thylissa.

"What is happening?" she whispered.

"Be silent."

We listened. I was aware of the subtle scent of the woman, and even felt the heat from her body, she stood so close.

There came the soft crunch of pebbles.

"Get behind me," I said.

Altrus appeared. He carried his sword high in his left hand. He stared hard at Thylissa.

"What did you see?"

"Nothing," he admitted. "I thought I heard something and went to take a look. That's when this happened."

He turned, and I saw that his back was rent by a slash across his shoulders. The blood that soaked his thawb looked black in the moonlight.

"I sensed something coming and crouched, but it still caught me with one of its claws. When I turned, it was gone. The thing is quick, Alhazred."

"We'd better get back to camp. Martala is alone."

The girl was relieved to see us. Altrus stripped himself to his drawers and she began to clean his wound. It was not deep, little more than a scratch, but it ran the full width of his shoulders.

"Just the tip of its claw, but it cut your thawb open like a razor." I told him.

He grunted. "If I don't stop getting injured, I won't be any use to you."

I turned to the woman. "Why did you leave the campsite?"

"I had to relieve myself."

"In future, when you need to relieve yourself, come to me or Altrus first. I don't want you to be alone at night."

She nodded.

"I'm surprised this leopard, if that's what it is, didn't try to take one of the camels or the girl while the rest of us were in the hills," I told Altrus.

"If I had been a bit slower it would have taken me. I felt the power of its foreleg. It is not a small beast."

"Why does it hunt us? It's not natural. The dead camel we left behind us on the road, to say nothing of Hassan, would feed it for a week."

Thylissa caught her breath at her lover's name. I paid no attention. I was not in a mood to humor her womanly weaknesses. Indeed, it was my strong inclination to bind her and leave her behind us, so that the beast could feast on her flesh while we distanced ourselves from it. Martala was watching me as these thoughts passed through my mind, and she frowned in reproach. Sometimes it seemed that the girl could read my very thoughts, so well did she know me.

For the rest of the night I stood watch. Altrus slept. I could tell by his snoring. I doubt the girl or the woman were able to sleep. Martala occupied part of the time by sewing together the back of Altrus's thawb. It was a relief to see the dawn.

9.

At first light we set off on our camels at a walking pace, following the faint traces of the caravan road through the hills. It was not a well-traveled road, since goods could be moved so much more easily by ship. Most of the larger towns in the Sinai were on the coast. The caravan road served smaller inland communities, such as the one that had grown up near the Mount Sinai Monastery, and the village at the Feiran Oasis.

"Last night was the first night in two weeks that the beast failed to make a kill," Thylissa said from her seat behind Martala.

"It wasn't for lack of trying," Altrus said.

"Do you think it is still following us?" Martala asked her.

"Oh yes, of a certainty. We never heard or saw it during the day, but at night it was always there, just beyond the light of our lamps. No matter what precautions we took, it killed something, and on most nights it took more than one."

"The way you describe its behavior, it almost sounds as though it is driven by some kind of malicious resolve," I said.

"I don't know about that," she said with a shrug.

"If we had left you beneath that ledge of rock, do you think it would have followed us?"

"It would have killed me last night, of that I am certain."

"Are you so sure?" Altrus asked, watching her from the back of his camel.

"Yes, I am," she said, and turned to me. "You saved my life. I can never repay you."

"I ask for no payment."

"Even so, I thank you with all my heart."

I saw Martala glance at Altrus and roll her pale gray eyes. Pity is not a part of my nature, but I almost felt pity for Thylissa, attempting to use her feminine charms on a man with nothing below his belly but scars and a hole. She would have been better advised to try to charm Altrus, not that it would have done her any good. His heart is even colder and more cynical than mine.

"We're approaching a village," Altrus said.

I looked at the hills ahead, and saw a thin line of smoke rising from behind one of them. A cooking fire. After riding a while longer, I smelled the smoke, and something more. Water. In the desert, water has a distinctive smell. I find that I lose the ability to smell it when I stay long in Damascus, but when I travel it returns to me.

We rounded the hill and came upon a Bedouin village built beside a small wadi. There were a few date trees and a patch of grass that grew where the water lay close beneath the surface. The huts of the nomads were made of flat stones piled up to make walls, with reeds plastered with mud for roofs. There were no more than twenty or so huts and other structures. It was a seasonal village. The Bedouin lived here for part of the year, and left when their herd exhausted the grass. We were fortunate enough to arrive while the village was occupied.

The wadi meant two things: we were not going to run out of water, and we could dispose of the woman.

The Bedouin accepted us with stoic fatalism. They could not control who came along the road, and were accustomed to dealing with all types of travelers. They fed us, cared for our animals, and gave us one of the huts in which to sleep.

The scattering of children who were not working stood at a small distance and watched us with solemn eyes. Among them was an ancient crone with a hunched back who leaned on her walking staff and stared unwinking. If ever a woman had the natural power of the evil eye, it was this shrivelled, toothless witch, swathed in black from head to toe. She seemed particularly interested in Thylissa. Her rheumy eyes seldom left the young woman.

"Why is that hag staring at me?" she asked while we sat in front of our hut, eating the food the women of the village had provided.

"She's old," Martala said. "Her mind is probably gone. Pay no attention."

5.

As twilight fell, the others entered the hut to sleep. I went aside to piss on a bush.

The crone approached me as I finished. "You are a man of the arts," she said in a voice like a rusty hinge.

"What arts would those be, old mother?"

She hawked and spat to the side, glaring at me. "The arts of magic. Don't play the fool with me, Alhazred. I have something to say to you."

I admit, I was startled when she used my name. Then I realized she had probably overheard it spoken by one of my companions.

"Magic is forbidden by the laws of the Prophet," I said.

"What has the Prophet to do with us? We worship older gods."

"Are you a witch?"

She cackled. "I have the sight, and you do not, for all your study and book-learning."

The intensity of her gaze upon me was disquieting. I resisted an urge to make the sign for warding off the evil eye. It would not have been polite.

"What do you wish to say to me?"

"Only this, necromancer: your company is cursed. A dark shadow follows behind the tails of your camels, and it will not be satisfied until you are all dead."

I wondered if anyone had spoken to any of the tribe about the leopard that hunted the caravan road.

"Cursed in what way, old woman?"

"You are hunted by a shape-changer."

"I do not understand you."

"You understand more than you will admit. A shape-changer, who has pledged himself to a demon in return for the power to become a predatory beast, bears your company a deadly malice that will only be sated by your blood."

"What kind of shape-changer are you talking about?"

She narrowed her eyes and squinted at the red light that lined the western horizon. The sun had already set behind the hills.

"I see teeth, a snarling snout. I see claws that drip with blood. I see fur sleek and shining beneath the moonlight. It stalks you even now. It will come while you sleep. Beware, Alhazred, for the Old Ones will not protect you from its wrath."

"Is this shape-changer human during the day?"

She nodded. "It has the power to change at will, but its power waxes greater with the moon, and is at its height when the moon is full, as it is this night."

"Tell me this, witch: how may we recognize this fiend?"

She nodded at me and chuckled softly in her throat. "It

will bear the mark of the beast it becomes somewhere upon its body."

"How am I to know this mark of the beast?"

"It takes the form of the footprint that the beast makes when it walks."

I did not reveal it to the old woman, but this information eased the worry in my heart. I had seen no such mark.

"How may we kill this creature?"

"Cold steel will kill it, if the injury is severe enough. It is best to sever its head from its body."

"Why have you told me these things?"

She grinned, revealing her toothless gums in the red light of the dying day. "There is one who concerns himself with your life, necromancer. He asked me to bear you this message."

"Who is this?"

But she had already turned her crooked back to me, and was walking away with the aid of her staff.

I did not pursue the matter. She had told me what she wished to tell me, and I had a sense that nothing I could do would make the old hag say more. It is true; I sometimes had dealings with the ancient gods and with the Old Ones, who were greater than the gods, but I could not imagine any of them caring enough about me to warn me of danger. If anything, the opposite was true—some of them would have enjoyed watching my violent murder, particularly the one I do not name aloud who is sometimes called the Crawling Chaos.

I entered our hut.

"What did the old woman want?" Altrus asked.

"She warned me that we are under a curse, and that a shape-changer will come tonight."

"A shape-changer? So that is what is hunting us."

"What have you heard of such things?"

"Only what is said in alehouses and around campfires. Men who can transform themselves into beasts to hunt and kill other men."

"Only men?" I murmured.

He glanced at Thylissa, preparing her bedroll in a corner of the hut. "Women also, according to the tales I've heard."

I nodded. We understood each other.

6.

"You get some sleep. I'll sit the first watch."

He went to his bedroll and stretched himself upon it to sleep.

It was not generosity that caused to me take the first watch. I knew Altrus, who was a battle-hardened mercenary, could sleep anywhere and at any time, whereas it would be impossible for me to fall asleep until I was reeling with fatigue, the old woman's words had set my nerves so on edge.

I sat upon my own bed and, as the last light of day left the sky, watched out the open doorway of the hut. The hut had a door that could be closed, but it was made from flimsy woven reeds and would not stop a leopard. I wanted to see what was outside.

One by one, the stars appeared. The small animal sounds of the desert reached my ears, carried by the night breeze. Altrus and Martala both snored, although the girl's snore was soft and intermittent. Thylissa did not seem burdened by this affliction. It was now so dark inside the hut that I could not see any of them. Outside, the rising moon seemed to frost the sand. Nothing could approach the open door without me noticing it.

As I shifted my legs to keep them from becoming numb, a pebble clicked against a stone outside. I stood up as quietly as I was able and drew my sword slowly so that its steel would not rasp against the brass guard of its scabbard. Listening, I waited. Again I heard a tiny click no great distant away from the hut.

I eased out the door and looked around. I even looked above me to the roof, but nothing lurked there. Wondering whether it was worth waking Altrus, I stood irresolute.

When nothing occurred, I finally returned to the hut and resumed my seat on my bedroll, which had seemed soft at the start of the evening but now felt as hard as stone against my bruised buttocks.

It must have been almost an hour later when a scream cut the night. It did not come from a human throat. I ran in the direction of the sound with my sword in my hand. It came from the camel yard of the Bedouins. One of the beasts lay on its side, making sporadic efforts to get its legs under it. Several Bedouin men had come from their huts and stood gathered around the agonized beast with daggers in their hands when I arrived. I saw that the belly of the camel had been torn open. It was dying, its life-blood spreading slowly over the sand. One of the men used his dagger to cut its throat while another man held its head. When they became aware that I watched them, they glared at me with hatred.

Altrus and Martala ran up behind me.

"What's going on?" he asked me.

"The leopard came into the village and killed a camel." I looked behind him. "Where is Thylissa?"

They both looked about.

"Maybe she was frightened and stayed behind in the hut," Martala said.

I looked at Altrus.

"I'll go back," he said. "You and the girl look for the leopard."

We searched the edge of the village but saw and heard nothing. By this time most of the Bedouin men had returned to their huts. I saw the old woman standing by the dead camel, watching me. Our eyes met, and she made the sign of warding away evil with her hand. I almost laughed. If anyone was casting the evil eye it was that vile old woman.

When I returned to our hut, the oil lamp burned inside, filling the little structure with a yellow glow. Martala and Altrus were there with Thylissa, who wore a bewildered expression. I shut the door behind me when I entered, and examined her closely. Her hair was disordered and her dress

179

wrinkled, but that was to be expected so soon after rising from sleep.

"Did you leave the hut?" I demanded.

She shook her head, her eyes wide. "Something woke me, I don't know what. I called out your names, but no one answered. I was too frightened to move; I just stayed on my sleeping mat."

"She was here when I came back," Altrus said.

I was in no mood to let things pass this time. Some hellish abomination was toying with us, stalking us, hunting us.

"Bring me your scissors," I told the girl.

"My scissors?" she repeated.

"Yes, your scissors. Get them."

She rummaged in her pack and brought forth a small pair of steel scissors.

"Bring the woman over to the lamp," I told Altrus.

He did not question, but grasped Thylissa firmly by her upper arm and forced her toward the lamp, which burned on a small projection of rock on the wall.

"What are you doing? You're hurting me."

"Help him," I told Martala.

She took the woman's other arm and pulled her nearer the flame. Ignoring her protests, I began to cut off her hair close to her scalp. She screamed and babbled and wept, but none of us heeded her. I did not stop until all the hair on her head lay scattered about on the hard-packed clay of the floor. Casting aside the scissors, I took her head in both my hands and examined every part of it, holding her skull only inches away from the flame. When I had satisfied myself that no birthmark was hidden there, I released her and told the others to let her go.

She crawled to a corner of the hut and folded herself into a ball, weeping like a small child. I ignored her and related to my companions what the old woman had said about the mark of the beast.

"It may still be there, hidden in some crevice or fold of her body," Altrus said.

"You look," I told the girl, who nodded silently.

We dragged Thylissa back near the lamp and held her flat by the wrists and ankles while the girl went over her entire body from the front, and then from the back.

"I can find no mark on her," she said.

Only then did we release her.

"Why are you doing this to me?" she asked, cringing back to the far side of the hut and trying to cover her nakedness with her hands.

I told her the words of the hag.

She snatched up her dress and quickly pulled it over her body. Her face was reddened and streaked with tears, but there was anger in her eyes. "The old woman is mad. How could I kill the camel? I never left this hut."

"You could have distracted me by tossing small pebbles out the window," I told her. "When I went out to look, you could have slipped out the door behind me. It was too dark inside the hut to see if you were missing. After you killed the camel, you could easily have come back into the hut when Martala and Altrus ran to investigate the noise."

She shook her head. "You are mad as well. You're as mad as the old woman. How could you cut off my hair? How could you shame me in this way? If my father were still alive he would have you whipped to death for this outrage."

I looked around the floor of the hut at the scattered strands of her dark hair. "I had to be sure."

"And are you sure now that I'm not a shape-changer?"

"No."

"I will go no further with you on the road. You are all mad. You all saw that I was the prey of this beast, yet you accuse me."

Martala went over to try to comfort her.

"Stay away from me. Don't touch me. You are as bad as they are."

We stopped trying to talk to her and let her sit in silence for the remainder of the night. I don't think any of us slept.

181

ר.

"You must go, all of you," the headman of the Bedouin said.

The men of the village stood around us, their hands on their daggers at their waists, their eyes hard and cold.

"We will go," I agreed, making placating gestures with my hands. "Yet it would be best for the woman if she stayed with you."

"No," he said emphatically. "If you leave her behind we will kill her."

"Please let me stay," Thylissa begged him. "These people are strangers to me, and they are all insane. They think I am a leopard. Don't make me go with them."

He ignored her as though she were silent and invisible. "There are your camels. We should take one for the camel that was killed last night, but we give them back to you. Take them now and leave this place. If you do not go at once we will kill you all."

"I beg you, don't send me away," Thylissa said with tears streaming down her cheeks. "They are mad, and they will kill me. My family has great wealth. You will all be rewarded if you let me stay."

The headman might as well have been deaf.

We strapped our belongings back on our camels. The Bedouins allowed us to get water from their well, but they watched us narrowly the whole while. After her outburst, Thylissa appeared to resign herself to leaving with us. Her face bore a fatalistic expression of despair. She allowed Martala to help her up on the back of her camel.

We rode out of the village as the Bedouin stood in silence and watched us. Even their children were still and silent. I saw the old woman at the back of the crowd, a malicious smirk on her wrinkled lips.

We rode north in silence, each of us alone with our thoughts. I eyed the crests of the hills, wondering if eyes watched us from one of them, or if the evil was here among us, sitting behind the girl. When Martala's camel chanced to stray some distance ahead, Altrus rode close beside me and leaned over to murmur in my ear hole. "If we're going to do it, we must do it before sunset."

"I know," I told him.

"The girl won't like it. You know how sentimental she gets."

"Martala will do what I tell her to do."

"Yes," he agreed. "But she won't like it."

Morning turned to afternoon, and the sun began to decline in the west. Still I hesitated, uncertain what action I should take. I wished that we had left the woman behind us beneath the ledge, or better yet, that the girl had never found her there, but this was idle gazing at clouds. The truth was that I did not want to take an action that would cause Martala to hate me. The shadows lengthened.

"You must decide," Altrus said. "If you want, I will do it."

"No. The decision is mine. I will do it, when I decide it must be done." I stroked the skull of Gor on my belt, as was my habit when seeking resolve to decide a difficult question.

The sun settled itself behind the hills and twilight came on. We came to a great upthrust of rock that was rounded on the top and seemed to loom over us like a dark cloud. The wall at its base was nearly vertical and provided good protection from any approach from the east.

"We'll make our camp here," I said.

We dismounted stiffly and Altrus led the camels away to see to their needs. Thylissa eyed me warily. She had put on her burka, and it was impossible to see that her hair was gone. I met her gaze, and she suddenly turned white in the face and began to tremble. I realized I had forgotten to renew the spell of glamour that concealed my true features. It seemed not worth the effort to do so, now that she had seen how I look. Even so, from habit I renewed the glamour.

"What are you?" she whispered.

I approached her silently. She cringed backward.

Martala stepped in front of her and faced me with a look of resolve that I knew only too well. "What are you doing, Alhazred?"

"We can't take the risk. It should have been done before this." I drew my dagger.

"No," she said. "We don't know that she is a changeling. She doesn't have the mark."

"It could be anywhere."

"I won't let you kill her."

"This is what I was afraid of," Altrus said, returning to us from where he had staked the camels. "I told you, the girl is sentimental."

"Don't kill me," Thylissa cried. "Don't let him kill me."

It was almost full dark. She ran a short distance, unmindful of the sharp stones on the bare soles of her feet, but I had placed myself so that the wall was behind her and she had nowhere to go. Altrus separated himself from me so that she would not be able to escape around us. He drew his own dagger.

"Alhazred, if you do this thing, I will leave your house," Martala said. There was an edge of steel in her voice and I knew she spoke the truth.

"If we let this changeling continue to stalk us, she will kill us all."

"We don't know that she is a changeling."

"We will know when we are all lying on the sand with our entrails hanging out of our bellies. I'm not prepared to wait that long."

The girl made her little dagger appear in her hand as though by some magic trick.

I stopped and stared at her. "Would you really use that against me?"

Before she could answer, the yowl of a big cat sounded in the gloom. It raised the hairs on the back of my neck and made the camels bellow with alarm and jerk against their tethers.

"Where did it come from?" Altrus said, turning all around.

"Over there, I think." I pointed to the west.

He sheathed his dagger and awkwardly drew his sword with his left hand. I transferred my dagger to my left hand and drew my sword in my right.

"Stay behind me," Martala told Thylissa, who cringed back against the wall of rock.

8.

In the dying light from the west, a leopard stepped out from behind a boulder at the side of a low hill and stood staring down at us. It was larger than any big cat I had ever seen at the palace of King Huban in Yemen, where lions and African leopards and cheetahs were kept as pets. From nose to tail it must have been at least six cubits in length. Its muscles rippled beneath its spotted coat as it shifted and stared at us with an intelligence that was more than animal.

Instinctively, Altrus and I both began to edge back toward the wall, in order to put the great rock behind us. The beast would not have so easy a prey as it had accustomed itself to while raiding the caravan of Thylissa's father. We prepared to sell our lives at a high price.

"It can be killed," I said. "A sword can kill it, or a knife."

The leopard stretched its back and lifted its head. It opened its jaws and made a coughing noise. I realized that it was laughing at me.

"Stand behind me," Martala said to Thylissa.

I glanced at the woman. She stood with her back perfectly straight, her head held high, staring at the leopard. Her pupils had expanded into pools of blackness that seemed to swallow her eyes. She did not appear afraid.

She met my gaze with her empty black eyes and laughed in a way that was disturbingly similar to the coughing laugh of the big cat. "You fools are so easy to manipulate and so much fun to play with," she said.

I looked at Altrus.

"You were right," was all he said.

We put our backs together.

"Move away from the woman," I told Martala.

She did not hesitate, but came to us and stood with Altrus on his weak side, facing the leopard.

"Are you in league with the changeling?" I asked Thylissa.

185

She took a gliding step toward me, but stopped when I raised my sword. "The changeling is Hassan, my mate."

"Then the dead man we found with you—"

"One of the men hired to protect the caravan from bandits. I never even learned his name."

"Did you kill your own father?" I said it in the hope that I could unsettle her nerves.

She merely shrugged. "When the blood-rage takes us, we forget ourselves in the beast and scarce know what we do."

"You are a hellish thing and surely damned."

She grinned, not like a woman but like a beast, and lolled out her long red tongue. On it I saw a mark that was like the footprint of a leopard. "So are you, Alhazred."

This truth I could not dispute.

"If you try to change yourself, I will put my blade through your heart. The old Bedouin woman told me that cold steel can kill your kind."

"She may be right, but we heal very quickly when we have fresh blood to lick. If you had been paying attention you might have noticed that my scratches healed, but I was quick to remake them when you were not watching me."

She took another gliding step toward me, barely seeming to move her leg beneath her dress, yet suddenly she was almost within range of a sword thrust. I held my blade at the ready, knowing I would get no more than one chance, if indeed I got so much as that.

"The leopard is coming nearer, Alhazred," Martala told me.

"When it leaps, stab for its eyes and its throat," I said.

With a languid twisting of her body, Thylissa plucked off her burka and pulled her dress over her head. She stood naked. I saw by the graying light that indeed her scratches had healed. Her ivory skin seemed to glow with inner radiance. As I looked at her smooth, rounded belly, it rippled. The fingers of her hands became longer, and the nails turned into curved claws. I looked back at her face. Her nose and mouth were extending themselves into a snout, and her eyes no longer appeared even remotely human.

Knowing I dared not hesitate any longer, I thrust with my sword point between her white breasts. She moved so quickly, I did not even see the motion of her arm, but my sword clattered on the rocks some distance away from where we stood. I transferred my dagger to my right hand.

Again, the leopard laughed its coughing laugh. The sound was much nearer than before but I did not dare turn my head.

"They are fast, Altrus. Very fast."

He made no answer. He was preparing himself to die and wanted to sell his life as dearly as he could.

"This is the end, Alhazred. It has been amusing to toy with you. We will meet again in hell, and then we can play another game."

Fur suddenly appeared on her limbs and belly, and in an instant she was no longer a woman with the attributes of a leopard, but a leopard that reared on its hind legs. I prepared myself for death.

The fletching of an arrow appeared as if by magic in her neck. Her eyes widened in surprise. More arrows sprouted from her body, and from somewhere behind me I heard the twang of bowstrings. The leopard that was Hassan roared in fury. I heard men cry out and scream, and the sound of battle, but did not dare take my eyes from the woman. Thylissa growled deep in her throat. Blood burst in clots from her jaws and ran down her neck as she tried to reach the arrow in her throat with her claws. She seemed to remember me, and suddenly lunged.

I buried my dagger in her chest and hugged her close, expecting to feel her claws rend open my back to my spine, but instead she sagged against me, a dead weight, and slid slowly to the sand.

Pushing myself away from her and dragging free my bloody dagger, I turned in time to see Altrus strike at the leopard with his sword. The keen blade cut halfway through the neck of the beast, and its snarling head dangled from what remained. It glared hatred at me and collapsed. I counted six arrows in its body.

The Bedouin came down from the hills with caution. Some of them carried hunting bows. The headman of the village nudged the leopard's head with the toe of his boot. As we looked at it, the body of the big cat seemed to shrivel in on itself and became that of a naked young man.

"I must apologize for our poor hospitality," he said to me. "We could not risk accepting the woman into our village. When you left, we followed you through the hills. We knew the changeling would attack at nightfall, but we never imagined there were two of them."

"We owe you our lives. I am called Alhazred. If you ever need assistance on any matter, send word to me at my house on the Lane of Scholars in Damascus, and I will come to you."

He nodded. "It is reward enough to rid the world of such foul creatures."

"How did you know your arrows would kill them?"

"The old woman who spoke to you is very wise. She told us to dip the tips of our arrows in molten silver. This we did, and the silver coated the bronze points."

"When you return to your village, give the old woman our thanks."

He smiled. "I will do so. She said I should tell you that people are not always what they seem."

To make certain the changelings were truly dead, we finished cutting the head from the man, and then did the same to the corpse of the woman. We buried the heads separately from the bodies a little distance off the caravan road. Their work done, the Bedouin returned to their village.

"You were right, I was wrong," Martala said to me as we prepared our bedrolls for the night.

"It's never wrong to have compassion," I told her. "But sometimes it is dangerous."

Ancient Evil

"**E**nough!" Harkanos roared.

The squabble of voices stopped. The men and women seated at the long table in my great hall stared at the necromancer in shocked surprise. Most of them had never heard the gracious man raise his voice in anger. He stood at the foot of the table, leaning forward with his hands upon its polished surface, glaring with his clear gray eyes at the eight who sat on its sides. There was silence.

"We have all agreed to let Alhazred arbitrate our dispute, and to accept whatever judgment he decides to render. The time for recrimination is over."

He sat down, and the eight pairs of eyes turned to me. As I stood, I tried not to let my intimidation show. These were the greatest necromancers in Damascus and they were not happy.

"The problem I was asked to investigate by you of the Council is the recent shortage of acids, essential salts, and other materials necessary to our art that has occurred in the city. As you know, most of it comes from Egypt and is brought in by caravan. You will be happy to hear that I have found no reduction in the amounts of supplies being brought into Damascus."

"We know what is happening," said a fat man with well-oiled hair and beard who was dressed in the robes of a merchant. He pointed across the table. "The Hound is buying up all the best salts for his own use."

189

The bald and clean shaven Egyptian named Chigaru el-Masri shook his head gravely. "Fayyad, you are mistaken. I am as much in the dark about these shortages as you are."

A handsome young man seated beside Chigaru pointed his slender hand indolently across the table. "Isn't it more likely that our materials are being hoarded up so that they can later be sold at much higher prices? Who better to do this than Fayyad al-Majid, the one they call the Merchant."

An elderly man with a long white beard that reached almost to the table raised his hand with the palm outward in a placating gesture. "It is not for you, Baligh ibn Nazari, to accuse your elders without evidence."

"I thank you, Abdul-Basir," Fayyad said. "Your wisdom is famed far beyond the bounds of the Lane of Scholars."

"If you will allow me to speak," I said.

"Let the young Alhazred speak," said the beautiful Kalila Salib. She smiled at me and nodded.

"Thank you, Kalila. I know tempers are hot, and many accusations have passed up and down the lane, jumping from house to house like fire in the wind. I have inspected the houses of all who are present at this table, and I have found no evidence of hoarding."

"Thank you, Alhazred," the Merchant said. "It pains me to have my honor questioned."

"No more than it pains me," the Hound told him.

"If the Egyptian shipments are not in any of our houses, then where are they?" Dannu the Celt demanded.

"That I have as yet been unable to determine."

"Then what good are you?" muttered Jacob Hazan, the Kabbalist.

"My companions and I made a thorough inquiry. We know the salts and acids are coming into Damascus. We know they are not being offered for sale at the usual dealers. We know they are not being hoarded in the house of anyone present at this table."

"Then where are they?" the Celt demanded, his red beard bristling.

I spread my hands. "We found no evidence that they are leaving the city. They are still somewhere in Damascus. We were unable to determine where they are, or who is stealing them."

"What makes you believe they are being stolen?" asked an elderly woman with graying hair and a noble bearing.

"No one is being enriched, Mahibah. If these materials were bought, someone who has handled them would come into money, and would spend it."

"You would know this?"

"My companion, Altrus, has many contacts in the alehouses and brothels of the city. He is certain."

"Are we to take the word of a drunkard who frequents brothels?" Fayyad demanded.

"There is more information circulating in the brothels than you would imagine," Kalila told him with a smile.

"Yes, we all know of your former profession, before you began to raise the dead so that they could speak last words of comfort to their grieving families."

"I'm not ashamed of it," she said. "I was a harlot, and a good one."

"In any event, I can find no fault with any of you," I said. "Therefore it is my judgment that we share the salts, acids, and other matter of the Egyptian shipments that remain available equally, until the next caravan arrives."

"There are not enough salts to go around," Chigaru objected. "How am I to continue my work?"

"Why should we assume that the next shipment won't be stolen?" Baligh asked.

"My companions and I will continue to investigate the matter," I told him.

"I hope you have better fortune than you've had thus far, Alhazred," he said with a vague smile.

There were grunts of affirmation from both sides.

I smiled to conceal my frustration and met the gaze of

Harkanos at the far end of the table. He shrugged, as if to say, *it went as well as I had reason to expect*. I sat down, and Harkanos stood.

"Alhazred has given us his judgment. I know I speak for all of you when I say we thank him for his efforts."

"Much good they did," Fayyad muttered sourly.

"If you are dissatisfied, find the thief yourself," Chigaru told him.

"I will be looking, don't believe otherwise. And if I do find the thief, he will rue the day he was born."

This was no idle threat. Any of the men and women at the table were capable of calling up horrors that were almost too hideous to contemplate.

2.

"That went well," Martala said.

"How would you know?" I asked.

"We were listening at the door," Altrus said.

The necromancers of the Council had left my house for their own houses along the length of the Lane of Scholars, even Harkanos, who stayed last to thank me for taking on the task of arbitrator.

"I only hope I was able to head off a feud," I told the mercenary as I poured golden wine from a crystal decanter into a goblet of smoky blue glass.

He came over and filled two goblets, passing one to the girl and sampling his own. He nodded at me with approval. It was better wine than he was accustomed to. He spent most of his nights gambling in the alehouses or whoring in the brothels. As I had tried to make my visitors understand, that was one of the reasons he was so useful to me. No one had a better grasp of the gossip of Damascus than Altrus.

He transferred his goblet to his left hand and worked the fingers of his right hand, clenching and opening his fist.

"Does the arm still trouble you?"

"It's almost back to normal. Every so often my fingers tingle, that's all."

It was over six weeks since he had suffered the paralyzing injury to his right arm at Sinai Monastery. I was relieved that it had not crippled him.

"Is there any news about the most recent caravan from Egypt?"

"Nothing." He drank half his wine in one swallow. "If anyone knows what happened to the necromantic supplies, he isn't talking."

"We need to discover what is going on. The necromancers won't be patient forever. Harkanos gained us a pause of hostilities, but tempers will become heated if there are not enough salts to work with, and each suspects the others of hoarding them."

"I wouldn't put it past that oily Fayyad al-Majid to be lying," Martala said. "If anyone knows how to conceal stolen goods, he does."

"Why would he do it?" I asked. "He deals mostly in potions, philtres, unguents and charms. He uses mummy dust and the bones of the dead, but I doubt he raises them to life very often."

"No one really knows what you necromancers get up to in your cellars," Altrus said. "You are a secretive lot."

"True. That makes our investigation more difficult."

"If I keep asking questions, eventually someone will talk."

"You can be very persuasive," I agreed.

"I think no one's talked because no one knows anything," Martala said.

"It makes so little sense," I told her. "Only we necromancers in the Lane of Scholars have any use for the essential salts of the dead and powdered mummy and strong acids that were taken. They would be useless to others."

"Useless, maybe, but not valueless," Altrus pointed out.

"But nobody's tried to sell them."

"That we know about. It may be that one of your friends at the table has already bought the supplies from Egypt, but is keeping quiet about it."

"I suppose it's possible," I agreed. "Well, we can't do anything more tonight. I'm going to bed."

"I'm off to the alehouse," he said, setting down his empty goblet.

"I'm coming to bed with you," Martala said to me.

The girl still maintained her habit of sleeping in my bed, even though she had her own room in my house. I had grown accustomed to her weight and warmth beside me. So much so that when she was not there, I would often lie awake. The fact that I had been made a eunuch by King Huban of Yemen prevented us from engaging in more energetic sports, but I liked having the girl sleep beside me.

We were both in the habit of sleeping naked when we lay in my large bed. A cooling breeze blew through the wooden screens over the windows, but the white cotton sheets were more than enough to keep us from being chilled. I lay on my back, staring into the dark with one hand behind my head. The girl lay on her side, facing away from me. I could hear her soft snores and knew she was already asleep.

Following the intrusion of the djinn Xhalarhinni into my bedroom, I had strengthened the protective wards around my house, and believed it to be near-impregnable against magical attacks. Imagine my surprise when an apparition began to form itself in the darkness above the bed.

I reached over and shook the girl by her shoulder. She did not wake. My sword and dagger were across the room with my clothing. Watching the glowing green tendrils twist and form themselves from the empty air above my head, I doubted steel would have any effect. I should have rolled from the bed to the floor but did not want to leave the sleeping girl unprotected.

The green glow formed itself into an inhuman face with hollow black eyes. It spoke to me. "Alhazred, do not pursue the matter of the Egyptian salts. If you do, the girl will die."

"Who are you who violates the privacy of my bedchamber and threatens me?"

"One you do not wish to anger."

I made a gesture of banishing on the air. "Be gone."

The face laughed. Its voice was distorted. I did not recognize it as the voice of anyone I knew. "Heed this warning. There will be no other."

The glowing countenance scattered silently into a myriad of pale green sparks that spread and faded, leaving no trace to show they had ever existed.

3.

"It's not often you accompany me to the marketplace," Martala said as we crossed the busy street between the carts and entered the walled city market of Damascus.

"I want to look around and listen to the talk of the merchants. Maybe one of them will mention the Egyptian salts."

"Unlikely."

I did not argue. My real reason for being with her was to protect her from harm. The apparition on my ceiling may have been insubstantial, but I knew its threats were not.

With half an ear and half a mind, I followed the girl from stall to stall as she purchased the things needed by any great household. Ordinarily she was accompanied by a servant, but I had told the man that he was not needed. Soon I was weighed down with parcels and bags.

I lingered in the shade of a striped awning while the girl haggled for pepper. She had a gift for bargaining and always paid the lowest prices of anyone I sent to the marketplace, which is the main reason I sent her so often. In any case, she enjoyed it and I would not deprive her of that enjoyment.

A scrap of conversation made me turn my head.

"—the walled garden of his house is filled with Egyptian jars. I never saw so many jars in one place before."

"What's in them? Anything of value?"

"Dust. Nothing but dust. I think he's mad. He has a mad look about him, as though he listens to voices no one else can hear."

Craning my neck and standing on my toes, I tried to find the men who spoke, but the throng of the marketplace crushed against me and turned me around, knocking the cursed packages from my arms. By the time I got another view, whoever had spoken had moved onward.

I knelt to pick up my wares. From the corner of my eye I noticed a kind of blurring of the air. It moved down the line of stalls. I stared at it in puzzlement. My eyes said there was something there but my mind said there was not. As I struggled with this conflict, the blur moved toward Martala.

The packages scattered as I ran toward the girl, shouting her name. The babble was so loud, she did not hear until I was close. It was enough. She turned, and as she did so a man dressed in black with his face wrapped in a black cloth so that only his eyes were visible beneath his turban seemed to materialize from nowhere beside her. He raised his dagger. The girl moved as quickly as a striking serpent. Her little dagger flashed out and sank itself into the assassin's side and back as she moved past him. He staggered and dropped his weapon. Then he melted into the air and was gone as mysteriously as he had come.

"Are you hurt?" I took her shoulders in my hands and stared into her pale eyes.

"The dog did not touch me. He was slow; I was quick."

Bending, I picked up the dagger and examined it. There was nothing remarkable about it, other than a bluish cast to the steel at the end of its curved blade. I raised it to my face. The odor was unmistakable.

"Poison. An extract of the black lotus."

"What does this mean, Alhazred?"

Reluctantly, I drew her aside beneath an awning and told her about the apparition in the night. "Whoever sent it means to get to me through those near me. He does not want me dead or he would have sent his assassin against me. He wants me to make a futile investigation, so that the one who stole the Egyptian salts will not fall under suspicion."

"Oh, the packages! Look at them!"

I resisted the urge to curse the packages, and instead helped her pick them up and dust them off. Only two were missing. The citizens of Damascus were either more honest than I believed, or the fatherless children who made their bread by stealing from the merchants were all on hajj.

٩.

"I want you to stay at Martala's side at all times when she is outside this house."

Altrus grunted at me with amusement. "From what you told me about what happened in the marketplace today, I judge the girl can take care of herself."

"I was able to shout a warning. That's the only reason she is still alive."

"Very well, I'll become her bodyguard. She won't like it. You know how independent she is."

"Until this matter of the missing Egyptian salts becomes clear, I want the two of you together."

It was fortunate the girl did not like to go out that often. She enjoyed overseeing the running of my household. My servants knew to go to her when they had a dispute between themselves. The house was her domain, and for an Egyptian street urchin who had lived most of her life in a dirty shack, it was paradise. Altrus would be bound to the house because she was in the house, which he would hate, but that could not be helped.

"Just keep her safe. And watch your own back."

"I always do, Alhazred."

The girl could not have a more able bodyguard. More than this, I could not do. It was necessary that I focus my own attentions on the matter of the stolen supplies. I had sent out messengers to ask all those I knew if they had heard rumors about a back garden filled with Egyptian jars. Thus far, all those who responded claimed to know nothing.

Borka, one of my manservants, entered my study as Altrus was leaving. "There is a man at the door who wishes to see you," he said.

"What's his name?"

"He said for me to tell you that the Hound has words for you."

This was interesting. I knew Chigaru el-Masri well enough to nod to him in the street, but except for the Council meeting of the previous day, he had never before come to my house.

"Show him into the study, Borka."

The bald Egyptian entered, his round, beardless face beaming a smile. After him trailed a boy of eight or nine years of age whose dark eyes had a hunted look.

"Thank you for seeing me, Alhazred. I know you must be occupied with the affair that concerns us all."

"I always have time to talk with a man of your accomplishments, Chigaru."

This seemed to please him.

I looked at the boy. "Who is this you have brought with you?"

He put his chubby white hand on the boy's head. The boy did not flinch. He merely stared at me.

"This is Abdullah, my seer. He goes everywhere with me. He is my eyes in the other world."

"You use a child for a seer?"

"It is an ancient custom of necromancers in my country. Children see into the spirit realm more easily than adults. When I work a ritual to call forth the spirits of the dead, Abdullah tells me what appears in the triangle, and what they say in response to my questions."

I remembered that when I first met Martala in Bubastis, she was being forced by an elderly street juggler to read the future in a pool of black ink which he poured into the palm of her hand.

"Do you wish to tell my future?"

The Egyptian laughed. "I doubt you could afford our services, Alhazred. Little Abdullah is in great demand in all the noble houses of Damascus."

The boy looked at me with empty eyes that had seen too much and no longer wished to see.

"Then why have you come, Chigaru?"

The Egyptian spread his chubby hands to show me their pink palms. "In every adversity there is opportunity. As you may have heard, there was been a falling out between myself and the Merchant."

"Fayyad al-Majid? What has he to do with anything?"

"He cheated me." His dark eyes narrowed. "He stole a rich client out from under my foot. Such impertinence must be punished."

"That is an affair between you and Fayyad. It has nothing to do with me."

"But it could have a great deal to do with you, Alhazred, if you wish it."

He took a leather purse from his belt and extended it to me.

"What is that?" I asked.

"This is a hundred gold dinars, which I will give to you if you blame the Merchant for the stolen supplies."

"I have no evidence against the Merchant."

"It was him," he said with impatience. "It has to be him. He intends to hoard the salts and sell them at an inflated price, claiming that he has found a new supplier from Egypt."

"Have you proof of this?"

He scowled, and shook his head. "Rumors, only rumors. But why should such rumors come to be unless there is truth behind them? I have never trusted that oily, fat maker of potions."

This interested me. "Where did you hear these rumors?"

"It was the boy who heard them." Chigaru tugged the child's sleeve and nodded toward me.

The child turned and began to talk in a toneless voice. "I was walking along the street outside the yellow door when the Merchant came forth with the Celt. They were arguing and didn't notice me."

The yellow door was the door to Fayyad's house in the Lane of Scholars. All the doors in the lane bore different colors, and by these colors their residents were known.

"The Celt told the Merchant that he knew what the Merchant had done, and that unless he confessed it to the Council, his secret would be betrayed."

"That's not a confession, that's an accusation, and it's not even at firsthand," I told Chigaru. "Coming from you, it carries little weight. Everyone in the Lane knows you hate Fayyad."

"It's true: I do despise that oily cheat and liar. He has shown malice toward me more than once, for no other reason than his unreasoning hatred of foreigners. The Celt cares nothing about him. What other thing would the Celt want Fayyad to confess, but the theft of the salts?"

He extended the purse of gold.

I waved it down. "Put your gold away, Chigaru. I will investigate what you've just told me, but I have sworn to the Council to find guilt impartially."

"This gold is not a bribe," he said with a forced laugh. "It is an inducement for you to examine the Merchant closely."

"I examine everyone closely, even you."

5.

The Celt's manservant was gone from his street door for so long a time that I was about to turn away, when the door opened and he ushered me in with the unreadable expression of all good servants. He was uncommonly tall, with a cadaverous face, close-cropped hair and a scant beard on the end of his elongated chin. Those who look after the needs of necromancers tend to be unusual. It is a position shunned by the average man or woman.

I looked around the courtyard with curiosity as he led me to the front door of the house. It was smaller than my own, received less sunlight, and had an air of neglect. The Celt's house was located at the far end of the Lane where the houses are less opulent and the grounds not so extensive. I wondered if this tall, silent man did all the work of the house.

200

Dannu had come to live in Damascus a month after my own arrival. This made him the most recent of the necromancers to take up residence in the Lane of Scholars. Rumor had it that he came from a distant land far to the west, beyond the Pillars of Hercules. He had made a living as a traveling juggler, performing a mixture of magic and deception for crowds in the marketplaces of all the larger towns, before taking up the serious study of the black arts. His primary discipline was said to be demonology. He had come to Damascus for the same reason the rest of us live here: it is the center of the world where the arts of magic are concerned.

The interior of the house told the same tale as the courtyard. It was well appointed, but the marble was unpolished, the wall hangings dusty. Minor damage to one of the window screens had gone unrepaired. Dannu was not nearly so prosperous as most of his neighbors.

I was led to the back of the house, into a little workshop. The Celt sat on a stool, bent over a small iron anvil on a work table. He was hammering a gold medallion with a tiny hammer that had a rounded end the size of a pea. The hammer made a *tink-tink-tink* as it struck the gold. The workmanship of the medallion was superb. All around its edge were intertwining creatures with long necks and beaked heads. In the center was set a large ruby cut with flat facets. It caught the light from the back window each time he turned the medallion on the anvil.

"What do you wish to say to me, Alhazred?" he asked without looking up from his work. "As you can see, I'm busy."

"It's a beautiful piece," I murmured in appreciation.

"A charm to bring good fortune. The man who commissioned it is wealthy. He has two houses, three wives, and a fleet of caravans. Why he thinks he needs more good fortune is beyond my ken, but the fool pays well, and that is all that matters."

"I've come to speak with you about the missing salts."

He set down his hammer and turned to study me with his

keen gray eyes. There was intelligence there, even though it lay half hidden beneath his bushy red eyebrows. "Why do you think I can add to the statement I gave you when you last interrogated me?"

"It was scarcely an interrogation," I said with a smile.

"Call it what you wish. What do you want?"

Taking a stool down from its peg on the wall, I sat upon it. "You were observed talking with the Merchant outside his door in the Lane. The one who overhead you claims that you told Fayyad that you knew what he had done, and that if he didn't confess it to the Council, you would be forced to betray his secret."

Dannu nodded. "There are spies everywhere in this pestilential city. Sometimes I wish I had stayed in Albion."

"Is the White Isle your home?"

"It is where I was birthed. I have no home. I have wandered the world since I was a small child, eking out a living by doing tricks for fools in marketplaces and at country fairs. The world is my home, or I have no home. I don't know which it is."

"Will you speak to me about the Merchant's secret?"

He hesitated long in thought, his expression stony. "Know this, Alhazred. When I came to Damascus, I had no friends. Fayyad made a loan of gold to me so that I could begin to make amulets and talismans to sell to the nobles. All that I have here, small though it is, I owe to that loan. I would not willingly betray him."

"Surely you have repaid the loan by now."

"Yes, the gold is repaid."

"Then you owe Fayyad nothing. He lent gold to you only because he judged you a good risk. You were an investment to him, nothing more."

"That may be so, but without his gold—without his trust in me—I would have nothing today. It is a serious matter to betray his secret."

"We must think of the well-being of all who live in the Lane. This affair has hurt us all, and it is not just the theft of the salts, it is the suspicion that grows between us."

He nodded and took his bristling red beard into his fist. "You are right. I have remained silent long enough, and I have given Fayyad many chances to confess his crime before the Council."

"His crime? So it was Fayyad who stole the salts?"

"I know nothing about the thefts of the salts."

"Dannu, I ask that you reveal to me what you do know. I will not use it against the Merchant unless there is no choice in the matter. We must resolve these thefts."

"Yes, I am decided. I will tell you what I know."

He rang a silver bell attached to the wall by pulling a cord. The manservant appears so quickly, he must have been listening just outside the doorway.

"Tea."

The man bowed and withdrew.

"While I was repaying my debt to the Merchant, I helped him with a few trifling matters. I acted not so much as his servant as his assistant. I procured the parts of corpses he needed for his potions. You probably know that Fayyad's potions and unguents depend for their efficacy on necromantic materials such as mummy dust, human hair, and human bone."

"I confess I know nothing of the Merchant's manner of working."

"Now you know." Dannu smiled. "I wonder how many rich ladies who drink his potions realize they are drinking the dead."

"A sausage-maker is wise not to tell his customers how his sausages are made," I observed.

"Indeed. In any event, my assistance to Fayyad brought me to his house on many occasions at odd hours of the night. His servants became accustomed to my comings and goings, and even started to leave a small side door unlocked so that I could enter without disturbing them."

"I presume you saw something," I murmured to encourage his speech.

"Yes, that is right." He hesitated, then took a deep breath

and committed himself. "I came upon Fayyad in his cellar, working the Egyptian ritual of Yog-Sothoth to raise the dead and reconstitute them into living flesh from their essential salts."

"Many of us have worked that ritual. I myself—" I stopped talking.

"Yes?" He studied me with curiosity.

"I myself have worked that ritual, but I confess I had no great success with it."

"It is a difficult necromancy," he agreed. "I have never even attempted it."

"Few of us have a need for it. Usually it is enough to raise the shade of the dead and feed it so that it can speak. It is unnecessary to rebuild the body from its salts."

He nodded agreement. "I have never found a need for it in my own work."

The manservant returned with a silver tray on which rested a tea service. He set it on the workbench and poured from the pot, and I saw that the tea was green.

"Green tea is one of my few indulgences," Dannu said. "I find it restores my concentration when I become weary."

I sampled the tea from the tiny cup I was offered, and found it hot and strong.

"What is the significance of the Merchant experimenting with the Egyptian ritual, when so many of us have attempted it?"

"With unmarked salts?"

I set my cup down before I spilled my tea. "The salts were not labeled?"

"They are less expensive to get when unlabeled," he said.

"Yes, but the risk. What precautions did Fayyad take?"

"None."

I stared at his gray eyes with incomprehension. "None? You mean, nothing? He took no precautions at all?"

"Nothing. When I came upon him, he was working the ritual without assistants, without a circle of containment, without magical wards."

It was difficult even to comprehend such recklessness.

"In the names of all the gods, why? Why would he take such a risk?"

The Celt shrugged his broad shoulders beneath his stained work shirt. "Who can know? Arrogance. Expediency. Reckless haste."

"Did you confront him?"

He frowned and dropped his gaze. "That is what I should have done. But remember, Alhazred: I was newly arrived in Damascus, and I was still in the man's debt.

"What did you do?" I could not keep the censure from my voice.

"May the ancient ones forgive me, I helped him. When he saw me in the entranceway at a critical moment in the ritual, he beckoned me to him, and I went. I helped him complete it."

"What was the result?"

"Nothing, I swear it. The ritual was not successful. The salts may have been contaminated with extraneous matter, for what we raised up was a misshapen monster. I killed it quickly with my axe and we buried it outside the walls of the city."

"I sense that this is not the end of your story."

"Would that it were. Would that Fayyad had taken my gentle advice and ceased his experiments with the unmarked salts. Would that I had made my objections more strenuous at the time, although I do not think he would have heeded me."

The sense of an ominous dark mass hanging over the room was almost palpable.

"What did he call up?"

"That, I don't know, Alhazred. I swear that I would tell you if I did. I arrived at his house one night, expecting to aid him in his ritual work, and found him almost dead. Something had blasted him with hellfire and burned more than his skin. His mind was gone as well. I have some leech-lore, gleaned from the Druids of my birthplace when I was a boy, and I know the use of a healing spell that few know. I felt it was my duty to try to bring Fayyad back from the brink of death. I worked over him for two days, and I was successful. His reason returned and his skin healed."

"You should have reported Fayyad's crime to the Council," I told him. "What he did was dangerous. Surely you must know what could have happened, if he chanced to call back into the body a mage of ancient Egypt."

"I know that there is no necromancer alive today who has even a fraction of the power of the ancients. I know that if the essential salts are old, the risk is great. But I was in the man's debt."

"Why did you have words with Fayyad outside his door?"

He grunted with uneasy laughter, and met my gaze shamefully. "I learned from the merchant's guild that someone is asking the dealers to procure unlabeled salts, and the more ancient the salts, the more that person is willing to pay."

"So you think Fayyad went back to his reckless experiments?"

He shrugged. "Who else?"

"What did Fayyad tell you?"

"As you would expect, he denied it all. He swore to me he was no longer attempting the Egyptian ritual. There was something in the way he said it that almost persuaded me to believe him."

"What was that?"

"He was terrified. I have never seen a man in the grip of such abject, shaking panic. Something has happened to him that made him fear not only for his flesh, but for the fate of his soul."

6.

The contrast between Dannu's house and that of Fayyad al-Majid was striking. The Merchant had lived in Damascus for two decades, and had prospered greatly. His house was one of the most splendid in the Lane of Scholars. It almost merited the title of palace.

The street door was black and had no design upon it. Only the best houses in the Lane had doors painted with simple colors. The doors of the lesser houses bore additional designs, since the number of colors was limited, and there were not nearly enough colors for all the doors in the Lane.

The grounds in the front of the house were landscaped with shade trees and flowering shrubs. They were more extensive than my entire property. A marble fountain bubbled up a constant stream of clear, pure water, fed by who knew what occult device or mechanical contrivance. Birds sang from the trees. I looked at them more closely as I walked past and realized they were made of metal, not living. Then I noticed that the flowers were made of colored paper. The entire initial impression of the courtyard bursting with life was an illusion. Even so, it was impressive; perhaps even more so than if the birds and flowers had been alive.

I was led into a bath chamber. The floor and walls were lined with marble slabs of the most delicate pinks, polished until they shone like mirrors. The center of the room was occupied by a square pool that was large enough to accommodate a dozen men. In it Fayyad al-Majid sat alone with the steam rising around him from the heated water. I could smell the mineral salts in the water, sharp and unpleasant.

"Would you care to join me, Alhazred?"

"I think not today."

He regarded me with shrewd dark eyes. "You sound so serious. I take it this visit is connected with your continuing investigation of the matter the Council has asked you to arbitrate."

"The theft of the salts."

He cupped his hands and raised them to pour water over his closed eyelids. "As I already told you, I know nothing of this theft."

"New evidence has emerged that requires me to interview

you again."

"Very well. I have nothing to hide, as you see. My house is your house. Ask what you will."

I began to walk slowly around the pool. "Did you raise an ancient one from unlabeled Egyptian salts?"

He laughed. "Who has been talking to you? The Lane is filled with such malicious gossip."

"I cannot reveal the names of those who provided me with my evidence."

"No matter, I can guess his name. It is that thankless, ungrateful Celt, isn't it? I should have known better than to trust him."

"As you know, Fayyad, raising the dead from unlabeled salts is strictly forbidden by the Council."

"Don't quote Council rules to me, young man. I was aware of them before you were born. Will you stop walking behind me and come where I can see you? You are making my neck cramp."

"Forgiven me, but pacing helps the flow of my thoughts."

"If you had any real evidence, you would be talking to the Council, not to me."

"Fayyad, I came here to appeal to your honor. If you have committed an indiscretion, I'm sure the Council will forgive it, but we must know what you have done."

"One necromancer schooling another about honor. That is a scene as rare as it is ridiculous."

I stopped in front of him and met his eyes. "Did you try to have my servant killed in the marketplace?"

He frowned at me, and his surprise appeared genuine. "Of course not."

"Did you make an apparition appear in my bedchamber?"

"No. What in all the realms are you talking about?"

In addition to his obvious confusion there was fear in his voice.

"I know you raised an ancient from his salts. If you persist in denying it, I will go to the Council with the recommendation that you be banished from Damascus."

This silenced him. Beneath the skin of his bravado, he was a badly frightened man.

"If you tell me the truth now, I will speak on your behalf in front of the Council."

I could see him weighing in his shrewd mind the courses of action I had laid before him. The facade dropped from his face. He looked at me as a man looks at another man.

"The salts were not labelled, but I was assured by the seller that they were no more than two centuries old. Why would anyone sell ancient salts for common salts, when the ancient salts are worth five times the price?"

"When the salts are unlabeled, such errors are inevitable."

He nodded heavily, his double chin jiggling under his stringy, water-soaked beard. "I was imprudent, I admit that. The price was so favorable, Alhazred. It was a gift from Fortuna herself. I ask you, would you have declined to buy?" He named a price that was absurdly low for essential salts, even those bearing no labels.

"I used the salts to perfect my working of the Egyptian ritual. I wanted to expand my horizons as a necromancer. As you know, the sale of health potions to the sick or dying is a rewarding trade, but it commands little respect among my peers. Do you think I don't hear them, speaking words of contempt about me behind my back? Fayyad the brewer. Fayyad the pill-peddler. Fayyad the charm merchant. Do you think I have no pride?"

"Just tell me what happened."

He sagged in upon himself, his shoulders slumping and his back rounding, so that his chin touched the surface of the bathwater. He stared at the water, eyes unfocused. "I achieved success with the ritual. He arose from his salts fully formed, a tall man, lean and hard. As you know, most of the dead who are returned to bodies reconstituted from their essential salts are confused and in great pain."

The memory of my own agony when Martala had raised me from the dead with my essential salts came strongly into my mind. It was like a second birth. The pain was indescribable. "So I have been told."

He shook his head in bewilderment. "This man was not confused. He was not in pain. From the first instant he knew exactly who he was and where he was. I perceived my danger and threw up a spell of containment around him. He walked through it as though it did not exist. He did not resist the spell, Alhazred, he seemed not to even notice it. Then I knew fear in my heart, and wondered what I had done."

"If he was so powerful, I'm surprised he didn't kill you."

"So am I. Why he let me live, I don't know, unless it was that I was too insignificant to notice, just as the containment spell had been."

"Did you summon your household staff to restrain him?"

He giggled and shook his head. "I tried to cry out but my voice would not work. Nor could I move from my place. Truly, I don't know if it was some spell that bound me, or only my own terror. He passed me without a glance and left the cellar. I never saw him again."

"Do you think he may still be in Damascus, stealing caravan shipments of essential salts?"

He lifted his hands out of the water. The tips of his fingers were wrinkled. "How can I know of such things? I know nothing about the theft of the salts, Alhazred. I told you that before, and it was the truth."

"Still, it cannot be coincidence that an ancient mage is raised up from his salts, and then salts begin to go missing."

"I know nothing of these matters. When you speak to the Council, tell them I intended no harm, only to deepen my skills as a necromancer. They will understand that."

I nodded agreement, but inwardly I was not certain the Council would be in an understanding state of mind when they learned of Fayyad's astonishing lapse of judgment.

"There is one more thing, Fayyad. May I take a walk around your back garden?"

"My garden?"

I nodded.

He shrugged. "By all means, tour my garden. You will find the fragrance of the orange trees delightful."

I found my own way to the back door of the house and explored the walled garden. It was much larger than my own, but not so well laid out. All the trees and plants were trimmed and tended to perfection. I looked in every corner, but there were no Egyptian jars.

ו.

"Did you know that someone is whispering rumors about you to the Caliph?"

I looked at Uto with surprise. In the dimness of the deserted street only the ghoul's large eyes were visible, reflecting the crescent of the waning moon. His naked black skin was hidden in shadow, even to my keen sight. A ghoul's skin has no sheen. It is a flat black, like black velvet. A citizen of Damascus could pass within touching distance of him and never know he was there.

"What sort of rumors?"

"That you secretly hate the Caliph and are plotting to kill him, as you killed his father."

"Absurd lies," I said, trying not to let my surprise show in my posture or movements.

It was true that I had killed Moawiya's father, Yazid, but only Martala, Altrus and my neighbor Harkanos knew of this.

"What would be the purpose of such a rumor?"

"To cause the Caliph to turn against you and order your arrest."

"Moawiya will never believe such a lie."

"I hope you are correct, Alhazred," Uto said. "After the great service you rendered to the White Skull Clan, I would regret to feast on your decapitated corpse."

He referred to my help in exposing a shape-shifting creature from another reality that fed upon the life-force of members of his clan, and would eventually have destroyed it had I not intervened.

"I, too, would regret feasting on your flesh, my friend."

He laughed the rasping laugh of ghouls that is sometimes heard in the night by lone travelers through graveyards or along remote pathways. Even though I was well familiar with it, still it chilled my blood.

"Where are you leading me?"

"We must approach the house from the back, along the access lane that allows for the removal of its refuse."

"Are you certain this house is the house I seek?"

"It is the only house in or near the Lane of Scholars that fits your requirement."

The rear wall was high and lined with iron spikes along its top. Fortunately, pieces of mortar had fallen from chinks between the large stones of the wall, allowing access for fingers and toes. I took off my boots.

"I will leave you now, Alhazred," the ghoul murmured. "I would accompany you, but I cannot afford to involve my clan in a feud between necromancers."

"I understand, Uto. You have a first responsibility to your clan. I thank you for locating the house."

"Have a care, my friend. If what you told me is true, I may yet have the honor of feasting on your dead flesh."

His voice faded as he spoke, so that the last words were almost inaudible, and I knew I was alone by the wall. I climbed the stones, eased over the spikes, and dropped to the lawn. The waning crescent of the moon was high above, indicating that dawn must not be far off. It enabled me to see outlines of the trees and bushes. The enclosure had a wildness to it. The grass was as high as my knees and its dryness indicated that it had not been watered for many days and was in all probability dead.

Following Uto's instruction, I moved toward the rear door of the house. Not far from the door I found the Egyptian jars. There must have been a thousand of the clay vessels, stacked on their sides in rows and piled one atop the other. The thought flitted through my mind on bat wings that Altrus should be at my side. I thrust it away. It was necessary that he protect Martala from further attacks, be they natural or unnatural.

I picked up one of the jars and examined its lead seal. Without a label, there was no way to know where the essential salts had been prepared, or the identity of the grave of the corpse from which they were extracted. Rolling the jar between my hands, I heard what sounded like fine sand shifting within it. That was all that remained of a human being, after the corpse had been completely prepared and rendered down. It was a sobering consideration, particularly under the present circumstances.

The back door of the house was unlocked. This was not unusual for houses in the Lane of Scholars. No thief was insane enough to try to rob the house of a necromancer. I entered the rear hall, moving silently as only ghouls can move. Had there been a dog, it would not have barked. The glow of an oil lamp drew me deeper into the house. I approached the open doorway of the illuminated room with caution and peered around its edge.

It was a small study, filled with books, scrolls and untidy clutter. At a writing desk sat the Celt, his broad back to me. His full red beard made him easy to recognize.

I eased into the room. "Dannu, I have seen the Egyptian jars in your back garden. There is no point in trying to deny them."

He did not respond. I edged closer, my hand on the hilt of my dagger. He was a large man with vast reserves of physical vitality.

Even when I stood beside him, he did not stir. I touched him on the shoulder. It was like touching a corpse, save that the flesh was warm. I waved my hand several times in front of his face, then grasped the back of his chair and forced him partway around so that I could look into his face in the light of the lamp.

His gray eyes were open but stared into infinity. There was a slackness in his mouth, and his breaths came slow and shallow.

Only when he moved did I notice the tall figure of the Celt's manservant, seated in the shadows beyond the circle of the lamp. It puzzled me that I had not seen him. As a ghoul I had learned to see into the darkness with a keenness that was more than human. Yet I had not seen this man.

He leaned forward, and for a reason I could not have articulated, his calm gaze sent a chill along my spine.

"Welcome to my house, Abdul Alhazred," he said. His voice was deep and carried a strange accent.

"This is the house of Dannu the Celt," I pointed out.

"This was the house of Dannu, before I took it for my own, even as I took the mind of Dannu."

A horrible suspicion arose within my mind. "Who are you?"

"At one time, very long ago, men called me Hemiunu. I was vizier for the Pharaoh Khufu, and did a trifling service for him as architect of his tomb. He found reason to question my loyalty and had me strangled in my bed as I lay asleep. Yet here I am." He spoke these words with a sadness that was almost poignant.

"What have you done to the Celt?"

"Very little." He made a gesture upon the air. "You may speak to him, if you wish."

"Dannu? Can you hear me?"

He turned his head to look at me. "Greetings, Alhazred. It is good of you to visit my house again, so soon after our last meeting."

I stared into his eyes. His pupils were tiny black spots on fields of gray.

"Dannu, do you know what has happened to you?"

"Nothing has happened to me," he said calmly.

"This man has entranced you," I said, pointing at his servant.

The Celt looked across the room, then back at me. "What man? We are the only ones here."

I stared at the man who called himself Hemiunu as though at a viper that had suddenly appeared in my bed. His thin lips quirked into a faint smile.

"You are the ancient mage whom Fayyad al-Majid raised from unlabeled salts."

"Indeed. It suited my purposes to pass unnoticed for a time in this city. It was a simple matter to take possession of this fool's mind and pose as his manservant."

"What are those purposes?"

His narrow countenance darkened. "Do you know why my Pharaoh built a great tomb of stone over the resting place of his dead flesh?"

I shook my head, wondering if I dared to lunge at him with my dagger. He did not appear powerful of body and I could see no weapon at his waist, but his complete ease of manner disquieted me.

"He did it so that his body should be undisturbed for eternity."

"Then he was a fool. No man can preserve himself forever."

The ancient Egyptian seemed not to hear my response. "The preservation of our honored dead is the most sacred duty of my countrymen. What the necromancers of your barbarous age have done is an abomination so monstrous that my mind recoils from its contemplation."

"You have been buying up and stealing the Egyptian salts so that they cannot be used to resurrect the dead," I said with sudden understanding.

This focused his attention on me, and I wished I had held my tongue. The malice deep in the blackness of his eyes was the same malice in the eyes of a serpent when it strikes its prey. I knew how the rat feels under the eye of the cobra.

"The salts, as you call them, are the sacred bones of my people, which thieves have stolen from their places of eternal rest. For this, you shall pay. I swear it, by the war god Horus and by his father Osiris, god of the dead, and by his mother, Isis, queen of all magic. For this outrage you shall pay with your lives."

8.

I drew my dagger and lunged toward him in a single motion. He raised one finger of his hand from the arm of his chair. One finger, and I stopped and hung motionless upon the air, like a fly in the web of a spider. My dagger dropped from my numb fingers. I heard it clatter on the floor.

"You will be the first of your age to face the fury of my wrath."

I found to my surprise that I could still speak. "Before you kill me, tell me why you spared my life earlier. Why did you target my serving girl instead of me?"

He shrugged his narrow shoulders beneath his white thawb. "I wished to remain undiscovered so that I could collect as many jars as possible. I hoped to discourage your investigation by intimidating you, but I see that I underestimated your perseverance."

"What do you intend to do with these jars?"

He frowned at me, and I felt my body tremble with a fear so primal, I could not begin to control it.

"Haven't you listened to my words? Your people have committed an abomination, the desecration of our sacred dead. I must return them to their resting places. For your crime, you must all die."

"Not all of the necromancers experiment with the essential salts," I said.

"All of you must die," he repeated.

"The men of the caravans, the merchants, they had no knowledge of the offense they were committing. Spare them in their ignorance."

"I said, all of you must die."

It was only then that I understood his words. I stared at him, my jaw slack, unable to speak, my mind frozen with horror.

In the depths of his black gaze there stirred amusement. "I have been studying your sacred texts. The Hebrew book regarding the plagues of Egypt is particularly fascinating. What it does not reveal is that the plagues were caused by magic, or that they represent the merest shadow of what may be unleashed on the race of men."

"My race is your race," I was finally able to say.

"My race is dead. I have nothing in common with the soulless hordes that infect this world in your barbarous times, when the true gods of the Black Lands have been forgotten and their temples defiled by dogs and harlots."

"Not everyone forgets the gods of Egypt," I said in desperation. "Bast is still worshipped at Bubastis."

He did not hear me. His gaze had gone beyond my face to some vista only he could see. "I will wipe the papyrus clean and write new symbols upon it. All that is here now shall be forgotten. I will strike your names off the obelisk of time. It will be as though none of you ever existed."

I could not decide whether he was mad, or merely filled with a terrible righteousness.

"You must die, Alhazred. I am not yet finished gathering the salts that have been stolen from my homeland. Come with me."

My body jerked like a puppet on strings, then began to follow him when he left the study. What chilled my heart as much as any other thing was the way he worked his magic with complete effortlessness and no display. It showed a skill far beyond any I had ever encountered.

"You will disappear. No one will know what became of you. By the time your Council returns its attention to the problem of the missing salts, I will be ready to call down the plagues."

"What joy will be yours, when you have destroyed everything?" I asked him.

He looked at me with contempt. "Do you believe I want to continue living in this degenerate age? When I have dealt with you all, I shall return to my salts in a suitable resting place for eternity. And there will be no one—no one, Alhazred—to disturb my rest."

He pointed toward the ragged open lawn. "Walk over there, so that I can kill you and get on with my work."

My body did as he ordered it to do and turned to face him. It was not that my resistance to his will was insufficient, but rather that I could not begin to resist.

"And now, farewell. I almost regret killing you, half-blood. You are the most interesting of your kind in this age."

"Wait. Before you slay Alhazred, you must deal with us."

The shadows along the back of the house wavered, and suddenly there stood the necromancers of the Council, and the ghoul Uto with them.

Hemiunu did not react. "I am impressed, Harkanos. Not many could veil their presence from me, even in my own age. How long have you been listening?"

"Long enough to know that you are mad. The second birth has unbalanced your reason, Hemiunu."

"On the contrary, it has made my mind as clear as water. You must all die."

A strange contest began, not a battle of physical weapons but a battle of wills. The ancient and the necromancers of Damascus stood still and silent. The battle revealed itself only by small twitches and involuntary grunts of effort.

A kind of halo appeared in front of Hemiunu. It had a faint blue glow that flickered. I realized that it was some kind of shield he had raised to turn aside the combined killing stroke of the Council. Alone, he stood against the eight of them, and he did not appear to be straining himself. I wondered why Uto did not attempt some attack, then realized Hemiunu held him in the same invisible bindings that he used to restrain my body. I never ceased struggling to free myself, but my efforts were useless.

From the open back doorway of the house came an animal roar like that of an enraged bear. Dannu emerged at a run, throwing balls of lightning from his hands. They burst against the ancient one's shield, and I saw him stagger for the first time. The Celt stopped as abruptly as though he had run into a wall. I felt him join the force of his will to the rest of the Council.

The effort to sustain his shield, hold the Council motionless, and also keep Uto from attacking with his claws had divided Hemiunu's will enough to weaken it, allowing

Dannu to free himself from whatever spell controlled his mind. Now the ancient one had recaptured him and held him with the rest.

I felt the invisible bindings around my body weaken and flicker in and out of existence. Was it possible that in his intense concentration, Hemiunu had forgotten about me? I was behind him. I did not dare try to burst free. He would have tightened his hold on me instantly. Instead, I contrived a distraction.

In the night sky above our heads burst forth a rainbow of brightly glowing bands of color, accompanied by a noise like the singing of many voices. For an instant, Hemiunu raised his head to look up.

I ran at him with the stealth of a ghoul and drove the point of my sword through his heart from the back. He cried out: the most dolorous wail I have ever heard. The blue shield before him vanished, and in an instant he was a smoking column of blackened cinders that crumbled and fell to the grass.

9.

Once again we were gathered in the great hall of my house around the long table. It was not a formal meeting of the Council. Martala and Altrus were there. My manservant Borka had brought up the finest of the vintages stored in the cellar by the previous owner of my house, a necromancer named Hapla, who despite his other faults had excellent taste in wine. People stood or sat talking in pairs or small groups that merged and broke apart as the topics of conversation changed. Emotions were light, almost cheerful. I realized it was the nearest thing to a social gathering I had ever held in the house.

"If Uto had not gone to you, I would surely be dead," I told Harkanos.

"Once I understood what we were facing, I knew it would take the combined magic of the entire Council to oppose this ancient mage."

"It would still not have been enough, had Dannu not broken his bonds."

"And had you not used your sword. For all our magic, Alhazred, a blade of good Damascus steel can still end our lives. It is a humbling truth that all necromancers do well to remember."

"It's something I always bear in mind," Altrus said, approaching with a cup of wine in his hand.

"I know you wanted to be in the fight, but it was vital that you protect Martala so that Hemiunu could not use her against me."

"She was safe enough," he said with a grin. "She lay snoring in her bed all night while I sat up and read a book."

"Boredom will make a scholar of anyone," the girl said. "And I do not snore. Alhazred, tell this oaf that I do not snore."

"Look there," I said, pointing behind her. "Chigaru is beckoning me."

I crossed the floor to where the Hound stood beside the Merchant.

"Alhazred, we were just remarking on how well you handled this terrible affair of the salts," Chigaru said.

"You have a wisdom beyond your years," Fayyad said. "Now that the danger is past, we have agreed that it would be wisest for us all to put this unpleasantness behind us. It serves no purpose for us to feud amongst ourselves. It's bad for business."

"I agree," I said, eyeing the two. "I have been talking with Harkanos, and we both believe that nothing would be served by seeking to place blame in this unfortunate series of events."

"Very wise, very just," Chigaru said, nodding his bald head.

"The Caliph's trust in you is not misplaced," Fayyad said.

"Provided Fayyad is willing to compensate us all for the money we lost while forced to purchase our supplies at inflated prices due to the shortages created by the thefts."

The smile fell from the Merchant's face, then gradually returned as he thought about it. "You are right, my dear boy,

I was the cause of this confusion, and it is only just that I pay restitution for my error in judgment."

Across the room, Baligh caught my eye and raised his glass. Kalila and Mahibah, who stood talking to the handsome young necromancer, turned and did the same.

"You are the hero of the day," Chigaru said, with just a trace of bitterness beneath his ingratiating tone.

"The hero is Dannu," I said. "If he had not burst forth from the house when he did, we would have lost everything."

"I never imagined an ancient mage could be so powerful," Fayyad said with awe. "Do you really believe he would have called down the plagues of Egypt?"

"I do. He was a man whose people, their customs, their gods, were lost in the past, and he knew there was no way to return to them. He would have destroyed this entire world, or at least made a good attempt."

Dannu approached, weaving as he walked across the floor, and the Hound and the Merchant drifted away. He slapped me on the shoulder. I saw that he was half-drunk, but at least he was happy in his cups.

"We saved the day, Alhazred, me with my lightning balls and you with your good Damascus blade."

"We all owe you our lives," I said sincerely.

"No, we owe *you* our lives." He frowned and seemed to sober. "He took all I could cast at him. He would still have defeated us all but for your sword. I never knew a man could move with such stealth and swiftness. You have hidden talents."

The chatter and the wine began to make my head spin. I excused myself and stepped out my front door into my courtyard. Dawn had not yet arrived, but it threatened on the eastern horizon. I stood leaning against one of pink marble pillars that supported the projecting upper story of my house, breathing deeply the cool air.

A shifting of shadow against shadow caught my eye. Uto approached in the customary crouching posture of ghouls.

"You should come inside," I told him.

He shook his hairless head. "The lights, too bright for these eyes."

"I think they are too bright for these eyes as well," I told him, pointing at my face.

"I did not mean to deceive you, Alhazred. Harkanos thought it best that we follow and watch you from a distance, in case you needed help."

"Everyone deceives everyone, Uto; you know that. You are a ghoul."

"And so are you, my friend." He patted me awkwardly on the shoulder with his clawed hand. "Why don't we ghouls leave this noise and brightness and walk together for a time while the night lingers."

I left my house behind me without a backward look.

Blood Ties

I.

ltrus stood in the doorway of the library, watching me play chess with Martala across the reading table. There was something about his posture that made me turn my head. He held one arm across his chest to hug his other arm, and leaned his shoulder against the door frame. In the light that slanted through the carved window screens, the red sear on his cheek looked almost black.

"Are you coming in?"

He shifted and took a step into the room. "I need to talk to you." The hesitation in his voice was uncharacteristic.

"What is it?"

He glanced at Martala, who studied him impassively with her sphinx-like gaze. Then he shrugged.

"I need to go away for a week or so. Maybe two weeks."

"For what purpose?" I put my hand on my sole remaining knight, hesitated, then moved it forward.

The girl smiled.

"It is a personal matter," he said. "It involves family."

This was a surprise. In all the time I'd known the mercenary he had never spoken of his blood relations.

The girl advanced her rook, putting pressure simultaneously on my knight and one of my bishops. There was no way I could protect both pieces without exposing my queen. I felt mild annoyance. When I had taught her chess some months ago, I had not expected that she would end up defeating me two games out of three.

"Are you visiting your mother?" Martala asked him. Her pale grey eyes remained fixed on mine with predatory intensity.

"My mother is dead."

"Who then?"

"Tell us, my friend," I said, advancing my rook to protect my bishop. "We have no secrets from each other."

This was a lie, of course. I have many secrets I would never tell them, and I assume they have secrets they are not telling me.

"My brother is being held for ransom. I must go to where they are holding him and buy his release."

I turned from the board to study his face. There were signs of strain in his usually impassive features.

"You never mentioned that you have a brother."

"It is many years since I last saw him. I thought he must be dead. Then this morning, a letter arrived from my mother's sister telling me of his fate. It was addressed to my mother."

The girl smiled and sent her queen diagonally across the full length of the board.

"Check," she said.

I studied my side of the board with bemusement, and not a little annoyance. I could not move my king. I could block her attack with my queen, but if I did so, she would simply capture my queen, and then it would be checkmate. With a grunt, I used my index finger to knock over my king.

"How much?"

"A thousand drachmas."

"That's a king's ransom," the girl said.

"Do you even have that much silver?" I asked him.

"Most of it." He looked at me seriously. "I was hoping you would loan me the rest."

"Of course," I waved my hand vaguely. "Anything you need."

"I intend to take a horse this afternoon and ride to the

meeting place the bandits named in their letter. They threatened to kill him in three days-time from today if the silver is not brought to them."

He felt inside a pocket of his quilted tunic and drew out a folded sheet of parchment. I unfolded it. There was dried blood on the lower part of the sheet.

"This came with the letter," he said, and handed me a severed finger.

It was the small finger from a man's hand. I turned it over and examined the fingerprint, then compared it with my own. From the slant of the fingerprint, it appeared that the finger had been cut from a left hand. The blood had dried on the stump, where a ragged piece of white bone poked through. Partially covered in blood, which acted as a kind of glue to stick it to the skin, a gold ring encircled the last segment. It was fashioned with the face of a roaring lion.

"You recognized the ring?"

"It belonged to my father. Before he was killed he gave it to my brother."

I read the letter aloud.

"We hold your son Gregorius hostage. As proof we send you this token which you will recognize. Have one thousand silver drachmas brought to the ruins of the Raj Fortress in the Red Hills before the setting of the sun on the tenth day of this month, or we will send you his head."

"We'll all go," I said. "Martala, tell Borka to get some horses ready and fill our travel packs."

She stood and left the library, her green-silk morning robe shimmering in the rays of sunlight from the screens, the Persian slippers on her feet making no sound on the floorboards.

"It is not necessary for you and the girl to come," Altrus said. "This is my problem. I would not even have mentioned it, except –"

"Tell Borka how much silver you need. Tell him I said to give it to you out of the strongbox."

He left the library. I sat studying the chess board, then

began to put the pieces away in their box. I had no intention of allowing my friend to give over a thousand pieces of silver to bandits, particularly since some of it would be my own money. The audaciousness of the demand puzzled me. Why would they believe the mother of a common mercenary had a thousand in silver? Unless, somehow word had reached them that the brother of their captive was in the employ of a wealthy necromancer living in Damascus?

The image of Sashi's beautiful face seemed to form in the air before me, but I knew it was inside my mind.

It is always best to be cautious, my love, she said in her golden voice that only I could hear. *I sense danger.*

"As do I," I said, rubbing the bleached white ghoul's skull at my belt meditatively with my thumb.

2.

"There it is." Altrus stood in his stirrups, pointing at distant reddish hills.

I squinted and made out a smudge of darker red that might have been the wall of a fortress built into the side of a hill.

"Right where the goatherd said it would be," Martala murmured.

We had ridden our horses hard over the past three days. Altrus had known the location of the Red Hills, but not where the ruins of the fortress stood. We had wasted hours the previous day searching for it before happening upon an old man who knew the way.

Setting our horses into a trot, we approached across the rocky sands. The sun glared down from a cloudless sky like the wrathful eye of some malicious god, but its rays have never troubled me. I rode with my head uncovered. My companions were shrouded to the eyes in white cotton, Bedouin fashion.

"When we reach the fortress, I ask that you allow me to

represent you," I said to Altrus. "Concern for your brother may make you rash in judgment."

"There's no need. I've dealt with ransoms in the past, on both sides."

"Even so, in matters of blood a man forgets himself."

"Very well," he said after a pause. "You do the dealings."

Strapped to the back of his saddle was a small box of ebony studded with brass nail heads. It clinked with each step of his horse. In it was a thousand drachmas, a mixture of older Greek coins and those more recently struck by the Caliphate. I wondered if the bandits, if indeed that is what they were, would want to count them.

We reached the base of the hills and began to ascend the slope of an ancient roadway that passed under the ruins of the fortress. Centuries ago, the local ruler had probably exacted tolls from caravans winding their way through the hills. The fortress was situated in such a way as to rain down rocks and arrows upon hapless travelers.

A harsh cry went up from the rampart of the ruin. It was echoed by another from within the walls.

"They've seen us," the girl needlessly observed.

"Keep your eyes on me," I told them. "It may be necessary to strike without warning. When the moment comes, don't hesitate."

"I don't want my brother killed," Altrus said.

"Trust me. I intend to do all I can to preserve his life."

A man dressed in ragged and filthy clothing scrambled down the hillside amid a rattle of loose gravel and stones, and pointed us toward a goat path that led off from the road. For some reason he felt the need to grin at us. His upper front teeth were missing.

The horses climbed the steep path single file with some difficulty, stones rolling beneath their hooves. Eventually the ground leveled and we passed through a brick archway. The walls on either side had crumbled to half their original height, but the arch, which was made Roman-fashion, had endured. On the other side was a small courtyard in which stood nine men, including the toothless fool who had led us up the path.

It was the sorriest band of brigands I had ever seen, but two of the men stood out from the others. One was a giant with a bristling black beard who wore his sword across his chest on a blood red sash of silk. A dagger hung from his hip on a silver-studded leather belt. He was dressed Persian fashion in trousers and high leather boots.

The man beside him stood with his arms bound in front of him at the wrists and joined by a length of rope to similar bindings that hobbled his legs. He was unable to straighten his back, and could only take small steps. His left hand was covered by a dirty wrap of linen stained brown with dried blood.

Altrus slid slowly from his horse, his charcoal-grey eyes locked on the bound man.

"I knew you would come," the man said.

The family resemblance was plain to see, but whereas Altrus had the leanness of a desert wolf, the tendons standing forth on his bronzed arms and neck like wires strung over a frame of wood, the captive was fuller of body, with fleshy cheeks and sensual lips. His eyes were lighter than his brother's, and I saw that were he able to straighten his back, he would have stood at least two fingers taller than Altrus. I wondered which of them was the elder.

"Time for talk later," the black-bearded giant said in a grating voice. "Do you have the silver?"

"We have what you demanded in your letter," I said, stepping in front of Altrus. I gestured for him to unstrap the strongbox. He and the girl pulled it off the horse and deposited it in the sand at the feet of the leader of the bandits.

He immediately fell to his knees and began to pull and pound on the box.

"Get hammer and chisel," he barked at one of his men.

"No need."

I tossed the key into the sand. He snatched it up eagerly and fitted it into the box. When it opened, a cry went up from every member of the band. They began to shout and make ululations like women.

"Silence," the giant demanded. He stepped forward and glared at me. "You are not his brother."

"I am his brother," Altrus said.

"And a happy day it is to see you, Altrus," the captive man said in a voice that was strangely lacking in emotion, given his circumstances.

"The family thought you were dead, Gregorius," Altrus said.

"It was better that way. I fell on hard times, and was forced to do things that were no credit to our father's good name."

"Our mother died believing you were dead."

"Our mother is dead? When was that?"

"Three years ago."

"May Allah give her peace. But the ransom note must have reached her sister."

"Yes. She knew enough to send it to me."

As they talked, the bandits began to inch around us with their hands on the hilts of their swords. I felt the eyes of Martala and Altrus on me, waiting for my signal. But I did not give it. Something about the tableau was not right.

"Take their weapons," the giant barked.

They fell on us in an instant and snatched away our swords and daggers.

"This one is a woman," the bandit who held the squirming girl said in wonder. The others laughed with delight.

"We'll soon find a use for her," another said.

"Do you mean to break your bond and murder us?" I demanded of the leader.

He laughed and glanced at his bound captive. "By Allah, no. You are much too valuable to us alive, Alhazred. That is who you are, is it not? Alhazred the necromancer?"

"How do you know my name?"

Altrus's brother hobbled forward. He flexed and twisted his hands, and the rope fell away from his wrists. He bent and quickly untied the rope from his ankles.

"I told Boulos your name," he said in a mellow voice, meeting my gaze. "It became known to me that my little brother was living with a wizard at Damascus, a wizard called Alhazred who was reputed to possess great wealth."

"What trickery is this?" Altrus demanded.

"I knew you would come, Altrus," Gregorius said, smiling. "I expected you to come alone, and then to use you as a hostage to extort a ransom from your master. I didn't expect you to bring him with you, but that is even better. His friends at Damascus are sure to pay the one thousand gold dinars I will demand for his release."

The giant called Boulos clapped him on the shoulder. "It was a fortunate day when we decided to make you our leader. Now we will all be rich."

Gregorius looked at him with thinly veiled distaste. "Yes, my friend, you will get what is yours as soon as the friends of the wizard pay his ransom."

He began to unwrap the linen from his left hand. To no one's surprise, he still possessed all five fingers. With a sneer he threw the dirty bandage away.

"Whose finger did you send to us?" I asked.

"Does it matter? It is enough to say that he will not miss it. Do you have the finger?"

I pulled from my tunic a packet of cloth and unwrapped it. He snatched up the finger and tore off the ring, then threw the dead flesh into the dust. The ring he carefully fitted onto the small finger of his left hand.

Altrus tried to approach his brother, but the men on either side of him held him back while another bound his wrists behind him.

"You shame our father's name by wearing it."

"He gave it to me, not to you. That's always been a burr in your flesh, hasn't it, little brother?"

"You don't need to do this, Gregorius," Altrus said. "Whatever has happened to you since we parted, we are still family."

"Family." The taller man spat it like a curse. "Where was

230

my family when I was enslaved on a galley for two years? Where was my mother when I starved and froze in the northern hills, hunted like a jackal? Where were you when I lay sick in a jail cell at Tyre, accused of something I didn't do?"

"You had only to send word. I would have come to help you."

"I don't need your help, little brother. I've always been better than you at everything, as you well know."

Altrus touched the sear on his cheek reflexively. "What's past is past. We are bound by blood."

"I reject the blood bond," his brother said, and spat on the sand. "I am a hawk, and you are nothing to me but prey. Never think otherwise, or it will be your undoing."

3.

They finished binding us and put us into a roofless room half-filled with blown sand. We sat in shadow, our backs to a brick wall, watching our captors pass back and forth in front of the doorless entry to the chamber. They were in a jovial mood and had begun to drink wine. Their voices and laughter grew louder.

"Soon they will come for you," I murmured to Martala.

"Let them. I have lain under worse pigs than these."

"It need not come to that. Do you have your dagger?"

"Of course."

The girl had a way of hiding her short-bladed dagger so that no search had ever discovered it. She could make it appear and disappear as if by magic.

"Cut our bonds. Our horses are still saddled. If we can reach them, we may be able to slip away."

"Not without the silver. I won't leave without it," Altrus said. His tone was dark.

"Forget the silver," I told him. "When we get back to Damascus, I'll hire a force of mercenaries and we will return and exterminate these vermin."

"I'm not leaving without the silver, and my father's ring."

"Who was your father, that his ring is so important to you?" the girl asked as she sawed through the bonds around her ankles with her dagger.

"He was half-Arab, half-Greek by birth," Altrus said. "He fought in the army of Uthman and gained distinction as a able and fearless leader of unimpeachable honor in the Persian campaign. It was ever his wish that Gregorius and I distinguish ourselves as soldiers in the army of the Caliphate."

"Why did your father give his ring to your brother, and not to you?" she asked as she cut at the rope around his wrists.

"Gregorius is the first-born son, and he's a better swordsman than I am."

"I find that difficult to believe," I said. "You are the best swordsman I have ever seen."

"Even so, it's true. I could never defeat my brother in anything. Not in swordplay, not in archery, not in running." He touched his cheek. "I got this when he rolled me into a fireplace while we wrestled."

"All the more reason for us to steal our way to our horses and ride away from this place. We are almost weaponless and outnumbered. You have nothing to prove."

Altrus shook his head grimly. "He will not treat me like a dog and steal from me, and from you, without paying a price."

The girl began to work on my bindings.

"When was the last time you sharpened your knife?" I asked impatiently.

"It's point is sharp enough," she said with a grin.

Sounds of drunken revelry came through the doorway from the open cooking fire, which was around the corner and out of sight.

"If only they would drink themselves unconscious," I murmured. "We could slit their throats one by one."

"Should we wait until morning?" he asked.

"Too dangerous. I have value to them. They won't kill me,

although they may cut off a finger." I chuckled in spite of myself. "I would like to see their faces when they tried to cut off an ear."

Two years ago King Huban of Sana'a had disfigured my face as punishment for lying with his daughter Narisa and getting her with child. I lacked ears and a nose, although a glamour I had picked up in my travels enabled me to give the illusion of my former appearance. As my hands came free from my bonds, reflexively I renewed the glamour, which only endured for a number of hours.

"The girl also has value to them," I continued. "They will not kill her. You, on the other hand, hold no value. Your brother has made that plain enough. We must escape or they will kill you."

The light began to dim in the sky, and the glow from the cooking fire painted the edge of the door frame with flickers of orange and red. Night was falling. I began to hope the intoxicated bandits had forgotten us.

The black-bearded giant named Boulos lurched into the doorway, holding its edge to keep from falling. He was very drunk. We sat in the shadow without moving, our backs to the wall and hands behind us, watching him. He staggered over to Martala and leered down at her.

"You're just a little slip of a thing," he said, slurring his words. "No need to untie you. I'll carry you out of here."

He bent down with his huge hands to pick her up at the waist. Like a striking cobra, her knife shot out, and he staggered back clutching his throat. Gagging sounds came from his gaping mouth. Dark blood seeped between his fingers.

"Catch him before he gets out the doorway," I hissed at Altrus. He was ahead of me and caught the arm of the giant, pulling him deeper into the sand-filled room. Boulos fell on his face and did not move. Blood reddened the sand around his head.

"Let's get out of here, before someone notices he hasn't returned."

We almost reached the horses. Had the bandits been as drunk as I had hoped, we might have escaped. A cry sounded. Two men with drawn swords blocked the archway that led out of the fortress. In moments we were surrounded.

9.

The body of the giant was discovered amid much ape-like hooting and howling. They led us into the fire glow. Gregorius approached and regarded us with an expression of disgust.

"I should not have been so kind, but generosity has always been my vice. We need the wizard," he told his men. "Kill the other two." He turned away.

"Wait," Altrus said. His voice carried an edge of command. His brother stopped and faced him. "I demand the right of all bandits. I will fight you for leadership of these men."

"You are not one of us," a man said. "You can demand nothing."

"Is your leader afraid to face me with a sword? It that the kind of man you want giving you orders?"

"Gregorius has done right by us," another bandit said, his words slurred with wine. "He brought us the silver."

He drew out a long dagger and approached the girl, who had both her arms held apart by men on either side.

"Our father watches you from heaven," Altrus said. "He knows you are a coward."

The drunken bandit raised his dagger to Martala's throat.

"Hold," Gregorius roared. "I will fight my brother. No man calls me a coward and lives."

The bandits cleared a space around the fire pit and stood in a circle. The brothers faced each other across the flames. The girl and I were almost forgotten, although the men who held us did not slacken their grip.

"My sword?" Altrus said.

Gregorius walked to where our weapons had been thrown and selected one of the two swords. He held it up. Altrus

234

nodded. Gregorius threw him the sword over the fire. Altrus caught it and spun it in his hand, making its polished steel flash red.

"No one is to interfere," Gregorius said quietly to his men. "But if by some mischance he kills me, kill all three of them."

They began to circle the fire, their movements catlike. In the sudden hush the crackle of wood burning in the pit was the only sound. When the clash of steel came, it was startlingly loud, like thunder on a silent night. Altrus wore a grim expression, but there was a smile on his brother's lips.

"You've learned a thing or two," the elder man said, dancing back to catch his breath.

Altrus said nothing, but darted forward to press him hard with overhand cuts that struck sparks from his brother's blade. As they fought, it gradually became apparent that Gregorius was only playing with Altrus. My heart grew cold as I watched their dance around the fire, for I knew it could have only one outcome. Altrus had always been the finest swordsmen I have ever known. Until this night. Gregorius was his master, and both combatants, as well as all those who watched, knew it.

I wonder if Altrus could bring himself to kill his brother, even if he found an opening in his defense to do so? He struck boldly but somehow I sensed his heart was not in the strokes. For his part, Gregorius was enjoying himself too much to end the duel quickly. He danced forward with a flurry of steel, and when he stepped back, there was blood on the shoulder of Altrus. It seeped down the sleeve of his thaub and glistened in the firelight. Again, Gregorius darted forward, and blood welled forth from his younger brother's sword hand. Altrus threw his sword across his body and caught it in his left hand. He could fight with either hand, but he was better with his right.

"You still remember that old trick," Gregorius said with delight. "You were just a boy when I taught you to fight with your left hand."

"We need to do something," Martala said.

She strained forward, and the two grinning bandits who held her arms pulled her roughly back.

"It's time to end this dance," Gregorius said, breathing hard. "As I should have ended it years ago, the day we parted."

"Do your worst," Altrus said between clenched teeth.

The fury of sword strokes raining down on him redoubled, driving him back, and back again. He stumbled and fell, but somehow continued to fend off the furious sword cuts of his brother, who seemed to have gone mad with bloodlust. Shouts of excitement rang out from the ring of bandits.

Sashi, I need you, I said in my mind.

I understand, she said.

I felt the fine tendrils of her being, which were like long strands of hair, withdrawing themselves from the muscles and nerve fibres of my body. They concentrated themselves in my chest in the region of my heart. Suddenly the djinn burst out of my chest in a flash of light and interposed herself between the fighters, just as Altrus lost his grip on his sword. Gregorius was in position to strike a death blow. The face of the djinn, so abruptly thrust in front of his own, froze him like a statue of bronze. His expression of blood fury turned to fear.

A silver-white light illuminated the edges of Sashi's transparent body. Her large round head with its bat-like ears and enormous black eyes stared into the eyes of Gregorius from no more than a hand's span away. She grinned with her wide mouth, revealing countless long, needle-like teeth. Her slender forelimbs with hands that were so much like the hands of a woman pressed on either side of his face. Gregorius made a sound of mingled disgust and horror and stepped back. He slashed at Sashi with his blade, but the steel passed through her ethereal body.

Altrus found his grip on the hilt of his sword. Sitting up and leaning forward in one motion, he thrust the blade of his sword into the space between his brother's left thigh and his groin, pushing it up and up with both hands on the crossguard until only a small portion of the blade was visible.

236

Gregorius staggered backward. His sword struck the stones with a clatter. He dropped to one knee, then fell backward with his head in the cooking fire.

Sashi danced on her long legs in an arc around the circle of terrified bandits, thrusting her leering face into theirs as she passed. They scattered like dry leaves on the wind and fled the fortress screaming. Returning to me, the djinn positioned herself along my body, and I felt her sink back into my flesh. I shivered as the warmth was drawn from my limbs and into the djinn, who had exhausted herself with the effort of making herself visible to human sight.

"They've all run away," Martala said in a wondering voice. Her dagger was in her hand.

I scarcely heard her. My eyes were on Altrus as he staggered forward to stand over his brother. With a grunt, he set his boot on his brother's belly and drew his sword from the corpse, its blade glistening scarlet along its length. Reaching down, he grabbed the corpse by its left hand and pulled. I thought he intended to drag it from the fire to prevent his brother's head from being further burned, but he only wanted to position the hand. With his sword he slashed down and cut off its four fingers at the knuckles. He picked up the small finger, plucked the gold ring from its stump, and tossed the finger into the fire, where the head of dead Gregorius was surrounded by a crackling halo of burning hair. Tucking his sword under his arm, he slid the ring onto the little finger of his own left hand. He realized I was standing beside him.

"We're done here," he said without emotion.

The girl stared at him with wide eyes and a curious expression, as though she had never seen him before.

"Find the silver and get the horses before those fools realize they were tricked and return to kill us," I told her.

Altrus wiped his sword with care on the tunic of the corpse and slid it into its scabbard at his waist. The stench of burning hair and roasting flesh was strong.

"Are you badly hurt?"

He glanced at his shoulder, then shook his head.

"You had no choice," I told him.

"It was fated," he said. "From the time of our boyhood, it could only have come out this way between us. I think that's why he left me – he knew that if he stayed, he would have to kill me."

"Families can be difficult."

"My father loved him. He was always showering Gregorius with gifts. Fine clothes. Jewellery. A horse. A sword and armor. One night Gregorius came home from the tavern drunk and took money from my father's strongbox. My father tried to stop him, and Gregorius killed him. He knocked me unconscious and left our mother kneeling over our father's corpse. That was the last she ever saw of him."

"You can't be blamed for what you did." I rested my hand on his uninjured shoulder. "You have avenged your father's murder."

Altrus shook his head sadly. "You don't understand. I hated my father. But I loved my brother Gregorius."

The One Who Walks

I stood in the marketplace with a wicker basket on my arm, enjoying the warm sun on my face and the variety of smells that floated in the air. Some were good, others foul, but they were all alive. Around me voices babbled in Arabic and Greek. Brightly dressed merchants hurried to and fro on business. Women draped from head to toe in black cloth waved their hands in the faces of the watchful proprietors of the stalls, while dirty and near-naked children crouched and waited for the chance to steal a piece of fruit. It was the exact opposite of the environment I usually sought, which was one of solitude and silence, but perhaps for that very reason, from time to time it drew me out of my house.

Martala's elevated voice reached my ear holes through the general din. I looked for her, and found her in front of a fruit stall, haggling over the price of lemons. She caught my eye and waved me over impatiently. Snatching the basket off my arm, she began to put lemons into it.

"We need to buy a chicken," she said.

"I am not carrying a live chicken through the streets of Damascus."

"If you were unwilling to help me carry what we need, you should have said so. I would have come to the market with Borka."

"I'll tell the vendor to kill the chicken."

"I want fresh chicken for our table, Alhazred, not rotting chicken. I'll kill it when we get it home."

I did not bother arguing with the girl. No doubt she was right. In spite of her youth, she ran my household with efficiency and economy. She handed me the basket and darted off toward the poultry cages. The birds inside them emitted a constant squawking that added itself to the general din. I began to follow her when a woman stepped in front of me and met my gaze with disquieting directness.

She was tall and slender, dressed in a black abaya tastefully ornamented with gold threads. A matching black hijab embroidered with gold covered her head and concealed most of her face. Her dark brown eyes met mine above her veil. I began to step around her, but she laid a hand on my arm.

"May I be of service to you?" I asked out of politeness.

"Don't you recognize me?" Her deep, rich voice was familiar. I realized she was the seeress who dwelt in the Lane of Scholars. Although she attended meetings of the Council of Necromancers, I had seldom spoken to her.

"Kalila Salib. Is this a chance meeting?"

"In part. I spied you across the marketplace and came to speak to you."

"Speak, then."

She looked around, and I saw that she was nervous.

"It would be better if we spoke in my house."

Martala cast me a foul look when I gave her the basket and told her I was going home with the beautiful seeress. Such jealously ill became her, and was foolish given that I possess no manhood to be unfaithful to her, or faithful either, for that matter. My prick and balls had been cut off years ago by King Huban of Sana'a, who fed them to me after having them roasted in front of me on a charcoal grill, along with other less palatable food. In addition to this hospitality, the King had my nose and ears cut off and my cheeks slashed before throwing me naked into the great desert known as the Empty Space to die.

How much of this history Kalila had divined, or guessed, I did not know. Gossip about my disfigurement had probably circulated up and down the Lane, but my true face was veiled beneath a glamour, which gave the illusion that I still possessed my normal features. It was a very good glamour – few practitioners of the black arts could penetrate it.

I followed the woman through the sun-baked, cobbled streets to the Lane of Scholars. Her small house was near the bottom of the Lane. It was completely hidden behind the high brick walls that bordered the narrow way on both sides. At intervals wooden doors of different colors interrupted the walls. She stopped before a gray door and tugged the dangling brass chain to ring a bell on the other side. After a few moments, an elderly housekeeper opened the door inward and admitted us to a courtyard of no great size and devoid of ornaments.

I allowed myself to be led into the house to a room with a round table in the center of the floor that was surrounded by a circle of chairs. In the middle of the table rested a silver bowl covered with black lace. Black drapes hanging from the windows could be drawn shut to exclude all light from the outside, but presently they stood open. I realized this must be her workroom, where she called up images of the dead for her clients.

She was said to earn her living by acting as a bridge between the souls of the newly dead and their grieving loved ones and family. Her style of necromancy did not deal with rotting corpses, as did mine, but only with their spirits. People came to her to give their departed loved ones a final message, or to receive communication from a spirit regarding things left unsaid or undone during life. Often these concerns related to business or money matters.

When I was seated in one of the chairs, she pulled off her hijab, extracted her hair pins, and shook down her glossy hair over her shoulders. She was extremely beautiful, even without cosmetics. Her eyes were large, and her eyebrows uncommonly dark and thick, lending her face a Persian cast. I wondered why she had given up her former profession of harlotry, which must have been quite rewarding for a woman of her beauty, to become a seeress for the dead.

"I need you to help me find buried treasure," she said without preamble.

"What kind of treasure?"

"Gold. Very much gold."

"And you learned of this treasure from a spirit?"

"I know what you are going to say. Spirits are unreliable. They boast, they make mistakes, and they lie."

"They do. That's why most necromancers prefer to raise the corpse. As you know, by manipulating its dead flesh, the spirit that formerly inhabited it can be persuaded to be cooperative."

"I have good reason to believe this spirit spoke the truth."

I waited for her to tell me the reason.

"It was powerful," she said. "Not confused the way most spirits are who have recently died. This one has been dead for over a century. In life he was Abdul Yaghouth, a pirate who raided ships off the ports of Alexandria and Tyre. When he grew old, he had his plunder traded for gold coins and carried to a small villa in the hills a few hours outside Damascus, where he lived until his death. He told me that he buried it in a cave near the villa, but died before he could make use of it."

I stretched my arms and laced my fingers behind my head, studying her with a bemused expression.

"If you know all this, why do you need me? Surely all you have to do is go to this villa, find the cave, and dig the treasure up."

"There are problems I have not yet mentioned," she said.

Aren't there always? I thought to myself.

"The descendant of this pirate, who purchased my services to call up his spirit, leads a gang of thieves in Damascus. His name is Rashid. They call him Red Rashid the Butcher. He came to me with a family legend that spoke of a great treasure. I think he suspects that I received more information during my session with his ancestor than I revealed. For the past few days I've seen men following me, watching me when I venture out. He is waiting for me to lead him to the treasure."

"If he is the descendant of the pirate, doesn't the treasure rightly belong to him?"

She surprised me by laughing out loud. It was a pleasant sound, deep and full throated. "After a hundred years? The treasure belongs to anyone who can pull it out of the ground."

I found myself nodding in agreement. "You mentioned problems."

"The spirit of Abdul Yaghouth intimated to me that he had set a guardian of some kind to keep watch over the treasure, and punish anyone who dared to disturb it."

"What sort of guardian?" I was growing interested in spite of myself.

"I don't know. But the spirit indicated that it would be very bad luck for anyone who disturbed the resting place of his gold. He had a most unsavoury laugh. I got the impression that he wanted the treasure to be found so that he could enjoy watching its finders die in horrible ways. That is why he talked to me about it."

I leaned back in my chair and looked at the ivory-colored tiles on the ceiling. She waited patiently without speaking.

"It's probably no more than a fool's errand," I said at last.

"I agree, it probably is."

"But I've been bored of late, and have no pressing business. I will help you retrieve this treasure, if such a treasure exists. I will rent horses for us at the east gate stable. Come to my house at twilight. We will slip out of Damascus under cover of darkness."

"You did not ask how the gold is to be divided."

"If the pirate gold exists, I'm sure we can come to some equitable arrangement for its division."

"I know you will not take advantage of a lone and friendless woman," she said sincerely, staring into my eyes.

No more than you would take advantage of a client, I thought. But I returned a bland smile and said nothing.

2.

When I rode through the eastern gate of Damascus, the rising moon had already begun to paint the ground with silver. I glanced back into the city as the gate was closing but saw no one who appeared interested in our passage. Kalila rode at my left side. Martala rode behind her, and at her side, Altrus, my bodyguard. We were robed in black to make our presence less conspicuous in the darkness.

"Are we being followed?" the seeress asked nervously.

"I see no sign of it."

The journey along the caravan road was uneventful. When we reached the little valley between fertile, rolling hills where the abandoned villa was located, the moon was high overhead. The tiled roof of the old house had collapsed in places and the front door was missing. We dismounted and tied our horses to a stone pillar with four iron rings in its sides that was almost hidden by tall weeds.

"This is a green place. There is water close beneath the surface," I said, sniffing the air through the hole where my nose had once been.

"How do you know this?" Kalila asked.

"Alhazred lived in the Empty Space before coming to Damascus," Martala told her. "He can scent even trace amounts of water."

"Nobody lives in the Empty Space."

"Alhazred did."

"Is that where you met him?" Kalila asked her with the curiosity of a woman.

"No, we met in Egypt. I was sent to kill him. Instead, he tried to kill me, and then we became ... companions."

"You are very young," the seeress said, appraising her face. Martala was dressed in her usual fashion as a boy, her hair tied up in her head covering and her breasts strapped close to her chest beneath her Persian tunic.

The girl did not answer.

Altrus scanned the land around the villa. "This is good farmland. Why would it remain empty for so many years, Alhazred?"

"People think it is haunted. I asked about it before we left Damascus. Any attempt to live in the villa meets with misfortune."

"Haunted by what?" the girl asked.

"They call it the One Who Walks." I shrugged. "From how it was described, I took it to be what the Greeks term a *genius loci*."

"What's that?" Altrus asked.

"A spirit bound by magic to haunt a specific place," the seeress told him.

"We'll stay well away from the villa." I peered at the surrounding hills. "How are we to find the cave where the gold is hidden?"

"Abdul Yaghouth told me how to find the cave," Kalila said.

"Why didn't you share this information earlier?"

"And have you ride off and leave me in Damascus? I wanted you to need me, and you do – you would never find the cave alone."

She looked up at the moon, than at the villa, and began to scan the horizon to the northeast.

"What are you looking for?" Altrus demanded.

"The cave is located by standing with your back to the entrance of the villa, and lining up two trees that grow in the valley, an almond tree and a thorn tree. I see the almond tree over there, but I don't see any thorn trees."

I walked over to the almond tree and searched the horizon. There were no other trees in that direction, only low bushes.

Look again, my love, said Sashi inside my mind. The eyes of the race of lesser djinn known as the *chaklah-i* are able to see in the darkness like the eyes of an owl. Although Sashi used my eyes to see while she was inside my body, her perception was keener than mine. I did as Sashi suggested. My true father was a djinn, so my own night vision is better than that of most men.

"I still don't see anything – wait, now I see it."

Walking away from the others, I picked my way across the valley floor to a jagged stump that stuck up from the earth. It showed signs of having been burned, and the bark had been blasted away from it. Altrus approached behind me.

"There's our thorn tree," I told him, pointing at the stump. "Decades ago it must have been blasted by lightning."

I made him stand in front of the stump, then went back to the almond tree and lined up its trunk with the mercenary.

"Run out past Altrus and stand where I tell you," I said to the girl.

She ran nimbly past the mercenary and turned to look back. I waved her to the right. She took a sidestep.

"Walk backwards toward the hill," I told her. There was no need to raise my voice – the still night air carried my words like the chimes of a brass bell. She began to walk awkwardly backwards by glancing over her shoulder, while keeping her gaze on me as I directed her to move a step to one side or the other.

"I can't walk any further," she called out.

"What do you see?"

"Nothing. Wait, I see a shadow on the slope behind some brush."

We began to walk toward her. "Is it a cave?" Kalila asked eagerly.

"It could be. It's dark, I can't see into it."

"Go back to the horses and get the brass lamp that hangs from my saddle," I told Altrus.

He turned, then stopped suddenly. I turned to see what he was staring at. A line of men stood in front of our horses, their swords and daggers drawn. Cursing inwardly at myself for failing to hear their approach, I realized they must have been hiding inside the ruined villa. I counted them. Eleven. None spoke or moved. They might as well have been bronze statues in the moonlight. One stepped forward. He was taller than the others and more richly dressed, with embroidered red baldrics crossing on his chest that supported his sword and dagger. A gold ring hung from his right ear. Another gold ring encircled his long beard, drawing it together beneath his chin.

"Red Rashid," Kalila said.

He smiled, revealing even white teeth that shone in the moonlight.

"You shouldn't have tried to cheat me, woman," he said in a voice that boomed across the night. "I would have paid you well for your service. Now I must kill you."

3.

"You can't kill me," Kalila told Red Rashid. "You will never find the treasure if you kill me."

"It's in the cave," he said. "Thank you for locating it. I studied these hills for years, trying to see where the treasure might be buried."

"Yes, it's in the cave, but where in the cave?"

He looked at her, then smiled. "There is no need for any of you to die just yet. You can help us recover the treasure."

One of the thieves lit an oil lamp and crawled into the cave on his hands and knees, holding the handle of the lamp between his teeth. The opening was broad but not high. At first glance it appeared to be nothing more than a shadow beneath a ledge of rock. Red Rashid must have gazed upon it many times in his search for the treasure without recognizing it for what it was.

"What do you see, Asif?" he called into the cave mouth.

"There is a chamber at the end of a long throat." The thief's voice came weakly from the shadow. "No, wait, I see a trunk of black iron in the chamber."

"That's not the gold," Kalila said.

"Open the trunk, tell me what it contains," Red Rashid called into the cave.

For many seconds there was silence. Rashid chuckled

nervously as he looked at the faces of his men, straining to listen.

"Soon we will be rich," he said. A few of his men nodded and grinned agreement.

A scream issued from the cave. It was a high-pitched shriek that rose higher toward the end before abruptly cutting off. I recognized it as the scream of a man dying in agony.

"The One Who Walks," Kalila said in the sudden silence.

The thieves stepped away from the entrance and drew their swords. They began to babble amongst themselves. Altrus and I also stepped back, but we had no swords to draw. They had been taken from us and cast on the ground near the villa. I was pleased to see Martala holding her little dagger in her hand. The man who searched her had not been able to find it. I drew Kalila further away from the thieves.

"Stand your ground," Red Rashid barked. "The man who runs is the man who dies."

Oily black smoke boiled from the cave entrance. It began to rotate in the moonlight, turning into a strange kind of dust devil. When it thickened, something stepped from its midst. It had a squat ape-like body covered in fine black fur. From this pelt projected hooked thorns or spikes. Two curved horns stood from its head, two similarly curved tusks hung down from the corners of its snarling mouth. Its eyes glowed red, like sooty embers in a fireplace. At the ends of its long, ape-like arms were enormous hands with hooked black claws on the fingertips. A long pink tongue unrolled from its mouth as it glared at us and roared.

"What in all the gods is that thing?" Altrus murmured, stepping back in spite of himself.

"That is an ifrit," I said. "The old pirate must have summoned it up from one of the seven subterranean hells."

"Can it be killed?"

"Not by any weapon these fools possess."

We continued to back away as the band of thieves stood shoulder to shoulder in a crescent to confront it. Red Rashid was not watching us. All his attention was on the ifrit. Kalila hugged my arm in terror.

"When the thing attacks, turn and run back toward the villa," I murmured.

We did not have long to wait. With inhuman quickness, the ifrit lunged forward and plucked a man from the line of swordsmen as easily as though it where snatching up a small child. The man dropped his sword and screamed. An instant later, his head was rolling across the sand. The demon put the neck of the corpse in its mouth and widened its eyes in delight as it sucked the still-pulsing hot blood.

We ran toward the villa, hearing the terrified shouts of the thieves and Red Rashid's bellowing voice behind us. It was some moments before we located our weapons where the thieves had dropped them. I felt better with a straight blade of good Damascus steel in my right hand and a curved dagger in my left, though I knew how little use they would be against an ifrit. They were reputed to be more powerful than the djinn. I saw Kalila pick up a long dagger.

"Did you notice that the horses are gone?" Altrus asked me.

I looked all around. There was no sign of our mounts. Bits of leather hung from the rings on the stone pillar where they had been tied. The emergence of the ifrit from the cave must have maddened them with terror. They had snapped their reins and run off into the darkness. The horses of the thieves were undoubtedly tied up somewhere nearby, out of sight, but there was no time to search for them.

"Into the villa," I told the others.

Inside the front room of the villa we found the old door lying in the dust where it had fallen from its hinges years ago. Altrus and I picked it up and fitted it back into the doorframe. The darkness was broken only by moonlight slanting into the rear of the structure through a hole in its roof. The room we occupied was empty save for a table and some stools. I made a quick circuit of the house and determined that there was no back door. All the windows were shuttered, but by peering close we could see out through cracks between the boards. Screams continued to sound across the valley.

"Maybe it will go back into the cave after it kills them all," Martala said.

"I fear your optimism is misplaced," I told her. "The ifrit has been bound by magic to this villa and this valley as a guardian. That is why nobody has been able to live here since the death of Abdul Yaghouth."

"He must have possessed skill in necromancy."

"Or he hired someone to perform the magic for him," I said. "Either way, binding an ifrit is no small task."

"What is an ifrit?" Altrus asked as he peeked out through one of the shutters.

"It is a type of djinn, is it not?" Kalila said.

"In a sense. The race of impure djinn known as the afarit dwell beneath the ground rather than in the air. Whereas the true djinn are composed of clear fire, the afarit are made of sooty fire that is filled with smoke. They are malicious in their natures. This ifrit has only one purpose, to kill anyone who seeks the treasure it was set to guard."

Frantic pounding came on the door. For a moment I thought the ifrit had come to kill us, but then I realized it was some of the thieves who had run away from the hopeless battle against the monster.

"Move the door," I told Altrus.

Kalila grabbed my arm. "We can't let them in. They'll kill us."

"We need allies who can fight." I shook off her hands and helped the mercenary to shift the heavy door aside. Three men squeezed through the gap. One of them was Red Rashid. We pushed the door back into place and used a wooden beam fallen in from the roof to prop it shut. The end of the angled beam pressed against the center of the door, and the weight of the beam kept the pressure constant. The door would not easily be breached.

"We need light."

"I have a candle," Altrus said.

"I have flint and tinder," Red Rashid said in his harsh voice. Sparks flickered near the floor as flint was struck on steel. Soon the glow of a candle illuminated a circle of anxious faces.

Rashid's upper body and left thigh were covered in blood. More blood seeped from his skull down his face. I thought it had stained his beard, then realized that his beard was a dark red color. The redness had not shown in the moonlight. His men were in even worse condition. One was missing three fingers from his left hand where the monster had bitten them off. The other had lost an eye and babbled weakly. He could barely stand. His companion, who propped him up with an arm around his shoulder, helped him to sit on a stool.

When I looked at Red Rashid, I saw that the fight had gone out of his eyes. He stared at me wildly.

"It won't die. We cut it a thousand times but it doesn't bleed."

"We need to remain quiet and wait for dawn," I murmured to him in a soothing tone. "It may be that it does not kill in daylight."

He seized my shoulder in his hand. "Do you know this?"

"Not for a certainty," I said, gently extracting myself from his grasp. "But it is in keeping with the behavior of such demonic beings."

"How many hours remain?" Kalila asked.

I pictured the position of the moon in the heavens and thought for a few moments. "A little more than four hours."

"You are a necromancer," Red Rashid said to me. "You must have prepared some magic when you came here for the treasure."

"I didn't know the treasure was guarded by an ifrit." I looked at Kalila. "Did you know?"

She averted her gaze and shrugged. "Something about a guardian was spoken by the spirit of Abdul Yaghouth. The spirit did not specify the kind of guardian."

"And you did not think to ask?" Martala said.

251

The seeress gave no answer.

"You knew I would never have agreed to help you if you admitted the nature of the demon that guards the treasure," I said.

"I needed your help," she said. "What else was I supposed to do?"

My reply was cut off by a thunderous bang against the door.

"It comes!" the thief on the stool cried out in terror. "The One Who Walks comes!"

9.

I made the sign of silence by putting a finger across my lips. The thief who had helped carry in the man on the stool cupped his good hand over his friend's mouth. The other struggled weakly against him, but made no further sound.

The door groaned as something massive and powerful pressed against it. In the flickering light I saw its boards flex and heard the scrape of claws across wood. The noises stopped, and the ifrit began to circle the house. It paused at each shuttered window and sniffed the air, but did not attempt to break through the shutters. The thought came to me that it might not perceive the windows as entrances. Symbolically speaking, a window is not a doorway. Three times it circled the house, then there was silence.

"Maybe it went back to the cave," Red Rashid whispered. His fingers were white and bloodless where he gripped the hilt of his sword, and his eyes darted from side to side when he cocked his head to listen. I knew he was on the edge of losing his reason.

I drew Kalila aside where I could speak to her without the others hearing.

"Can you summon the spirit of Abdul Yaghouth?"

"What?" She looked around. "Do you mean here? Are you mad?"

"It may know how to unbind the ifrit from this place."

"Even if it does, why would it tell us? It wants to watch us being torn to pieces by that monster."

"Never mind that. Can you do it?"

She thought for a time. "Yes, perhaps. I don't know."

She found a chipped plate and set it on the table. We moved the babbling one-eyed thief away so that she could sit on the stool. Drawing her dagger from its sheath, she used its blade to cut herself on the inside of her left forearm, than allowed her blood to drip onto the plate until it formed a puddle. Closing her eyes, she rested her head against her hands with her elbows on the table and began to chant in a low monotonous voice.

Faint wreaths of smoke began to arise from the blood. They entwined themselves in the air above the plate and formed a face. As it became clearer, I saw that it was the face of a man with heavy cheeks and full lips. Its black eyes peered out from the smoke and glanced from one to another of us. When they fell on me, they pierced me to the heart. The face smiled with satisfaction.

"Abdul Yaghouth, do you hear me?" I said.

The eyes flicked back to lock with my own. I felt their power, and their malice. The spirit of the dead man wanted us to die.

"Do you know how to unbind the ifrit from this place?"

"Yes."

The word came not from the face in the smoke, although its lips moved, but from the throat of Kalila.

"Tell us how to unbind it."

"I will not." The face smirked at me. "I will watch you all die."

"What good is the gold to you? You have been dead for more than a hundred years."

"No one else shall have my treasure."

I pondered how I could persuade the spirit to show mercy, then pointed at Red Rashid. "This man is of your own blood. The treasure is his rightful inheritance."

The face studied the thief with interest, than shook from side to side. "He is a weakling. He does not deserve my gold."

Red Rashid lifted his sword. I raised my hand to press down his sword arm.

"I am a necromancer," I told the face, and pointed at Martala. "This woman is also a necromancer."

"What is that to me?" Kalila murmured as the lips of the face moved.

"I will dig up your corpse and render it down to its essential salts, then reconstitute them to bring you back to life. I will torture you until you scream for death, but death will not be given to you."

"Idle boasts," the face said contemptuously. "You do not know where my body was buried."

"I know it," Red Rashid said suddenly. "I know the very gravestone in the Place of Skulls where your bones lie."

An expression of uncertainty passed across the face in the smoke.

"It makes no difference. The guardian will kill you all."

"Rashid, describe the grave where your ancestor lies buried."

The thief described the location of the grave with precise detail. I was familiar with the burying ground called the Place of Skulls and knew I would have no difficulty finding the grave.

"Now we all know where your bones are buried," I told the face. "If even one of us escapes, that person can have your corpse dug up and render it down to its essential salts, or hire a necromancer to do the work. Are you willing to take the risk that none of us will survive this night?"

The arrogance was gone from the face. It contorted, torn between a longing to watch us all die and a fear that there might be a shadow of truth in my words.

"Very well, I will tell you the incantation that will unbind the guardian," Kalila said tonelessly.

A clatter of tiles came from the roof, followed by a series of thuds. There was a great crash.

"It came through the roof," Altrus shouted. "It's in the other room."

I snatched my sword from its scabbard, determined to sell my life as dearly as I could. Altrus stood at my left side and Martala at my right. The thieves shrank back and pressed themselves against the wall.

In the flickering glow from the candle the nightmare creature entered the room and stood savouring our terror. Its horned head brushed the ceiling beams. It snatched up the one-eyed thief and killed him by breaking his neck, then threw him against the wall like a discarded doll. Red Rashid screamed like a madman and rushed forward, cutting furiously at the ifrit with his sword. His sole remaining man came forward to fight at his side.

Suddenly I heard a deep voice sounding barbarous words of power that made the very air itself tremble. Kalila, whom I had forgotten, stood confronting the monster. It ceased to be interested in the thieves, but stood watching her. As she uttered the last words of the incantation, it nodded and turned to black smoke that swirled around the room and found its way out through cracks in the window shutters and under the door.

After a while, we removed the beam from the door and opened it. The first light of morning had paled the stars. Birds were singing. We went out with wondering eyes, like voyagers landing upon the shore of a new world.

"It is gone," Kalila said at last when nobody spoke for several minutes.

"Are you certain?" Red Rashid asked.

She nodded, and turned to me. "I heard the words of the unbinding in my mind."

"Well, for us you did. We would all have been torn apart."

"Now we must go into the cave and get my gold."

"My gold, you mean," Red Rashid said, raising the tip of his sword.

"Our gold," Altrus told him. There was warning in his voice.

"Do you think you can best me, little man?" Rashid asked. The other thief moved his hand toward his sword hilt. From the corner of my eye I saw Martala inch nearer to Altrus.

I stepped between Red Rashid and Altrus with my palms upraised.

"What we passed through together on this night has made us one company. I propose that we divide the treasure into equal shares, one share for each of us."

There was reluctance. Most of it came from Kalila, who did not want to give up any of the treasure. The thief who had lost his fingers was in favor of the bargain, knowing it would bring him more gold than his master would ever have given him. After some bickering, all agreed to the pact. Red Rashid was not happy, but neither did he wish to fight Altrus and myself on his own. He probably discounted the girl, which would have been his fatal mistake. Martala is more deadly than either of us.

"This night has cost me dearly," Kalila said to me as we all made our way toward the cave. The others walked in front of us.

"On the contrary, the night has been kind. You have your life and a share in the treasure, if such a treasure exists. Be content."

"I suppose you are right. None of us got everything we wanted, but we kept what is most important."

"Any night one can say that is a good night," Altrus said over his shoulder.

"You are right, my friend," Red Rashid said, clapping the mercenary on the back. "And we have a story to tell our grandchildren."

"One they will never believe," Martala said.

As they talked, the seeress and I fell some distance behind. I let my gaze glide over the low bushes and rocks around us. I had no doubt that the ifrit had been released from its binding to this place. What I could not help wondering was if it might voluntarily choose to come back. No sane man wanted an ifrit for an enemy.

"I am not coming back," Kalila murmured in a monotonous tone.

I looked at her. Her eyelids were fluttering as she walked. She did not turn her head.

"You are an interesting man, Alhazred. I bear you no ill-will. But at some future time, we may meet again."

Kalila stumbled, and I caught her before she fell. We continued after the others in silence.

Day of the Dead

1.

Sashi woke me.

There is a presence in the room, my love.

Against the darkness of my closed eyelids her beautiful face floated. It wore an expression of concern.

What kind of presence? I thought to her without opening my eyes.

I don't know, but it isn't human.

Parting my eyelids cautiously, I saw a faint greenish glow in the air of my bedroom. I turned my head on my bolster to peer past the foot of the bed. The spectre of a naked woman regarded me impassively. For a time she simply stood there, her long hair floating around her head as if borne up upon some otherworldly breeze. She was young and very beautiful. I shivered. The air was unnaturally cold. Beside me on the bed, Martala lay sleeping. I heard her soft snores.

The spectre beckoned me with her hand, then turned and seemed to glide rather than walk to the open doorway of the bedroom, where she paused and turned to look back at me. Her expression had changed. Now it was anguished and imploring. She passed silently into the hall.

I rolled onto my back and stared at darkness on the ceiling, wondering how the spirit had managed to penetrate the occult wards around my house. They were designed to keep such beings outside the walls. It was obvious the spectre wanted me to follow her. I debated whether to wake the girl, then decided to let her sleep. With care so as not to disturb her, I slipped from under the single white cotton sheet that covered my naked body and went on bare feet from the room.

The lambent luminosity of the woman led me along the corridor and down the main staircase to the entrance hall. As I descended the steps I caught a glimpse of her gliding toward the kitchen at the back of the house. Following across the chill marble tiles in the entrance and along the hallway, I came to the door that led to the cellar. It stood open, even though I always keep it closed. My work is down there, and at times my work can be dangerous.

In the kitchen I found a candle stub by touch on the shelf where I knew they were kept, and ignited it on an ember that still smouldered in the ashes of the cookstove. I cupped my hand around its fluttering flame and descended the steep stone steps. My cellar is a network of Roman arches supported by stone pillars. Between the pillars brick walls were erected to divide the space into separate but connected rooms.

She had paused to wait for me at the bottom of the stairs. When I drew near, she turned and glided through my workroom and into a storage room where I kept the materials I used in my necromancy on shelves. She stopped before a blank brick wall and regarded me intently. I stood examining her. The glow that emanated from her translucent body highlighted every curve, every detail. She could not have been older than twenty, but had an exotic beauty that made her appear ageless.

Her expression saddened. She turned and walked into the wall. Her body passed through the bricks as if they were made of air.

For some time I stood, waiting to see if she would re-emerge. A rat skittered in the shadows behind me. I found the familiar sound comforting. When it became evident that she would not show herself, I retraced my steps out of the cellar and returned to my bedroom.

Martala lay on her stomach in her usual sleeping posture,

her head turned away, her arms and legs sprawled. Blowing out the candle, I slid back under the sheet and was soon asleep.

2.

"I saw something strange last night," I told the girl in the morning while we were both getting dressed.

She listened as I related the incident. She did not appear surprised, or even very interested.

"You saw the ghost," she said from the side of the bed, where she sat pulling on one of her boots.

"The ghost?"

She stopped and stared at me with wide crystal-gray eyes.

"You mean you didn't know about the ghost?"

"I have no idea what you are talking about."

"Everyone in the house has seen the ghost, even Altrus, and you know what a tree stump he is when it comes to matters of the spirit."

I digested this for a few moments. "You are telling me that our house is haunted?"

"Of course."

"For how long?"

She shrugged and thought about it. "I suppose it must have been haunted before we got here."

"How could the house be haunted, yet I never see the ghost?"

"You are always so preoccupied with your books and your experiments. Maybe you just didn't notice."

"It was a beautiful woman with no clothing who glowed in the dark. I believe I would have noticed."

"She doesn't always come that way. Sometimes it's just a knocking on the walls, or a cold touch as you walk along the hall. Once, I saw her hand extend up through the top of the dining table."

"And you never thought to mention it?"

"It never seemed important."

"And Borka has seen her? The cook? The maids?"
She nodded.

"What about the gardener?"

"He's never said anything to me, and you know how poor his eyesight has become. You'll have to ask him."

I finished dressing and went down to breakfast. Altrus was already there at the table. A serving maid set places for me and the girl.

"Have I told you how happy I am to be a bad Muslim?" Altrus said cheerfully.

"Frequently."

He rolled up a strip of bacon and popped it into his mouth. "I'd rather go to hell than give up bacon. To say nothing of wine."

Impatient with his good spirits, I told him about my spectral visitation.

"So you've seen the ghost at last?" he said, chewing.

"Martala tells me you've seen it."

He nodded. "Only twice. Once it was just her face. The other time I glimpsed the back of her body as she passed through a wall."

"What do you make of it?"

He looked at the girl, who said nothing, and shrugged. "I suppose the house is haunted, as many houses are."

This was not enough for me. My interest had been aroused. Here was a mystery, and I intended to solve it.

"Why do you suppose she came to me last night?"

"Who can fathom the mind of a ghost?" Altrus said.

"Maybe it's the season of the year," the girl suggested as she nibbled a stick of cheese. "The Christians call today the Eve of All Hallows. In Egypt they used to celebrate it by wearing masks shaped like grinning skulls."

"What is the significance of this day?"

"The Christians claim that this is the time of the year when the separation between the world of the living and the world of the dead is at its weakest and can be crossed over. They say that on this night, the dead walk the earth."

For the rest of the day while at the reading table in the library, or working in the cellar on my latest experiment, I remained alert for appearances of the spectral woman. None came. I retired to bed perplexed and disappointed. The girl had already forgotten about the apparition and was asleep before I could talk about it.

Alhazred. It was Sashi's silent voice in my mind.

My eyes snapped open, and I realized I had fallen asleep. The spectre stood leaning over the side of the bed, her face inches away from my own. Cold radiated from it as if it were sculpted from a block of ice. She laid her hand on the sheet where it covered my lower belly, and a mingled sensation of cold and pleasure washed through my veins and ran along my nerves to every part of my flesh. It was different from the pleasure I received from Sashi when we made love. This sensation was sharper – darker in some indefinable way.

"Show me what you wish me to see," I whispered.

The spectre moved back from the bed and waited for me to arise, then led me out of the bedroom as on the previous night. Again we descended the stairs and went into the cellar. I had no candle, but the green glow emanating from her body was enough to guide my way. She stopped in front of the brick wall through which she had vanished the previous night.

"Are you just going to disappear again without telling me anything?"

She raised her hand and began to trace a pattern on the bricks. Where her finger touched, the bricks glistened with a glowing green line that was like the slime trail left by a snail. When she was done, I saw that she had drawn a kind of seal composed of two squares rotated on each other to define a star of eight points. In the center was a pictogram, but I did not recognize it.

She bowed her head in sorrow and stepped into the wall. The pictogram vanished with her.

Cursing under my breath, I felt my way back to the

entrance hall and went to my library. There I struck a lamp alight and drew the symbol from memory on a sheet of papyrus using a reed pen and dragon's blood. The red ink made it stand forth vividly.

When morning came, I sent Borka with a note to my neighbor Harkanos asking if he had time to speak with me. He sent a note back with the manservant inviting me to breakfast.

He was waiting to greet me at the front door of his house, smiling and cheerful as was his usual manner. I did not know his true age, but I knew he had lived for centuries. Yet he looked scarcely forty. His beardless face was without blemish, his eyes clear grey, and his curling brown hair, which he wore short after the Greek fashion, shone with gold highlights in the morning sun. It was said in the Lane that he had discovered the alchemical secret of eternal youth. I saw little reason to doubt the rumor.

We ate a light meal in his sunlit dining hall, which faced eastward. He wore a loose-fitting morning robe of blue silk embroidered with salamanders in gold thread. His young daughter did not sit at the table with us, but flitted around like a bird, snatching bits of food from the table and putting them in her mouth while she watched what we did. As was her usual custom, she was naked. Harkanos had given up trying to keep her clothed. She was a fey child, of greater than average intelligence but disinclined to speak. Through the back of a chair she watched me eat with solemn eyes, holding onto the rungs with her little hands as if they were prison bars.

I smiled at her. She drew back. I wondered if she could see through the spell of glamour that concealed my mutilated face. Harkanos himself had that ability, but he was the greatest mage in Damascus.

"Anisah grows quickly."

He glanced at his daughter. "I can't seem to persuade her to wear a dress. She takes it off as soon as it is put on her. To be honest, Alhazred, it troubles me. Eventually she must go out from this house, and she can't go out naked."

"Perhaps a glamour?"

"I will use one as a last resort, but I would prefer the stubborn child simply put on some clothing." He rose from his place. "Let us go into my library where we can talk."

As always, I admired his celestial and terrestrial globes, which he had constructed himself from hammered brass inlaid with silver. He was an astrologer who took his own measurements of the motions of the stars from an observation platform he had constructed on the roof of his house. He used them to draw up nativities and horary charts for the nobility and wealthy merchants of the city, who paid him handsomely for his services. He had even done charts for the caliph, Muawiya the Second.

"What is it you wished to talk about?" he asked.

I showed him the drawing on the papyrus. His interest was immediately quickened. He carried it to a window and threw wide its screen to let in more light.

"Where did you get this?"

"I drew it myself early this morning. Do you know what it is?"

"It has been many years since I last saw this writing." He traced the lines of the central symbol with his fingertip. "It is used in the land of Chin, which as you know lies many leagues to the east of us, beyond the great mountains. The necromancers of that land practice an art they call the tao. They work their spells by drawing word pictograms that are stylized versions of their common writing script. By this means they can call up or put down the dead. They place them on the foreheads of corpses to prevent them from wandering out of their graves."

"Is this the symbol for calling them up or laying them?"

"That I don't know. It may have an entirely separate function."

"Can you read it?"

He studied the symbol for a time. "I'm not sure. I believe it is either the pictogram for liberation or the one for dissolution."

When I returned to my house, Martala and Altrus were waiting for me in the front sitting room. I told them what had occurred the previous night and related the conversation between myself and Harkanos.

"What does it mean?" Altrus asked.

"I don't know. But twice the ghost led me to the same wall in the cellar. I am going to take up hammer and chisel and find out what lies behind it."

3.

With the blade of a cold chisel I pried out the brick I had loosened and set it down with the others. I peered through the hole I had made in the wall.

"What can you see?" Martala asked.

"There's a space on the other side, but it's dark. Borka, bring the candles nearer."

My manservant, Borka, extended a silver candelabra that shed a bright light into the hole. His hand trembled, and I realized he was nervous. I regarded what lay beyond for several seconds.

"What is it?" she asked.

Without answering, I resumed chipping at the bricks of the wall. Now that several had been removed, the work was easier. In the end, the mercenary and the girl helped me while Borka held the light. What the irregular opening revealed was disquieting, even for my cynical temperament.

The desiccated, naked corpse of a woman was bound at the wrists and ankles upright to iron rings embedded in the rear stone wall of a shallow alcove. There was little left of it but leathery skin stretched over bone. Most of the long hair had fallen from the skull and its eyes were shrivelled into their sockets. Its jaw gaped down in an endless silent scream.

"She was walled up while still alive," Martala said in a small voice.

"How long has she been in there?" Altrus asked.

I studied the condition of the corpse. It was mummified. The dryness of the air had caused it to shrink in upon itself without decaying, but all the moisture had gone from the tissues, leaving it hard as wood.

"Decades, at the least."

"Here is a mystery to solve," Altrus said. He was mildly interested rather than horrified. In his work as a mercenary he had seen many forms of death. He peered close at one of the wrists.

"She's bound with some kind of silken sash or cord. The knots don't look very tight. I'm surprised she didn't wriggle out of them."

I motioned for Borka to bring the candelabra closer and studied the binding. He was right, the cord and the knots were not very tight, but over them had been impressed a seal in red wax. It clung to the knots. The symbol on the seal was unfamiliar to me. It did not resemble the tao pictogram I had drawn. There was one of these wax seals on the bindings of both wrists and both ankles. The cords passed through massive wrought iron eye loops that had been set between the stones of the wall with mortar. Each loop looked sturdy enough to hold back a raging elephant.

"What are you going to do with her?" Altrus asked, stepping back.

"I don't know."

"We could reduce her to her essential salts, then reconstitute her and ask her what happened," Martala suggested.

I thought about it, then shook my head. "I don't want to waste materials. She's probably just some poor servant girl Hapla, the former owner of this house, walled up to be rid of her." Even as I said the words, I knew they were false. There was a quality about the spectre I had seen that

267

suggested something more than a common servant girl. Her manner had been graceful, even aristocratic.

"We could just wall her back in," the girl suggested.

"No. I don't want a ghost wandering around my house. I'll remove her."

"I doubt that Uto will want her."

The girl was right. The ghoul would not want a corpse the flesh of which had dried as hard as stone. There would be no nourishment in it.

"I'll bury her, or burn her. It doesn't matter, I just want this thing out of the house."

I reached to the bindings on the left wrist of the corpse and broke the wax seal with my thumb so that I could untie the cord. The corpse jerked and arched its back. Its bony fingers clenched into fists and its head began to thrash back and forth.

I stepped away quickly, bumping into the girl. Altrus drew his sword. We stared in fascination at the twitching corpse. Its rolling head and beating fists made a kind of drumming noise on the wall behind it. The silk cord binding its left wrist stretched and strained but did not break.

Altrus approached it with caution. He glanced at me and I nodded. He struck at its neck with his sword, intending to lop the head from the body, but the steel glanced off the hardened skin as though it were armor plate. He began to cut and hack at different parts of the body. The blade did no damage to the thing's limbs, but by chance he struck the cord around its left wrist. Its arm came free and extended to clutch the air in front of his face.

"Keep back," I said in warning. He glanced at me as if I were a fool, and I realized my words were unnecessary. He had no intention of getting anywhere near that clutching hand. Its bony fingers clattered together like a bundle of dry sticks at it grabbed for his throat. The entire corpse was trembling with power that surged through its limbs. It leaned into the room, pulling to the maximum extent against its three remaining bonds, which held it in place.

"It cannot reach us," Martala said. She had her dagger in her hand.

As if the corpse had heard and understood the girl's words, it ceased to strain forward, and instead fumbled blindly at its right wrist. I realized it was trying to find the wax seal so that it could break it.

"Strike off its arm if you can," I told Altrus.

He tried again and again, but he might as well have been trying to use his sword to cut down an ironwood tree. It bounced off the hardened skin of the forearm. The corpse did not seem to notice the blows. After several minutes its flailing left hand struck the red wax seal on its right wrist, and its right arm snapped the silken cords that bound it like rotten strings.

"It's getting stronger," Martala said in a voice filled with dread.

The corpse was bending and fumbling with its hands at its ankles.

"We'll have to burn it," I said.

On one of the shelves there was a glass jar half-filled with pure alcohol, which I sometimes used in my work lamps because it burned so cleanly. I snatched it down, drew out the broad plug of cork, and dashed its clear contents over the flailing corpse. It straightened its back and seemed to glare at me with its blind eye sockets. A kind of rattling hiss of fury escaped from its gaping mouth.

"One of the candles, quick," I told Borka. "Don't get too close."

He understood and pulled a burning candle from one of the sockets of the candelabra, then stepped toward the niche and tossed it at the corpse.

With a great *whoosh* of heated air it was entirely engulfed in flame. It writhed back and forth, kicking with its legs to free them, but whatever magic was in the wax seals held fast the bonds around its ankles. We watched it burn. Its skin blackened but was otherwise unchanged.

After a time the flames began to die out as the alcohol that fueled them was consumed. Neither the remaining wax seals nor the cords that bound the ankles of the corpse appeared to have been touched by the flames.

"It didn't work," the girl said. There was something in her voice I had never expected to hear – fear.

The corpse bent down and once again began to strike blindly at its ankles with its fists. The seal on its right ankle broke, and it snapped its leg free with a hiss of triumph. It turned its full attention on its left ankle.

"It's going to get free," Altrus said. "We need to leave."

The words were scarcely from his lips when the final wax seal shattered. The cords around the left ankle of the corpse snapped and it stepped out of the niche and stood swaying with its bony arms upraised.

Borka chose that moment to drop the candelabra. The cellar plunged into absolute darkness.

٩.

"Stay where you are," I told the others.

I took my tinderbox from my pocket and struck its tinder into flame. Without even glancing at the corpse, I bent and searched the flagstones for the fallen candles. I found one and touched its wick to the tinder. In the flare of the flame I saw that the grotesque face of the corpse was almost touching my own. Before its arms could close around me, I jumped backward.

"Get out of here," I told the others.

Borka needed no urging. He stumbled and fell to his knees in his eagerness to reach the stone steps that led up to the house. Altrus backed away from the shambling corpse with his sword held at the ready, but he knew it was useless against this hellish thing. Martala came to me.

"Alhazred –" There was concern in her voice.

"Get out while you can. I'll follow."

270

The corpse seemed uninterested in the others. It continued to shuffle toward me as I moved back and to the side with the candle raised between us. Just in time I drew the flame back from its flailing arms. The only reason it did not fall upon me at once was its blindness. Some instinct drew it toward me, but it did not know exactly where I stood. It was like the game that children play in darkened rooms, where one seeks to find by touch the others who hide.

I circled it and circled it again, just beyond the reach of its clutching fingers. I wondered what drew it to me, and not to the others. Then I remembered the charm I had inscribed on the sheet of papyrus. Pulling it from my pocket, I unfolded it with one hand and glanced at it. I was tempted to burn it with the candle. The corpse was drawn to it, so I reasoned the charm must hold some power over it.

What had Harkanos said about the necromancers of Chin? The words he had spoken returned to my mind. With a quick motion, I spilled molten wax from the candle over the back of the papyrus, then thrust it forward between the flailing arms and pressed it against the forehead of the corpse.

I jumped away quickly. The corpse ceased its spastic motions and stood still. Something was happening to it. The limbs, the torso, even the head began to glow. I felt heat radiate from it and realized it was burning, but this time the fire was inside it. I took another step back and shielded my face with my arm from the intense heat. The heat washed upward over the barrel arch that formed the ceiling of the cellar. I heard a brick crack. It was fortunate the ceiling was not made of wood.

As quickly as it started, it was over. The corpse collapsed upon itself into a pile of glowing ash. Whatever internal fire the tao charm had kindled within its bones had consumed it utterly.

Standing over the ashes was the same naked woman who had come to my bed in the form of a spectre, but this time her body was more substantial. Her white skin glowed with a pale radiance that was like the lustre of pearl. She regarded me with a mild expression on her beautiful and exotic face.

"Thank you for freeing me," she said. The language she spoke was unfamiliar, but somehow I understood the meaning of the words.

"Who are you?"

"Many years ago I traveled from my homeland in the east to study the necromantic arts at the feet of Hapla, a great mage of this city. In return for his teaching I became his concubine. Eventually he grew frightened by how quickly I understood his lessons. He knew he could not kill me. I was protected by powerful magic. He tricked me into drinking a potion that entranced me, then bound me in this place using tao magic I had taught him. Only my spirit was free to move from this place, and even that could not leave the boundary of this house."

"What will you do now?" I asked.

"I will seek Hapla out, wherever on this earth he may reside, and punish him for what he did to me."

Her body began to glow more brightly.

"I am no longer bound by the limitations of the flesh. You have transformed me into something greater than I was. I have become a goddess. Know this, Alhazred. I am in your debt. If your need is dire, you may call upon my name, and I will come to you."

"What is your name?"

"Ho-sien-ku."

She spoke it once, then rose slowly into the air. Her glowing body became sparks of light that began to swirl in a vortex. In moments this vortex passed up through the bricks of the arch and was gone.

I stood pondering her words for several minutes. Martala approached me cautiously with Altrus close behind her. Of poor Borka there was no sign. I hoped the man would find enough courage not to flee the house.

"She's gone," I told them.

"She didn't kill you," Altrus said with surprise.

"No. She never wanted to kill, she only wanted release."

I walked back over to the niche where she had been bound for so many years and examined it with the candle.

"What are you looking at?" the girl asked.

"I think I will put a set of shelves in here," I told her. "I can use them to hold my jars of essential salts."

DONALD TYSON was born in Halifax, Nova Scotia. He writes a broad range of fiction and nonfiction based in the Western esoteric tradition. He is the author of the novel *Alhazred*, and the nonfiction works *Grimoire of the Necronomicon*, *The 13 Gates of the Necronomicon*, *Necronomicon: The Wanderings of Alhazred*, and the *Necronomicon Tarot*, all by Llewellyn. Most recently, his short novel *The Lovecraft Coven* was published by Hippocampus Press. He lives in Cape Breton, Nova Scotia, with his wife, Jenny, their American bulldog, Ares, and their Siamese cat, Hermes.

Colophon

The text was set in Clavo Book. Caliph, **Harquil**, Matura MT Script, and qurban feast were used for titling; Mohammed was used for drop caps.